THE

SHADOW

BOOK

OF

JI

YUN

EMPRESS WU BOOKS

THE SHADOW BOOK OF JI YUN

THE CHINESE CLASSIC OF WEIRD TRUE
TALES, HORROR STORIES, AND OCCULT
KNOWLEDGE

EDITED AND TRANSLATED
BY
YI IZZY YU & JOHN YU BRANSCUM

Copyright © 2021 by Yi Izzy Yu and John Yu Branscum

All rights reserved.

No part of this book may be reproduced in any form or by any electronic or mechanical means, including information storage and retrieval systems, without written permission from the translators, except for the use of brief quotations in a book review.

Published by Empress Wu Books

Library of Congress Control Number: 2020952354

ISBN 978-1-953124-03-6 (hbk)

ISBN 978-1-953124-01-2 (pbk)

Cover: Based on *Everywhere Eyeballs Are Aflame*, 1888, by Odilon Redon

平生心力坐銷磨紙上烟雲過眼多擬篆書嫌今老矣祇應說鬼似東坡 前因後果驗無羌瑣祀蔸羅鬼一車傳語洛閩門弟子稗官原不入儒家 觀奕道人自題

The Yellow Emperor visits me in my dreams.
It is there that he has passed on the secret teachings.
I have been warned not to reveal them to you.
If I did, the mountains would fade away,
The forests would dissolve.

—Shi Tao, artist and poet
(1641–1717)

*For Francesca Branscum, Vivianne Tabbutt, and 赵羿如.
We hope these stories from the past cast light on the paths in front
of you.*

CONTENTS

Introduction ... xv

Part I
STRANGE NONFICTIONS
On the Jiangshi and Other Returns ... 3
Twice Goodbye ... 10
The Secrets of Hanlin Academy ... 12
Meat Vegetables ... 14
Guests from the Sky ... 17
The Appearance of the Sha ... 21
Windows That Were Not Windows ... 26
The Delicacy ... 29
The Slope of Tigers ... 31
The Ringing of the Western Beast ... 34
The Powers of Early Childhood ... 36
Checkpoints ... 38
The Forest That Was a Nest ... 42
A Dog in Exile ... 45
The House on Zhuchao Street ... 48
Real Life in the Capital ... 51
A God of Our Own ... 55
Red in Darkness ... 59
The Shadow of the Old City ... 61
The Fields in Which We Wander ... 64
Rulai's Great Reversal ... 68
The Visitors ... 71
The Rat in My Friend's Room ... 74
The Setting of a Clock ... 76
Roof Walker ... 78
Jade Chicken ... 80
The Repeater ... 84
A Note on Conjured Spirits ... 87
Revenger ... 89
Beneath a Green Coat ... 92

The Shard and the Hunter	95
Playmates	98
What Things Become	100
Yeren Stones	102
Remembering Those Whose Names Are Forgotten	105
The Secret of the Whole Design	111
Houses at Night and of the Mind	114
The Red Sect	116
How to Speak a Spell	122
Circumstances in Court	124
A Messenger Rides From One Camp to Another	127
What Qi Becomes	133
A Spell for Dice	136
Horse in Snow	138
The Marked Pears	140
A Thing Done in a Moment	142
Water and the Objects Within	146
That Which Remains	150
Women Without Names	153
Road Ghost	156
The Swap	159
Peonies	163
The Realness of Paintings and Demons	165
Mistress Chen's Devotion	168
One Extra at a Wedding	170
The Second Trick	175
A Speaker for the Dead and the Discarnate	178
The Future in the Past	181
Spirits in the Belly	185
The Shao Yong Method	189
The Bloom	193
On the Double Nature of Written Characters and Spirits	195
Paper Horses, Wooden Houses	197
A Qing Dynasty Near-Death Experience	200
A Question Put to the Office of Ghosts and Yin Realm Matters	202
The Scroll of Ghosts and Fiends	204

Every Body is a Word; Every Word is a Future	207
Different Maps of the Same Places	213

Part II
FABLES AND PHILOSOPHIES

Yellow Leaf	221
Not That Maid	225
The Fire That Burst into Flames Far from Where It Was Set	228
The Stone That Bounced	231
In a Coat You'll Recognize	234
Crab Song	237
The Dogs That Follow	241
Ill Winds	243
Spring Storms	244
The Girl with Flowers in Her Hair	247
Apricot Spirit	249
Turtle Treasure	252
A Huli Jing Takes off the Mask	255

Part III
THE END OF THINGS

A Conversation with a Friend About the End of Things	261
Story Notes	267
Reading Group Discussion Questions	287
Timeline of Ji Yun's Life	291
Interview Excerpts	295
Further Reading	305
Statement on Translation	307
Acknowledgments	309
Translator Biographies	311

INTRODUCTION

Imagine if a national political figure like Benjamin Franklin was also a paranormal investigator, one who wrote up his investigations with a storytelling flair that reads like a combination of M.R. James, Lafcadio Hearn, and Zhuangzi—with a dash of the bureaucratic absurdism of Kafka sprinkled in, alongside a healthy dose of H.P. Lovecraft's weird antiquarianism.

In China, at roughly the same time that Franklin was filling the sky with electrified kites, there was such a figure. He was Special Advisor to the emperor of China, Imperial Librarian, and one of the most celebrated scholars and poets of his time. His name was Ji Yun (纪昀).

Beginning in 1789, when he was sixty-five years old, Ji Yun published five volumes of over 1200 tales. In one stroke, they revolutionized Chinese horror and creative nonfiction, revitalized Chinese occult philosophy, and offered the reader a vision of China never before depicted: one poised between old ways and new, where repeating rifles shared the world with Tibetan black-magic shamans and ghosts, Jesuit astronomers rubbed elbows with cosmic horrors, and a vibrant sex trade of the reanimated dead was rumored to be conducted in the dark of night.

Such tales would be unsettling enough if they were simply presented as fiction. But that was not how Ji Yun saw them. Astoundingly, he claimed some were autobiographical or the experiences of people close to him. Literary cousins to Michel de Montaigne's "Of a Monstrous Child" and Mark Twain's infamous *Harper's Magazine* essays on his paranormal experiences, they were meant to record first-hand encounters with the numinous, the inexplicable, and the odd.

To be sure, a handful of the stories—while terrifying or gruesome—remain plausible in a materialist paradigm: a famine-struck town that sells butchered women like livestock, a pear-stealing cat out for revenge, a poet's dangerous, rat-exploding aphrodisiac. Others though directly challenge our understanding of reality: precognitive dreams, sentient fogs that linger after the execution of rebels, abductions by flying orbs, and a research center where everything is so mystically connected that an opened gate can cause the death of one's parents.

There are also accounts of the terrifying "sha" (the strange entity into which the soul transforms after death), the "jiang-shi" (the Chinese vampire), the yeren (the Chinese yeti), a roof-walking Chinese variant of Spring-heeled Jack, the occult secrets of the red sect of Tibetan Buddhism, and nightmarish tales of soul swapping.

Ji Yun's claim that such stories are true, or largely so, is of course as unsettling as the stories themselves—especially given his position as one of the most respected scholars of his time, one who was moreover a leader of a particularly materialist and anti-metaphysical variety of Confucianism.

What brought a leading Confucian intellectual to decide at the height of his career to write a type of literature held in contempt by many of his peers? What brought him to not just neutrally record the incredible claims of others, but also to make his own?

As with most explanations for mystifying human choices, Ji Yun's motives were many.

One, while his work was in many ways unique, he was far from alone—even among Confucians—in reacting against his age's anti-supernaturalist streak by developing an interest in the occult. In fact, public appetite for such material during his life was nearly insatiable.

Two, the idea that educated skepticism and paranormal beliefs are necessarily opposed is false. Even today, roughly half of scientists hold spiritual or supernatural beliefs, and there are several credible research centers that investigate anomalous phenomena, such as the Division of Perceptual Studies at the University of Virginia School of Medicine. Even among Nobel laureates in science, you find several who have expressed an openness to (and experience of) the paranormal. For example, Marie Curie was a faithful attendee of séances; Nobel-winning quantum theorist Wolfgang Pauli believed in synchronicity and poltergeists; Nobel-winning chemist Kary Mullis wrote about his and his adult daughter's encounters with interdimensional entities; and Nobel laureate physicist Brian Josephson believes that water has memory and that quantum entanglement and paranormal phenomena stem from similar underlying cosmic principles. An ability to be skeptical and also adhere to supernatural beliefs was even more prominent during the Qing dynasty when most of the general public saw the spiritual realm as an extension of the natural world, similarly to how we view the microbiological or subatomic realms today.

But the most likely reason that Ji Yun took up his project is the most straightforward. He had experiences that didn't neatly fit into the Confucian worldview of many of his colleagues, and he was courageous enough to write about them. To fully appreciate this courage, it's useful to step back now and take a big picture look at his life.

Rise and Disgrace

Ji Yun was born to a Hebei Province government official and his wife in 1724—the same year that the philosopher of the sublime, Immanuel Kant, was born in Germany. By age four, he was reading at an advanced level and entertaining guests with his photographic memory and adult-like conversational skills. Add to this a fiendishly clever sense of humor, a genius for freestyling rhymes, and an uncanny ability to see in the dark as if it were day, and you have someone who seemed destined for greatness. Indeed, Ji Yun's early adult life is marked by countless awards for literary and scholarly achievements and, while still quite young, he ranked near the top on the national Chinese civil service exams—a steppingstone to his then occupying some of the most important positions in the Qing empire.

But in 1768, when Ji Yun was in his early forties, he made a serious mistake. Breaching confidentiality rules, he warned an in-law that his business was about to be investigated. His political rivals in the imperial court took advantage of this miscalculation to topple him from the emperor's good graces. Soon thereafter, he was banished to Urumqi in Xinjiang Province, a borderland of warring tribes, merchants, and state farms thousands of kilometers from the capital.

Urumqi was a radical, even traumatic change. Demoted to low-level military administrative positions, Ji Yun spent his days and nights with foot soldiers, prisoners, and travelling merchants rather than the empire's elites. While the material comforts of his lifestyle were much diminished in this new environment, Ji Yun benefited intellectually and artistically. More specifically, Urumqi increased his awareness of the suffering of everyday people and his disgust at the moral and intellectual rigidity of the Confucian scholars of his time. Here too, his interest in weird tales truly took off.

Urumqi brought strange stories and folklore from all over the world to Ji Yun's attention. As a result, he began to reflect upon his own weird experiences—and noted how certain themes, patterns, and categories of strangeness occurred repeatedly, as if providing hints about a hidden metaphysical order.

The Great Project

In 1771, three years into Ji Yun's exile, Emperor Qianlong abruptly pardoned him and ordered him back to the capital. Not only was Ji Yun forgiven his trespasses, but he was also promoted to his most important position yet: one of the lead editors for the *Siku Quanshu* imperial library project.

This nearly two-decade-long project was a massive undertaking. It involved acquiring, annotating, cataloguing, and editing the largest collection of Chinese literature ever attempted—over 10,000 works which dated back to China's beginning.

Overseeing such a project as a lead editor and supervising the efforts of over 4300 scholars working on it was a daunting enough task, but Ji Yun was eventually made chief lead editor as well and charged with a special task that profoundly influenced his own work: co-writing and editing an annotated guide to the *Siku Quanshu*, a 200-chapter series of reviews and critical synopses of its holdings. Ji Yun's work on the guide uniquely acquainted him with China's entire literary history, including the evolution of the genre of "zhiguai" to which he felt a particular affinity. As a result, this work was highly rewarding. His second appointed task was far less so.

Emperor Qianlong ordered Ji Yun to savagely edit or outright destroy literary works that were politically problematic or intellectually heretical. He had no choice but to comply.

Thus many classical works were lost forever outside of the impression they made on Ji Yun. But this radical act of censorship, alongside his other work on the library project, added to emotions generated from a lifetime of Ji Yun underplaying his own strange experiences, ignoring those of friends and family, and forcing himself to walk conventional intellectual pathways.

Consequently, in 1789, the same year that the French Revolution began, Ji Yun made a decision that had profound implications for Chinese literature to this day. He wrote the first volume of his famous strange tales, *Personal Accounts and Records of Others: Written During a Luanyang Summer*, the title's plainness belying the shocking contents therein. Four more volumes followed. In total, they contained a little over 1200 tales, which were later gathered together in one book, *Yuewei Caotang Biji*, by Ji Yun's student Sheng Shiyan.

The Occult Technology of the Zhiguai Tradition

To fully appreciate Ji Yun's achievement, it's necessary to understand a little about the strange tale genre in which he was writing: "zhiguai" (志怪).

While the term "zhiguai" can in part be traced back to the Taoist philosopher Zhuangzi, who used it to refer to tales of strange and exotic dimensions of reality outside the everyday, zhiguai first rose to popularity during the Han dynasty (202 BCE–220 CE) and flourished thereafter.

Initially, they took two primary forms. The first was personal or historical accounts and records too odd or heretical for the emperor's official library archives. These were catalogued as "shadow histories." The second form was personal accounts AND fables or parables used by Taoists, Buddhists, and others to illustrate metaphysical concepts. These were catalogued as philosophy.

The word "zhiguai" (zhi=record; guai=strange) during this

time functionally translates to "true weird tales." But this description glosses over zhiguai collections' typical inclusion of diverse materials.

These materials range from eyewitness and hearsay testimony about paranormal encounters, debunking of the same, reports of exotic cultures, and urban legends to discussions of scientific phenomena and physical and mental prodigies, fables or parables intended to convey allegorical rather than literal truths, lyrical essays on philosophical and legal matters, and narratives that liminally sit between these genres and consequently challenge our literary classifications—especially those drawn between the broad categories of fiction and nonfiction.

Despite this diversity, however, many classical zhiguai share commonalities. They are short-shorts that blend spare, evocative narratives with brief and frequent meditations on the strange. Furthermore, they were not usually meant to be stand-alone pieces but to convey their truth inductively and cumulatively through functioning as part of larger collections. This is to say that they're meant to work like multiple eyewitness reports. While perhaps individually flawed due to misremembering, deceit, gullibility, or exaggeration, collectively they testify to deep truths and metaphysical principles.

Thus, ultimately what unites zhiguai is their aesthetic use as occult technology, their incitement in readers of a sense of sublime weirdness that alerts them to previously unseen and frequently unsettling dimensions of reality.

In his 1791 introduction to the zhiguai collection *Qiudeng Conghua*, the scholar Hu Gaowang puts it this way: "Zhiguai are to be respected because they possess the power to awaken readers to the deep principles of reality. They do this by fixing their attention on that which they previously looked away from, while filling their hearts with fear and awe."

This is not to say that all zhiguai writers adhered to such

lofty goals. By Ji Yun's time, in fact most authors simply used the genre's strangeness to entertain and consequently fictionalized at will. A harsh critic of this development, Ji Yun actively worked against it. While he embraced fables that functioned as philosophical parables or satires, he was most invested in recording literally true accounts based on eyewitness or secondhand testimony—including most shockingly his own—expressed skepticism when called for, and was as interested in depicting social and concrete details from the real world and the psychology of fraud as he was in sharing accounts of the strange. Ironically, by virtue of their fidelity to truth-telling, Ji Yun's tales proved vastly more popular with Chinese readers than those of many of his contemporaries—a popularity that continues to our day.

The Shadow Book's Contribution to Contemporary Literature

Ji Yun's tales are easily the equal of other legendary collections, such as *Arabian Nights*, *Kwaidan*, or *Strange Stories from a Chinese Studio*—in terms of artistry and influence—while remaining very much their own thing. They include groundbreaking pieces that develop the mythology of the "jiangshi" (Chinese vampire) and the "huli jing" (fox spirit); predecessors to contemporary alien parasite and abduction tales ("Turtle Treasure" and "Guests from the Sky"); and accounts of astral travel and body swapping that presage modern narratives about journeys through computer simulations and downloadable minds (e.g. "The Fields in Which We Wander" and "The Swap"). Thus they prove themselves to be foundational works of Chinese horror, fantasy, and science fiction—even as they stretch how these genres are understood.

Astoundingly, their contribution to creative nonfiction is just as striking. Ji Yun's corpus contains masterful examples of flash, lyrical, meditative, and montage forms, as well as forays into crime writing. It showcases the Chinese tradition of occult writing too, particularly of the paranormal and speculative creative nonfiction varieties—in its exploration of events related to possession and hauntings, precognition, near-death experiences, and non-physical entities. As if all this wasn't enough, it is also ultimately a significant work of highly accessible metaphysical philosophy and sheds light, via Ji Yun's scattered commentaries, on such matters as Chinese theories about dreams and other dimensions of reality, spiritual development, magick, and the mysterious workings of "ganying" (the mystical resonance between things).

In the end though, Ji Yun's voice is perhaps the most enthralling thing in his tales. It is not a loud, showy voice. Its power is found in its emotional restraint and subtlety, in its suggestiveness and the quiet application of a Confucian's skeptical rigor to traditionally Taoist and Buddhist metaphysical concerns.

It lies behind all these stories like a red flag rippling in the wind, like a quality of odd light spreading over an early morning field, crossing time and space and translation.

Everywhere, there are flashes of Ji Yun's fierce and restless intelligence, his dark wit, his humility before the vast mysteries of reality, and his frustration with the limitations of the human mind. As well, one feels his horror at the suffering visited on the defenseless and the silenced, his sorrow over a nephew's madness and a daughter's death, and his troubled questioning of his times. In all of this, as much as his stories are explorations of the weird and the strange, they are equally explorations of human grief and struggle. His ghosts reveal themselves to be very much human, and his humans turn out to be as mysterious and haunted as ghosts.

The power of this collection is such that you will not walk away from it unchanged.

PART I

STRANGE NONFICTIONS

ON THE JIANGSHI AND OTHER RETURNS

1. Exhumation

Sometimes, when a Taoist is exhumed or digs himself out of the grave, he has no skin. It has rotted away. However, the organs are still plump and whole, and everything else beneath the skin as if fresh. This is because these individuals have cultivated the three treasures of essence, breath, and spirit so well that they can slow their respiration and the beating of their hearts to less than whispers, and thus enter a coma in which they can remain for years, even if buried—as well preserved as if submerged in a coffin full of mercury. This is what is said.

2. Treason

I have not been a direct witness to this Taoist miracle of inner alchemy. However, my friend Dong Qujiang told me that just as the bodies of saints may be preserved so may the bodies of their opposites: criminals.

For example, his neighbor saw the body of the writer Lü Liuliang dragged from his grave fifty years after his death in

Zhejiang so that his bones might be incinerated—the result of a posthumous sentence passed against him for inspiring, through his books, treasonous talk about returning the Chinese empire to Ming rule.

However, when Lü Liuliang's body was pulled from the ground, it was not that of a dead man, but fresh and lifelike—as if the gods had refused his admission to the yin realms. Thus the emperor's men decided against consigning him to the flames right away. Instead, their knives went to work on his flesh.

Blood soon oozed and trickled from his lacerated body, giving the impression that Lü Liuliang were somehow still alive—and feeling everything although unable to move.

3. Imbalance

Neither of these preservations is particularly dangerous. The Taoists mean no ill will. Criminals, imprisoned in their own bodies, can do none.

There are other cases, however, that concern far more vicious beings. Those creatures of the night known as jiangshi (僵尸), for example.

Jiangshi are living corpses who feed on the qi of living things, and sometimes their blood and flesh too.

There are two main types. The weak type occurs when a freshly dead body, one that hasn't had the necessary burial rites performed, temporarily reanimates and becomes violent. Like a guttering flame, these creatures are easily subdued and generally turn quite dead once placed in their coffins.

The strong type of jiangshi is far more dangerous. They are corpses that have been dead long enough to be buried in their coffins but then have become reanimated by an outside agent (a spell, lightning, a pregnant cat walking across their grave).

However, the deceased are not what they were. While in

the grave, their emotions have soured, their thoughts gone feral, and their rank bodies have fermented and stiffened into more monstrous possibilities. If freed of the dirt, these fiends will spread terror in the night—killing, infecting, feeding, and leaving the dry husks of their victims in their wake.

As depraved as they are, there is a complexity to these creatures. Sometimes, a lingering attraction to family and friends remains—albeit in a perverted form.

In his *Tales Forbidden by the Master*, for example, the zhiguai writer Yuan Mei tells of a government official who encountered a deceased friend while on a stroll at night.

The official, following his Confucian training, kept his emotions steady and registered neither surprise nor fear—as if it were the most natural thing to come across the dead in the midnight hours. His formerly stoic friend though manically cycled through several extreme emotions: chattiness, gratitude, and finally a deep sadness—a state from which he suddenly emerged with ferocious energy to launch himself at the official—snarling and clacking his teeth as he tried to sink them into his former friend.

4. Hun and Po

Many have shared stories of such things with me. It is difficult to make sense of them.

In the normal course of life, a person's spiritual essence leaves after death, just as smoke drifts from a fire that has gone out. Therefore, how could a body be active enough to attack and strangle?

Then there is the even more perplexing question of why a person, who for the entirety of their life was virtuous, should suddenly turn evil after death—so twisted that they'll attack their sons and daughters, or mothers and fathers.

Yuan Mei explains such accounts through the possession of

two souls by human beings: the bestial po, which drives the body and its appetites; and the heavenly hun, which is responsible for our more refined thoughts and emotions.

During life, the hun controls the po, moderating its primal impulses. When a person dies, however, the hun goes onto the nether realms to reincarnate or to explore other heavenly states of being. The po at this time is supposed to sink into the earth and dissolve.

But sometimes, it refuses. Instead, it witlessly clings to the body and uses it to rage, rampage, and steal life from others so that it can linger. Such abominations, Yuan Mei maintains, are nearly unkillable because they're already dead and can only be defeated by the spells and rituals of the most powerful magicians.

This theory has bits and pieces of truth in it. Certainly, jiangshi show that stray memories and habits from a body's former inhabitant remain accessible—even if rotting. But in the end, I find myself more persuaded by the view that it is not the po that animates the corpse at all, but rather the case that the deceased body has been opportunely possessed by a nonhuman force or wandering spirit that has snatched it up like a thug might snatch up a club.

5. The Mysterious Dr. Hu

When I was around six or seven, my father had an acquaintance named Hu Gongshan.

Dr. Hu was reserved about his past. So, many rumors circulated. One of the most popular held that he served in Wu Sangui's rebel army under the family name of Jin, and that upon Wu Sangui's defeat, he changed his family name to Hu to escape punishment.

No one offered proof of this, and Dr. Hu neither confirmed nor denied it. However, he was an extremely skilled martial artist and would have been a valuable member of an army. Even when he was in his eighties, he remained limber—with hands and feet as quick as a macaque's. Once, some bandits tried to seize control of his sailing vessel, expecting a helpless old man. But he snatched up a long-stemmed smoking pipe and whipped it around like a fishing pole to fight them off, jabbing its tail-end up into their nostrils and eyes repeatedly.

Dr. Hu was brave when it came to fighting men. But he wasn't entirely fearless. As soon as the sun set and the moon rose, he'd tremble like a child at the wind's moans and flinch at the flickering of shadows.

And on those nights where he had no one to keep him company, he would lock himself inside his house and refuse to come out until the sun was back.

When I first became aware of Dr. Hu's dramatic change in behavior toward evening, I couldn't understand why someone with his skills would act afraid of the dark. But then he shared two episodes from his past.

6. Two Episodes to Consider

Jiangshi, Dr. Hu said, were not just monsters made up to frighten children. They were actual creatures. At least, he had encountered two entities in his long life that corresponded to jiangshi legends.

The first attacked him in the dark of the woods one evening when he was a young man. As with the villains in the boat, he fought back. He could barely see what he was fighting, other than that it was person-shaped and oddly stiff and spastic in its movements—as if missing half its joints. Still, he felt hopeful because he was so good at fighting men. But this time his martial skills meant nothing.

Although he punched and smashed his knuckles against the figure, Dr. Hu might as well have been punching a wooden door or a rock wall. At last, he rushed to a tree to scramble as high as he could on its swaying branches. He was sure the creature would follow, but it turned out that its weirdly rigid body was no good at climbing—although he could hear it trying like a bird beating itself against a window.

The creature tried to reach Dr. Hu all night. Its dumb, stubborn arms hugged the tree stiffly, as it circled it in broken little skips, trying to gain the momentum to launch itself upward.

Exhausted and terrified, Dr. Hu clung to his perch until morning came, bringing with it the yang light of the sun. At this point, the figure's movements slowed until it stopped moving altogether—as if it had abruptly died while holding the tree and now adhered there like a cicada shell.

Despite the apparent death of the creature, Dr. Hu remained afraid to move until he heard jangling sounds. They belonged to a procession of belled camels and their owners. The numbers of the travelling group gave him the courage to scramble down from his sanctuary.

On the ground, Dr. Hu got his first close look at what tried to kill him. Man-shaped, yes, but not a man, although it looked like it might have been at one time. Covered with a snowy something resembling fur or mold, and possessing blood-colored eyes, talon-like hands, and pointed teeth so long that they jutted past the lips, the deep wrongness of the creature—which managed to be both aesthetic and moral—disturbed Dr. Hu to his core.

* * *

As bad as this first encounter was, Dr. Hu's second proved worse. It happened at a guest house in a remote spot in the mountains. He was sound asleep when a movement beneath his sheets woke him.

Thinking a rat or a snake had found its way into his bed,

Dr. Hu refrained from sudden motion to avoid getting bitten, and lay still to watch the progress of whatever it was, at least until it poked its head out of the sheets and could easily be caught by the neck.

However, before his widened eyes, the thing beneath the sheets began to impossibly swell until it was the size of a human head, and then the sheets inflated further as the rough form of a body formed around that. When the thing did poke out of the sheets, it was indeed a head, a woman's, and it stretched its way onto his pillow as its owner's naked body turned to him, feverishly warm.

Despite the woman-thing's beauty and the silky heat of her flesh, Dr. Hu felt no lust. But he was so paralyzed with fear that he did not fight her either when her impossibly long arms wound around him and crushed him close. Nor did he fight when she forced her stinking mouth against his in a kiss so pungent with decay and blood that he gagged and passed out. He was unconscious during what happened after that.

His blackout would have been a mercy except for one thing. He couldn't be roused from it when he was discovered later. In fact, he would have likely died without ever opening his eyes again if a physician hadn't been found with the good sense to treat Dr. Hu with anti-toxins and reversal agents. These were massaged down his gullet until he regained consciousness. It was after this that the dark began to make Dr. Hu tremble because he knew it was not empty.

TWICE GOODBYE

My son Ruchuan's wife, Lady Zhao, was a sensitive and enchanting young woman—one of those people who make you glad to be near them.

My wife Mistress Ma continually boasted to others about Lady Zhao's character and literary talent, as well as her needlework. She said that Lady Zhao talked with such charm that one could happily listen to her for a whole day. This was all true. We could not have hoped for a better daughter-in-law.

So when Lady Zhao died at only thirty-three years of age, I received a wound that still aches when I think of her. But my pain was nothing compared to what Ruchuan suffered. For many years, he mourned pitifully. Then, one year, he was ordered to temporarily move to Hubei to undertake some professional duties. While there, he entered a new relationship.

The first time I saw this woman upon Ruchuan's return, I was too shocked to speak. She looked just like Lady Zhao—the shape and length of her limbs, the flicker of her smile, how she moved—everything exactly the same. Ruchuan's co-workers were as stunned as me and drilled him about the woman's relatives and her birth details, suspecting that she was a reincarnation. But it turned out that the woman was born well before Lady Zhao died.

That two women should so resemble one another—down to marrying the same man—is a coincidence with a pulse and meaning. This is especially apparent when you consider their last point of similarity, which is this: only a few months after joining Ruchuan's household, this new woman also died very young and unexpectedly.

What can one make of these women's similarities? Why does Heaven copy some things and then introduce them into our lives repeatedly so that we continually meet the same person or experience the same disaster? Surely, there is some conclusion we're meant to come to.

THE SECRETS OF HANLIN ACADEMY

The center outside door leading to Hanlin Academy's main hall has been closed for so long that it's sealed shut with a crust of bird feces, rust, and autumnal debris. It will remain so into the future no matter what because if it is opened it is said that tragedy will fall upon the school's senior scholar.

Only once since I have been involved with Hanlin has this prohibition been tested. During a 1773 inspection, Prince Zhi Jun refused to use a lesser door and demanded that the large center door be unsealed. Soon thereafter, both Director Liu Wenzheng and his assistant died.

Then there's the sandy embankment built in front of the academy to protect its scholars and manuscripts from flood waters. Whoever built it planted strange smooth balls of hardened earth into the dirt as if they are occult artifacts of some kind—or maybe the balls formed themselves over time through a mysterious alchemical process—perhaps one related to thwarted flood waters or drownings.

Whatever the case, if the stone-like balls are broken—even by accident—harm too will befall the teachers in the academy. During the flood season that ran from the summer of 1763 into early 1764, the waters that hurled themselves against the embankment exposed a ball. A child then—perhaps innocently, perhaps not—flung the ball against the ground where it cracked open like an egg. As a result, my senior colleague Wu Yunyan abruptly died. Since then we've all been careful to shoo interlopers away from the embankment.

Opening certain things. Breaking certain things. These have both been proven to be great dangers at Hanlin, and the distinction between the teachers, the land, and the architecture to be far less than one would imagine.

As well, where one sits at Hanlin can also be fraught with peril. For example, if a faculty member's parents are still living, he should avoid the southwest corner of the Yuanxin Pavilion. The scholar Lu Ershan laughed when he was warned of this, thinking it nonsense. He sat in the pavilion without the least bit of concern. But when his father died not long afterwards, his cries were heartbreaking.

These are just three examples of the many taboos associated with the academy. Sometimes, I think that perhaps the taboos are the main point of Hanlin. Or, to put it another way, I sometimes think that the connections between things that initially seem to have no connection and the generation of rules based on the perception of these connections may be the deepest lesson taught. Indeed, similar institutions also have their lists of unexpected relationships and consequent taboos.

This is not to say, however, that I fully understand the principles involved. But it's not necessary that I do to know the connections are there.

MEAT VEGETABLES

When I was a boy, I went on a journey with our family servant Shi Xiang. While we were passing a village outside of Jingcheng, Shi Xiang pointed at some mounds in a field to the west. "Those are graves," he said. "Zhou graves. Long ago, one of their ancestors did a good deed that allowed their family line to persist three generations longer than it would have otherwise."

I asked Shi Xiang what kind of deed. He said that the ancestor did not eat a certain piece of meat. He then told me this story, which I now tell you:

As the Ming dynasty limped toward its conclusion and gave over to the Qing when the rule of the Manchus took effect, the Henan and Shandong provinces were decimated by drought. This drought withered everything to dust. As if the drought wasn't bad enough, a vast swarm of locusts next descended on the provinces.

Many villages died out due to starvation during this time. But a few cursed villages refused to accept extinction. They ate every animal or insect they could catch and scoured every twig or stem of anything edible that the drought and the locusts had not killed off. They even ate the bark and roots of the trees and bushes. When these things ran out, they moved onto each other.

Officials, who had previously spent hours debating the inherent goodness of human nature as put forth by Mencius, or who had enthused about the elegance of Confucian insights into the cultivation of human emotion, did not try to stop this. Instead, they joined in, unable to see the sense of rules of propriety that would see them dead. In this new social order, women and children from the poorest families were sold by relatives or taken by force. They were then bound and gagged and sold at street markets as "cairen"—meat vegetables—an ancient term that occurred in the historical records every couple of centuries in times of extreme hardship.

This was the state of affairs that met a travelling Zhou ancestor when he stopped to rest in the restaurant of a small Shandong village and ordered a pork dish. At first, the Zhou did not understand what was going on. Then he gave his order to the cook, and the man told him that the kitchen was out of meat.

"Give me a minute though," said the cook, "and I'll cut you some fresh meat myself." He yelled to the kitchen, "You're taking too long back there. We have hungry customers. Drag me some pigs out so I can chop off a hoof."

That was when the Zhou's world turned upside down. Because after the cook spoke, his assistant dragged out two young women from a back room, bound in ropes and gagged.

Before the Zhou knew what was happening, the cook grabbed one of the women, yanked her to a butchering area on the kitchen floor, and hacked off her arm with a cleaver. Gushing blood from the fresh stump, the woman flopped, writhed, and screamed against her gag. The other customers acted like nothing unusual was taking place, but the Zhou rushed forward.

Both women saw him. The one with the severed arm cried

for him to kill her. The other woman, trembling pitifully with a face drained of all human color, screamed against her gag too—but her plea was to be saved. Waving money, the Zhou yelled at the cook to stop cutting and sell him the women's freedom. After he saw how much money the Zhou was offering, the cook agreed.

The first woman had lost too much blood to have a chance at any kind of freedom but the kind she was begging for. So, the Zhou plunged a knife into her heart. As for the second woman, she remained by his side as they travelled away from the village. Later, she became his concubine and bore a son. It was this son that allowed the Zhou's line to continue three generations longer than it would have otherwise.

When the midwife wiped the afterbirth from their son, the Zhou and the woman saw that the boy was marked by a bright red line—a birthmark that looked like a cut. It ran from the edge of the baby's armpit and around his shoulder blade—so that it looked exactly like the wound the other woman had sustained. This shows how deeply we are marked not only by the previous lives we've lived but also by those we've encountered during those previous lives.

GUESTS FROM THE SKY

One day I received a letter that was written in my language but seemed to be written in a foreign one. The thoughts it expressed were odd, confused, and almost impossible to decipher. The letter's poor quality especially surprised me since my friend Shen Tiechan, who was highly intelligent and highly articulate, had written it. The letter was disturbing too because its tone was nostalgic and sorrowful, as if it was written as a final goodbye—this even though I knew that Tiechan had just begun a probationary post in Shanxi.

Not long after that, I received word that there would be no more letters. Tiechan was dead.

Life is filled with strange happenings that are hard to fit into our understanding of the world. Many we let pass in order to get on with our days. But this was not something I could let pass. I talked to Tiechan's neighbors and his friends, his family members and his enemies. Slowly, I pieced together what had pushed my friend to his tragic end. This is what I discovered.

That summer, Tiechan went hunting in the Xian mountains to restore his spirits after a long illness. The hunting trip proceeded unremarkably, with one notable exception: something followed him out of the woods.

This something took the form of two orbs in the sky, turning like windmills. No one else could see the orbs. Even Tiechan didn't see them in the way that one normally sees, which is to say that he could see them when he looked up even if his eyes were closed.

For several days, the orbs silently followed. Then suddenly, without warning, they broke open. From inside, two young women emerged, floated down, and delivered a message. Their mistress, a xian nü fairy, wished to meet Tiechan.

Knowing that he could not reject such an invitation, Tiechan agreed to meet the xian nü. Instantaneously, he was transported to a room. It was unlike any he had ever been in. Its dimensions were dizzying, and its massive jade walls were eccentrically decorated with odd, purple seashells.

The room's strangeness made Tiechan tremble, but its effect paled compared to the appearance of the xian nü mistress. She was beautiful, yes. But it was not a peaceful beauty. It was the kind of beauty that disturbs because it exceeds limits.

Her words exceeded limits as well. Shocking Tiechan, the xian nü asked him to become her lover.

When he refused, saying that he felt too overwhelmed by his strange surroundings to comply, the xian nü became angry and waved him away. The next thing he knew he was waking up on the road where the xian nü's servants first approached him.

Tiechan hoped that was the end of the matter. But several weeks later, the two rotating spheres reappeared. So did the two female servants. They did not ask him to come with them this time. They just took him. But they took him to a new place —smaller, homier, less exotic in furnishing and colors. It was much easier on his mind. When the xian nü asked Tiechan if he felt more comfortable now, he had no choice but to say yes.

This pleased her, and she declared he no longer had any reason to reject her. He agreed.

From then on, they met regularly—during both waking and dreaming states. "Tell no one," said the xian nü.

Tiechan promised not to and didn't for a long time—not even when he got sick.

But finally, the severity of his illness convinced him to visit a doctor who specialized in matters of both the spirit and the body. However, it was too late. Tiechan couldn't keep the red pills the doctor prescribed down, nor anything else. Everything was vomited back up. He died during one of these vomiting fits, and his last letter to me was written during these weeks of illness.

I will not forget Shen Tiechan. His qualities were simply too admirable. He wrote poetry that moved the heart and opened the mind. His calligraphy dazzled. He was witty, fun, and generous. However, no one is without secrets or vices, and I discovered one more fact about Tiechan during my investigation—one that might provide a clue to how all the weird events began.

In Tiechan's middle age, he had begun to mourn the passing of his youthful looks and obsess about death. This launched his pursuit of a formula for immortality. He acquired books of occult knowledge and sought out alchemists and sorcerers who were rumored to dabble in forbidden magic. It is no surprise then that something inexplicable occurred that ultimately led to his death. However, it is a shame. While spiritual entities of many kinds exist, they usually won't molest human beings unless a person goes out of their way to make themselves known.

Through my investigations, it seems to me that the manifestations of such entities, and the tragedies that follow in their wake, are prompted not by events in the external world but mysteriously conjured by events in one's internal world: the desires of the heart and what one dares imagine. If only Tiechan had guarded these inner borders better.[1]

---

1. This tale is nearly identical to modern accounts of alien abduction in several respects—from the appearance of a circular sky-craft inhabited by a mating-minded humanoid entity to episodes of teleportation and the infliction of the abductee with a strange illness (which in contemporary accounts would be interpreted as radiation sickness). Further similarities are discussed in the "Story Notes" section at the back of this book.

THE APPEARANCE OF THE SHA

Many Confucian scholars admit to believing that the soul survives the body's death.

What's more, like the Buddhists, many also believe that it is rare for the soul to return to earth once it ascends to the heaven realms—outside of reincarnation.

Nevertheless, accounts exist that testify the soul does sometimes return, newly strange, in the early days after a person's demise. It does so to take one last, lingering look at what it has left behind.

This is called "the return of sha."

These final visits are rare.

Still, they are reported with enough of the same details, and with enough regularity, that they seem the product of a natural law or process.

For example, if a child dies too young for its teeth to have grown in, its sha never returns to visit. And just as seers use books of charts and records to predict eclipses and other celestial phenomena, some specialize in predicting the exact time and day when the sha will make its goodbye visit, the direction from which it will come, and in which it will depart.

Does this sound ridiculous?

When I was young, I thought so. But I have learned over the years that my prejudices do not determine what events are permitted to occur.

Besides, I've had the opportunity to witness the appearance of the sha myself.

It happened like this. A village seer told my neighbor that her father's sha would return on such and such date, at such and such time. A believer in such things, she performed the proper protective rituals and then invited me over to wait with her family for the designated hour to arrive.

I expected nothing. Nevertheless, something came. The sha.

Striking terror in us, the transformed soul that had been my neighbor's father drifted through the rooms of her house, a blur resembling white smoke or translucent fabric.

Round and round it swirled—as if committing people and curios to memory or deciding how to dispose of each one—before it finally ducked into the chimney, swooped up its narrow throat, to then be glimpsed through the windows, disappearing in a southwestern direction.

The evidence of this event could not be doubted. Trusting in the seer's forecast, the family had even covered their floors in ashes. The prints of bare feet and hands were visible in these ashes throughout the house. I even got on my knees to make sure the prints were what they looked like. They were. Moreover, when questioned, the family members swore that they matched the size and shape of the deceased's extremities.

So my choice was this: to believe what I saw or to believe my theory of what it was possible for me to see.

* * *

When souls leave the body in the days after death, they can resemble many things.

Sometimes, people see mists or blurs. Other times, they see

something black and quick. A few people say the quick, black things look like enormous black birds folding themselves out of the body before taking flight. In the collection *Notes from the Hall of Records*, the Tang dynasty writer Zhang Du writes about several cases of the sha appearing in this bird-like form.

He records: "During the Wei dynasty, a man by the name of Zhang saw something that looked like a glossy black bird made of smoke—the size of a large child. He threw his hunting net on the creature. When he took the net away, there was nothing underneath. Afterwards, he went around his village telling everyone what happened. In this way, he discovered that about the time he'd tried to net the black thing, the sha of a recently deceased person had been forecast to return."

* * *

The thought that the spirit continues to exist after the body's death is not as comforting as one might first suppose.

Freed of the measurements of the human body, and the affections and limitations of the human mind, the things that the soul transforms into after death are radically different from who it once was—in the same manner that an animal freed of domestication might return to its wild nature. Consequently, the sha is dangerous.

A story in Xu Xuan's classical collection, *Historical Accounts of the Otherworldly*, illustrates this threat. It concerns one Peng Hu, a towering young man, with a reputation for being brash and skeptical. When his mother died, Peng Hu grieved deeply yet scoffed at those who warned him to take precautions in case her sha returned.

A seer said to Peng Hu: "Don't be foolish. I've done the calculations. Your mother's sha will soon visit. So you should prepare sacrifices for it, and have spells written and rituals performed to tame its savage heart. If you do not do these things, you shouldn't be here when it comes. It will not be your mother as you remember her."

While Peng Hu shrugged off the seer's advice, his family took the seer's words to heart and left to visit relatives. Thus, Peng Hu was home alone when his front door blasted open late one night.

Peng Hu was shaken to his core by the abrupt violation. But his reflexes were quick. In one breath, he leapt across the room to a large earthen pot and jumped inside, pulling the cover after him.

There he waited and hoped, even as he felt a shadow flicker across the pot. He knew the shadow belonged to what his mother had become in the same way children know when their parents are near. And there was something with her. He felt it in the room—moving around, a flood of darkness, an impossible thought. This something said to the sha of Peng Hu's mother: "Is somebody hiding in that pot?"

Peng Hu experienced then the longest pause that he'd ever known. It seemed to stretch on for weeks, for months, for years.

Finally, the sha of his mother said, "No. There is nothing in the pot. Let us leave. I have seen enough."

* * *

I have seen the sha, yes. And I know many others who have as well.

Just recently, the wife of our family servant, Song Yu, died. Shortly thereafter, whispers and shufflings came from her room—right before something that resembled her appeared to her children.

However, I also know that there are false stories told about the sha. Two of our family's other servants, for example, one Sun Wenju and one Song Wen, charge high fees to forecast the date of a sha's return. Certainly, there are those who have such skills. But these two scoundrels are not among them. For I have looked at their grimoires and found them to contain nothing other than generic charts of the seasons.

Likewise, the protective talismans and incantations sold to calm a sha or render it powerless are largely hokum. Their only power lies in depriving one of coin. This includes the currently popular "ghost-killing" rites sold to those too poor to move away from a haunted room.

So, as with everything, from the practice of medicine and scholarship to political service, the genuine and the fraudulent coexist and blur into each other.

What should one do then?

Simply this: be skeptical of what you hear. Yet also have enough humility to accept the world contains more than what you can see or imagine.

WINDOWS THAT WERE NOT WINDOWS

Qiu Wenda confided to me that when he was Head of the Office of Imperial Education, he set out for the Summer Palace one morning, around five, to get an early start on work. He thought hardly anyone else would be out at such an hour. But when he turned down a particular stretch of road, he saw a lamp-bearing crowd gathered around a willow tree. They were jostling against each other as if excited by something hidden in the tree's branches.

Coming closer, Qiu Wenda discovered that what commanded the crowd's attention wasn't in the branches but hanging from the tree. A city guard had hung himself, and a man from the crowd was frantically sawing through the rope around his neck trying to free him before he ceased kicking.

When the guard finally spilled to the ground, he was asked why he had hung himself. He rasped that he had not in fact done it—not on purpose. He had been on patrol when he saw a small house lit from inside—presumably by lamps. Its cozy look made him feel friendly toward it. As for the face of a pretty young woman staring out of the house's round window, that made him feel friendlier still.

Nevertheless, the guard was about to apologize for staring

when the young woman smiled. She then shocked him by gesturing for him to come inside by way of the window.

Embarrassed, the guard admitted to everyone that he tried to do just that. But as he ducked his head inside the house, someone roughly grabbed him by the neck and yanked hard. The next thing he knew, he was dangling from the tree.

The young woman in Qiu Wenda's account is a classic example of a substitute-seeking ghost. Such spirits are people who took their own lives while in distress. But their distress and their desire to die did not end with death as they hoped. Instead, these emotions keep them bound to earth. Consequently, they try to trick or persuade others to kill themselves, hoping their victim will take their place in the spirit world so that they can go on to reincarnate.

There are many records of similar incidents in the imperial library. However, the ghost who Qiu Wenda encountered was unique by virtue of her skill. It is hard even for a ghost to conjure the form of a house and even harder to disguise a noose as a window full of promise.

* * *

I personally witnessed a second example of the substitute ghost phenomenon when I was between thirteen and fourteen years old. The incident occurred at the shore of a lake, swollen from floodwater, that was south of The Shrine of the Literature God and northwest from The Altar of the Farm Gods.

I was passing by the lake when I suddenly saw a man, fully clothed, calmly march into the muddy water as if strolling down the street. He forged ahead with a blank look as I and several other people gaped disbelievingly. I didn't break from my paralysis until the water was lapping against his chest, but thankfully several other bystanders reached him in time to keep him from drowning.

It wasn't easy. The man struggled against the bystanders as if he wanted to drown and continued to thrash forward. But there were more of them, and they managed to wrestle him back to shore, where they forced him to the ground and held him there until his senses returned.

"Why did you do it?" someone asked.

"I was thirsty," the man told them.

The man's answer made no sense to anyone until he went on to explain that he hadn't seen the lake. Instead, he had seen a new teahouse near The Shrine of the Literature God. Enticed by the floral scent of tea, he had stepped into the teahouse's shadows to order a drink.

"So, I don't know how I wound up in the lake," the confused man said. "The teahouse was real. I'm sure of it. Its details weren't hazy at all—as you would expect them to be if it was a phantom house. It even had a sign hanging in front with the name of the teahouse handwritten in greenish-blue: A Face Toward the Sea."

Qiu Wenda and I experienced something very similar in nature. There is no doubt of that. However, ultimately my phantom was the more literary of the two. A Face Toward the Sea. That's a fine name, the product of someone with a poet's flair. Because of this obvious talent, I wonder sometimes about the man to whom the ghost at the lake belonged and about what unlucky event turned him from the noble pursuit of inventing literature to the dishonorable one of inventing murder.

THE DELICACY

Among the most sought-after dishes from those served at the famous Great Imperial Banquet are the "Eight Mountain Delicacies."

It is rare these days that anyone can obtain all eight delicacies. Some of the more exotic ingredients, such as leopard fetuses and rhinoceros' tails are almost impossible to track down because of the distances and danger involved. Camel humps of the kind served at the feast (which were from the one-hump camel and not from the more common two-humped version) are similarly scarce. Therefore, I'd only managed to try two dishes myself—bear paws and deer tails. Then, in the fortieth year of Emperor Qianlong's reign, General Min Shaoyi with great solemnity presented me with a box.

The box was made of red silk threaded with silver, the type of container usually reserved for expensive jewelry. But this one held no bracelet or necklace. Instead, inside I found the peeled face of an ape. The whole thing, from forehead to chin, and from ear to ear, had been scalped and cured. Everything was there: nose, eyebrows, eye holes, two drooping lips, an open hole of a mouth. It was like an actor's mask.

I asked my chef what could be done with such a thing. He

did not have a clue. So I kept the box with its face tucked inside until eventually passing it on to a friend. I later learned that the friend passed on the face too.

I have no idea where the face is now or what's being done with it. I have no idea how one cooks such a thing, nor how one feels after eating it.

THE SLOPE OF TIGERS

My student Ge Zhenghua shared with me an incident that occurred in his village of Jizhou. It is a unique incident that resists classification because it does not fit what is presently known about the behavior of spirits. It begins like this:

Several merchants were leading their mules through the mountains via a main road when they heard someone call out.

They turned to see a man in a black robe and a palm-leaf hat—the typical dress of a Taoist monk. The man was standing on a faint path that branched off the main road and led deep into the woods.

"Hey," the man said, approaching all of them, but speaking to one merchant in particular. "What's your name? Where are you from?"

After the merchant surrendered this information, the Taoist smiled. "Yes, indeed. It is you! But I see that you're still confused so let me explain. You have lived your whole life thinking you are like everyone else. This is not so. You are actually an immortal who was banished to the human realm as punishment for breaking a divine law. However, your sentence has now been completed. As your former mentor, I have been charged to lead you back to the heaven realms. Come. We must hurry."

The merchant did not hurry. As his companions gaped, he thought over what the Taoist had said. There was something off about his claim.

While not particularly deep or reflective, the merchant had a strong sense of who he was. He was stubborn, slow-thinking, unschooled, and much more interested in the next meal than beauty or poetry. In other words, there was nothing about him that indicated he was an immortal in disguise.

Therefore, the Taoist monk was mistaken. What's more, even if he had believed the monk's claim, he still wouldn't have gone with him. His elderly parents needed him far more than some far-off heaven realms.

After being refused by the one merchant, the monk turned his attention to the others. They had listened to the whole exchange with mute amazement, feeling as if they'd found themselves in the middle of the kind of situation you read about in the ancient tales. Now, they became even more amazed because the monk loudly proclaimed, "My friends, it's your lucky day! A balance must be maintained between the heavens and the earth. Your companion's decision means there's still an empty spot among the immortals that needs to be filled. One of you is destined to fill it. This may have been the real reason that I was directed to meet with your band today. Which of you is going to ascend with me?"

No one spoke up to accept the offer. Nor did they give in to the monk's follow-up attempts to persuade them. Eventually, the monk insulted the men for their stupidity and angrily slunk away.

That night, the merchants stopped at an inn and told everyone about the incident. Some guests thought they were idiots for blowing a chance to join the immortals. Others were convinced the Taoist monk was a demon impersonating a man.

All the guests, however, were deeply struck by the tale and curious about what was really going on.

The next day, one of the more curious guests, the nosy sort who likes getting involved in the business of others, retraced the merchants' steps and found the side path. He then circled the area, hunting for clues, and gradually moved up the mountain. Eventually, he reached a grisly slope.

The slope was black with rotting blood, covered in tiger hair, and decorated with the remains of people in various states of decay. These bodies had obviously been fed upon by tigers. Frightened, the guest fled the grim scene to make a report to the authorities.

How does one make sense of such a story?

Perhaps the Taoist monk was actually the ghost of one of the tigers' early victims whom the tigers had found some means of binding to their service after his death. Perhaps he was something else entirely. It is hard to understand such a person. But there is a lesson here that is clear. Good luck that seems to come out of nowhere makes the stupid joyous but the wise wary. The merchant who refused to accompany the monk considered himself a simple man. Certainly, he was the rough sort. However, because he knew his own nature, he was in fact very wise.

THE RINGING OF THE WESTERN BEAST

About 150 years ago, a Western nation gifted Emperor Kangxi with a mysterious creature called a "lion."

No one in the emperor's circle had ever seen such a creature before, and it immediately featured prominently in the poetry and paintings produced by members of the court.

It also featured in many tall tales. One story that made the rounds detailed how the lion escaped the palace one morning by snapping its chains in half and galloping so fast that it reached the far end of the Great Wall, 2800 li away, by noon—a feat well beyond even the fastest horse.

This is obviously a made-up tale. There are, however, true tales about the lion that are equally striking.

For instance, one summer the emperor visited the southern regions and displayed the lion as a show of power. While sailing back home on the Wei River, he temporarily docked in the village of my maternal grandmother, the Madame Cao. This gave her the opportunity to observe the lion firsthand from her family's home, the deck of which faced the riverside.

Madame Cao reported that the creature's torso was like a pony-sized yellow dog's, its tail tiger-like but longer, and that its face was disturbingly human—much rounder and flatter than that of other animals.

For the entirety of its stay, the lion was kept tethered to the main mast on the boat's deck, and that's where it was when a pig was dragged from the village to feed it.

According to my grandmother, the pig squealed and struggled all the way to the lion, but then—as soon as its hooves struck the ship's deck—all the fight left it, and it fell silent and limp.

By the time the lion's handlers used long poles to shove the pig toward the lion for it to sniff, the pig had died of fright.

One must marvel at such a creature and the effect that it has on other creatures. The great painter Alibai, whose skills were as great as those of the ancient artists, tried to capture this presence after encountering the lion in person. I eventually managed to buy his painting from my superior Bo Xizhai, whose grandfather received it as a gift from Alibai himself and passed it on to him.

Unlike his other work, Alibai did not sign this painting with his name, nor give it a title.

There is one final detail to add to this account. While the emperor's boat was leaving my grandmother's village, the lion let loose a pealing roar that echoed like hundreds of gongs. At the sound, the eleven horses in my grandmother's stable trembled and lay down in the shadows for hours afterward, not daring to make any noise.

This is why the lion is called a king.

THE POWERS OF EARLY CHILDHOOD

Yuan Shoutong and I knew each other for most of our lives. As children, we were close. As adults, we became in-laws upon our own children's marriage.

From the very beginning, Shoutong was a practical and hard-working sort, a trait that saw him promoted to one of the nine highest government positions in the country by the end of his career—Administrator General for the four provinces closest to the capital. Nearly everyone acknowledges that he was a clear-sighted official in this position. Even his enemies. What is less well-known, however, was that his clear-sightedness extended to his knowledge of a previous incarnation.

When we were young, Shoutong told me that up to the age of four years old he had very clear memories of his previous life—including specific events, friends, and family members. But around the age of five, these memories began to slip away—tree by lover by co-worker—until, in a few years, he only recalled that his former life's hometown was close to Changshan village and that he had been a good enough student to be accepted by the Imperial Academy.

When Shoutong shared his story with me, I did not find it difficult to believe. For I too had lost parts of myself as I grew older. As a very young child, I could see in the dark as if it were daylight. While others stumbled around in shadows, I could sit in a windowless and lampless house in the dead of night and have no trouble seeing anything. Everything looked as bright as it did in the day. By the age of seven though, this power weakened considerably. I still had keener vision than others, but objects began to dim and blur—as if I was losing the power to see their inner light.

By ten, I could see nothing well without a lamp once the sun went down.

Occasionally—just frequently enough to make me ache for my lost ability—the world will flash brightly like it used to, and the darkness will turn to day. Such a moment occurs once every year or so. But it always happens so quickly that my eyes don't even have time to settle on a single, illuminated object before the power is gone again.

Why did Shoutong lose his powers?

Why did I?

Why should so many young children know or perceive things that adults cannot? Is it that the more attached we are to this world, the less we can draw upon our inner clarity and see into other worlds?

CHECKPOINTS

In the early days of my assignment in Urumqi, one afternoon an army clerk came to me with a brush and ink, along with a pile of papers that he requested I sign.

"What are these papers?" I asked.

"Passports," he replied. "You see, most of the soldiers here are from far away. So, if they die, we have to ship their bodies back home for burial and funeral rites. Living people must pass through many border checkpoints when travelling. What you may not know though is that there are also spiritual checkpoints along the way for the souls of the dead. Thus, the dead must too be accompanied by the appropriate papers. If they don't have them, their spirits are blocked at invisible checkpoints set up to prevent souls from getting lost or causing trouble. Surely, where you come from you have documents like these."

I said that we did not and could barely contain my laughter when the clerk showed me a passport template and explained the details that must be present on every document.

Their wax seal had to be black. So too the ink. Even more importantly, he said, was the following directive, written on each one:

> To All Spirit Guards:
>
> On this day of _____ in _____, Master/Mistress _____, age _____, died in _____ from _____. Do not hinder the transport of this body to the deceased's hometown, or the spirit that hovers near it still. Furthermore, see to it that all possible aid is given the speedy arrival of this traveler.
>
> Signed _____, Presiding Official

Upon reading this directive and hearing the details about the ink and seal, it seemed immediately obvious to me that the spirit passports were one of those ploys that officials invent to collect envelopes of money and that only the superstitiously gullible believe. So after I dismissed the clerk, I sought out the general and strongly advised that he forbid the practice. Gullibility is not a trait that one wishes to encourage in one's forces.

I hoped that was the end of the subject since I had more pressing matters to attend to. But it wasn't.

A few days later, the clerk informed me with an air of urgency that reports were coming in that restless spirits were gathering near the western border of Urumqi: rustling through the grasses and the trees, wailing and frightening the horses and the pigs. People were upset not just at the spirits but at me too—since my refusal to give them documents had caused the spirits to be turned away at border checkpoints.

This time I was not amused by the subject of the passports, and I yelled at the clerk to bother me no more with ridiculous tales.

That particular clerk did not. However, to my surprise, in the following days several other people came to me. Reports were coming from all over the city now—not just from the border—about spirits running amok.

I racked my brains trying to figure out why all of Urumqi was succumbing to a plague of lie-telling. It made no sense.

And then I heard it myself late one evening: the hollow crying of ghosts. The noise seemed to come from the other side of the wall around my estate.

Even then, I resisted believing. I admitted that the sounds were real, yes. But I speculated that they weren't coming from ghosts but living colleagues who were trying to trick me. Probably, I surmised, even the original concept of the ghost passports was part of a larger and elaborate practical joke.

But that theory was short-lived because the ghostly cries were suddenly just outside my window.

I looked out.

There was no human source attached to the wailing, disguised or otherwise. Just empty air over a patch of ground —lit up by moonlight as bright as a lightning flash.

Deeply disturbed, the next morning I sought out my friend Guan Cheng, a higher-up in the Department for Supervising the Conduct of Government Officials.

"Here's my advice," he said. "It was sensible of you to initially forbid passports because they do seem absurd. But since then, the crying and complaints of stranded spirits have been heard by many witnesses, including yourself. Therefore, even if the spirit passports were originally a hoax cooked up by greedy officials, the spirits have become convinced that they need them. Why not have a few drawn up and see if it makes a difference?"

I did as Guan Cheng proposed. I even had passports made for bodies that had previously been shipped out without them. The following night was peaceful.

* * *

Paper creates a great many things. Marriages, official positions, educational degrees, residency. All of these states of being require documents and indeed are not considered real or valid without them. In fact, civilizations owe their existence not just to physical things but to things created by the drawing up of papers. Because the people believe it so, these things are as real as physical artifacts. It is interesting that both spirits and documents direct the physical realm without themselves being physical.

One further incident I witnessed makes this connection evident as well. The eyes of my assistant, Song Jilu, suddenly rolled up one day while we were working, and he fainted. When he came to, he told me that he had fainted because he saw his mother's spirit float into the room and gesture toward him. A few minutes later, a runner came in with a document that informed Song Jilu that his mother had died on her way to see him.

The rules that govern our world include many that are known but many more that are unknown or only half-understood. While people are eager to invent explanations for why the world is the way it is, at best their explanations can only account for the visible, physical world for that is the part of the world sensible to human eyes.

Years later, I wrote the following poem on this subject:

> *The seeded grass rustles beneath*
> *the rustling clouds in the sky.*
> *Who sets the boundaries*
> *between thoughts and things,*
> *between mountains and borders?*
> *Ghosts and people travel where*
> *thoughts and papers allow.*
> *This is a subject about which*
> *a chapter should be added*
> *to Han Yu's On the Ways of Spirits.*

THE FOREST THAT WAS A NEST

In the summer of 1768, a large group of criminals in a village near Urumqi were collectively sentenced to exile.

Their sentencing date coincided with the start of the annual Mid-Autumn Festival. So that night, the soldiers assigned to watch them hosted a going-away party in a nearby meadow.

Everything was going well, and the prisoners seemed happy with their captors' gesture.

But a few of the rowdier soldiers got drunk and started roughly flirting with the prisoner's wives and daughters—going so far as to command them to sing and dance like good-time women.

At this point, the atmosphere shifted.

A prisoner furiously said he would allow no one to dishonor his family in such a manner.

A second and third added their voices to this angry declaration. When the offending soldiers refused to admit wrong, the prisoners turned violent and bludgeoned them to death.

You would have thought the prisoners would then have promptly escaped the village with their families to start anew. But no. Their hearts were too poisoned with rage. Instead, they looted the village's armory and marched through the streets—

strangling, stabbing, hacking, shooting—until they had killed every soldier or official that they could lay hands on. Over the ensuing days, they subsequently used their newfound power to terrorize the village, only deciding to flee when they heard rumors that the emperor's forces were fast approaching. By that time, it was too late.

A small but well-trained, ferocious, and smart military force had already strategically stationed itself over a tight passage that threaded through a series of steep hills. Upon the flapping of a red flag held by their commander, these soldiers shot the legs out from under the prisoners' mounts—causing them to be hurled into the dirt and gravel from which they were easily plucked.

Not too long after that, the rebels were marched into a dense forest west of Urumqi and executed.

This series of events is appalling and gruesome, to be sure. But what happened next proved even more disturbing.

The forest where the executions took place was odd, so odd that it was locally known as "the nest," a name bestowed because inside its shade one always felt watched by something terrible just out of sight. This something was said to somehow encourage bad things to happen within its boundaries.

Sure enough, almost immediately after the rebels' execution, black clouds appeared. Low to the ground, they did not move like clouds. They moved like living things, like hunting things. Word quickly spread that if you were unlucky enough not to be clear of the forest by evening, these cursed clouds would swallow you whole.

Most who disappeared in this way were never found. But a few survived their envelopment. They said that the insides of the clouds were like the mind of a mad man, an endless, ethereal land—thick and reeking with vapors that caused panic, disorientation, and lost chunks of time.

I was the supervisory official for a large region that

included the nest during the period these events unfolded. Therefore, I launched an investigation into the sentient fogs. After interviewing survivors and witnesses, and scanning historical accounts for parallels, I eventually connected their appearance to the execution of the Mid-Autumn Festival rebels. I concluded that the clouds were made not of water vapor but of yin energy—the dark type that manifests as bodily illness or evil intentions.

Usually, upon the body's death, its yin spiritual components disintegrate into the earth. This time they had not done so. Instead, they seeped into the forest, darkly infecting it: similar to how the venom of certain toads, snakes, or spiders can infect the vegetation they touch.

The nature of the problem identified, I mulled potential solutions. I finally decided that since dark yin energy disperses when confronted by yang energy, I would recruit the help of soldiers known for their bright courage—indications of strong yang energy. I instructed them to hide in the forest on a night when the moon was especially well-lit to await the clouds' appearance. Once they sighted the mists, they were to fire their guns since the loud explosions would be strongly yang in nature as well. This was a universal trait of explosions of all kinds, whether from fireworks or guns. It made them deeply attractive, as well as useful for driving away sadness, wetness, and mental sluggishness. My hope was the surplus of this yang energy would counteract the excessive yin energy of the mists, just as the heating light of the sun clears morning fog.

The soldiers did as ordered. As I suspected, their energy, when combined with that of their guns and the shining moon, caused the clouds to cough apart with small, bright detonations and disperse.

After that, the clouds were never seen again.

Nor was any other sign of the rebels.

A DOG IN EXILE

My former student Master Zhai gave me a puppy as black as soot shortly before the emperor exiled me to a remote military garrison in Urumqi. I named him FourthSon.

FourthSon and I quickly became attached to one another, and he was ever at my side. He was with me when we entered the red gates of Urumqi. He accompanied me on my rounds to army encampments and from this village to that. And after I received the emperor's pardon, he trotted beside me when we passed back through the red gates three years later to return to Peking.

Initially, I flirted with the idea of leaving FourthSon in Urumqi.

The four-month journey back would be hard and dangerous. Three thousand miles of deserts, mountains, bandits, and tigers. But FourthSon stubbornly refused to be chased away and appointed himself as a guard over my possessions.

If someone drew near my bundles when I wasn't around, he would go wild, barking alarm and growling and flashing his teeth.

Although our journey began during summer, when we reached the Bizhan mountain range it was as icy as winter because of the elevation. One night, we came to a place so steep and narrow that we could only drag one cart up at a time, and only then by having it pulled by all the horses simultaneously.

We hoisted two carts up this way. But by then it had grown too dark to continue, and two other carts had to be left behind until morning. FourthSon occupied a shelf of rock between the carts for the whole night—glancing at one and then the other, back and forth.

I checked on him several times. Each time, the lean of his shivering body showed that he longed to run to me. Yet, his desire to protect what was mine was even stronger.

After the trip was over, and we were in our new home in the capital, I wrote two poems in FourthSon's honor:

1.

In Urumqi, you carried letters—an easy task—
but traded this for vicious days and tiring wind.
While the rest of us slept in the dark,
you watched over the carts.

2.

Ice and stone for months
wore your body down like a tooth:
Your nails torn, your coat patchy.
My titles vanished, but you remained.

A little over a year from the day we returned to the capital, late one night FourthSon ate a piece of poisoned meat in the courtyard and died.

A few members of the household speculated that a would-be thief must have thrown the meat over the gate to clear the way for a robbery later that week. But one of the servants later told me privately that she suspected another servant as the culprit.

"Some were jealous of the love you showed FourthSon and your long history," she said. "They resented FourthSon too for always alerting you if someone tried to slip out at night."

After FourthSon's body was washed and prepared for burial, I ordered a plaque for his grave. It read: "Here Waits FourthSon, Loyal Still." I also spoke to a craftsperson about carving figures of the four servants who accompanied us on our journey from Urumqi, with their names engraved on their chests. I thought I could place them on FourthSon's grave so that they seemed to be bowing to him to show the esteem in which he was held. However, a friend persuaded me that this was a bad idea because FourthSon would not want anyone other than me standing so near. Therefore, I had a plaque hung over the servant's hall.

It read: "A Dog Too Can Be a Master."

There is one more detail I should add to this account. On the night before FourthSon was given to me, I had a dream. In it, my late servant Song Yu bowed and said, "I humbly offer my services to my master who has been conscripted into the army three thousand miles away."

Therefore, when I received FourthSon, I understood exactly who he was.

As a man, Song Yu was so criminal and treacherous that I was relieved to be rid of him when he died. That he should choose to become such a loyal dog in his next incarnation speaks to the value of the perspective one gains after death, as well as to a genuine talent for remorse. It is hard to know what things will become.

THE HOUSE ON ZHUCHAO STREET

After three years of exile and military service in Urumqi, I finally came back to the capital in the summer of 1771. I settled down in a rented house on Zhuchao Street. Directly next door to me was a similar home occupied by Chief Magistrate Long Chengzu.

While the house initially seemed like a good one, it soon turned out to have serious problems.

The door curtain of one of the rear rooms on the house's southern side acted as if alive. Although there was no source of open air near it, and although the door curtains of adjacent rooms were perfectly still, this room's curtain would flap and flutter and lift several handspans from the floor—as if blown about by wind.

Neither I nor the rest of my family could think of any process that could account for this.

If that was the only indication that something was amiss, perhaps we could have grown used to it. But of the oddities associated with the house, the restless curtain was the least disturbing.

Far more unsettling was how my children burst into tears when entering that room and only that room. Sobbing, they would point at the empty air and claim to see a fat monk with dead eyes smiling at them from the bed and signaling them to come near.

There was one other thing too. Frequently at night, the keening of a woman would be heard. To us, the sound seemed to come from Magistrate Long's. But he swore that he too heard the sound—except it came from our house.

No matter how much I thought on these matters or dug around, I could not understand how these phenomena were connected to one another. Nor could I account for any of them individually. However, one does not need to fully understand the nature or history of something to know that it is dangerous. Therefore, we moved from that house to the Double Tree residence.

Magistrate Long later confided to me that his home had also been plagued by strange occurrences, causing him to also move. As for those tenants who rented our homes, they subsequently suffered a series of misfortunes, too tragic, strange, or coincidental to think natural. Bai Huanjiu, for example, the Head of the Department of Penalties and Justice, suddenly collapsed dead one day in Magistrate Long's house—although he was neither elderly nor ill.

Some people are skeptical that there is such a thing as a cursed house or even entire areas that are "off." However, my former teacher Chen Baiya made a good case when he argued the following:

"Those who live on cursed property are sooner or later visited by tragedies. This is no more surprising than saying that exposure to cold or poisonous air will eventually cause one to get sick. Indeed, the principles of the supernatural world are similar to those of the natural one. To give another example, curses and unlucky places are more powerful than blessings and lucky places. Similarly, a dose of healing medicine doesn't heal one immediately, but a dose of a toxic medicine can immediately result in violent diarrhea."

My teacher Chen Baiya's take on the subject is wise, and ample reason to stay far from cursed spaces. Although some people take unnecessary risks because they reason that everything is predetermined by fate, this is a poor understanding of reality. We too are part of the mechanism of fate. As Mencius taught: One who truly understands destiny will refuse to rest under a wall likely to collapse.

REAL LIFE IN THE CAPITAL

1.

The citizens of the capital city have perfected the art of deception.

Take the sixteen ink slabs that I once bought at what I thought was a bargain price. The craftsman who sold them assured me that they were made by the illustrious Ming dynasty manufacturer, Luo Xiaohua. Certainly, they looked the part. Arranged in a lacquer box that appeared faded with age, they gave the impression of being valuable.

When I returned home, I ground a cake against my inkstone, eager to see the stately blackness of the ink. But there was no ink. The ink slabs were just clay bars painted black. The thin coating of white on them, which I had taken to be a mark of age, was a covering of mold due to their long storage in a dark and damp place.

Another time, I visited the capital to take the provincial level exam and bought some candles. When I tried to light them, they refused flame. Upon examination, they turned out to be mud coated with mutton tallow to look like a candle.

My cousin was similarly victimized.

One night, while looking for something to eat, he bought a roast duck at a night market. At home, he cut the "duck" open to discover that someone had taken the skeleton from an already-eaten duck, stuffed it with filth, pasted it over with paper painted to look like roasted skin, and then smeared the whole thing in oil. Only the orange feet and neck were real.

Another time, my servant Zhao Ping paid out the substantial sum of 2000 wen for what he thought was a superior pair of leather boots. Soon thereafter, he wore them to town—eager to show them off—and got caught in a downpour. He returned home with bare, muddy feet. The boots were less than they seemed. The upper was oiled paper, creased and wrinkled to look like leather, while the sole was made from trash cotton, temporarily glued together inside a cloth shell.

2.

Such frauds are startling, but minor compared to others that have been perpetrated in the capital.

For example, I know a royal official who moved to the capital to take up a new position and became infatuated with a young woman who lived nearby with her mother. He soon learned that this young woman was married and only staying with her mother while her husband was on assignment outside the capital. So, he left her alone.

Several weeks later, the woman's house abruptly filled with loud sobbing, and its front gates were draped with white funeral paper.

It turned out that a messenger had come with the news that the young woman's husband had died. After that, a stream of people visited the house to pay their respects and participate in memorial ceremonies, the official among them. A wooden funeral altar, inscribed with the late husband's name, was set up inside. It was covered with offerings of food, drink, and burning incense while Buddhist monks knelt around it and chanted sutras to ease the transition of the husband's soul to the spiritual plane.

Not long after the conclusion of the funeral rites, the young woman was seen all around town, trying to sell clothing and furniture in order to feed herself and her mother. Recognizing an opportunity for mutual benefit, the official proposed himself as a marriage match. After the wedding, he moved in with the woman and treated her mother like his own. They seemed a settled family, but a few months later the "dead" husband suddenly appeared at the door, not so dead after all.

Discovering the official, the husband screamed wildly and swore he would take him to court and see him destroyed. But the young woman threw herself to her knees and begged her first husband to have mercy. He finally agreed. On one condition. The official had to leave his belongings behind and pay a hefty sum.

Half a year later, the official was in court on a work-related errand when he learned that his former "wife" and her alleged real husband had been arrested for adultery. Upon questioning the magistrate, he learned too that the man to whom he had paid compensation wasn't the woman's real husband but her lover. This is not to say that there was not a real husband. There was in fact one—a man who had been away on a long military expedition far from the capital. It was his unexpected early return that had revealed the deception.

Since what he had felt for the young woman seemed so real, this was all very confusing to the official.

3.

Another case I came across involves a compound in the Western District.

It was a lavish compound, made up of several houses.

Between them, the houses collectively contained almost fifty furnished rooms. The compound's monthly cost was consequently steep—more than twenty taels of silver. Nevertheless, a stranger approached the landlord eager to rent the estate. He even agreed to sign a contract to lease it for over half a year and pay his rent early. More than happy with this arrangement, the landlord left the man alone.

A little over six months into the tenant's stay though, he suddenly quit appearing in public, and the houses in the compound went dark. Worried that something bad had happened, the landlord investigated and discovered that the houses in the middle of the compound, which were hidden by the front and rear homes, had been secretly dismantled and reduced to rubble.

Over the next few days, it came to light that tenant had diligently taken the middle houses apart, door by window, pillar by post, and chair by table, and had sold it all off outside the back of the compound, near where he had opened a shop facing an entirely different street.

4.

In all these cases, greed for a bargain or an advantage led to a victim's deception. Therefore, we all can be seen as accomplices in our downfall. No one does anything alone—and this is as true for downfalls as it is for triumphs. But if this is so, is there a way to escape deception and delusion? A way to prevent one's life from being filled with clever frauds that one takes as reality?

My friend Qian Wenmin probably has the most sensible advice I've heard on this issue: "One should be wary when dealing with residents of the capital. All the bargains in a place inhabited by swindlers are naturally traps."

A GOD OF OUR OWN

One wonders about the gradual disappearance of gods. In the old days, households made sacrifices to five minor gods that guarded the home:

God of the gate
God of water springs and wells
God of the toilet
God of the estate
God of the stove

Today though, most households recognize only one god—the god of the stove.

There are many gods whose domains are larger than the stove god's. Some like the fire god see to the whole world. Others like the water and land gods are assigned to an entire village or city and are sacrificed to at a communal shrine.

If the stove god was of the sort assigned to an entire city or village, there would be such a communal shrine for him, but there is not. Sacrifices to him are made at one's home and one's home alone. This means that stove gods are likely devoted to just one household. Since this makes them very intimate gods, we naturally desire to understand them better. After all, the stove god is the only deity who is ours and ours alone.

When you think about the number of kitchens, the number of these gods must be as great as the grains of the sand in the Ganges. Recruiting and supervising this vast number of gods thus must be an unfathomably arduous task—so much so that one is moved to wonder what superior god appoints them and where this god finds candidates for the position.

Further, how do these candidates qualify?

And what do stove gods do if their families move away or die?

* * *

The work of stove gods is largely hidden, their habits mysterious. Still, they make themselves known sometimes.

When I was a child, my maternal grandfather had a cook who sometimes foolishly and lazily tossed garbage into the fire compartment of the stove—endangering the family to save a little effort.

One night, she dreamed a man in black smacked her face while telling her to never burn trash in the stove again.

When she woke up, her cheeks were covered by red boils. These swelled to the size of teacups, and their roots opened into the inside of her mouth so that pus flowed into her throat whenever she breathed, causing her to choke and vomit so harshly that she felt that she was going to die.

In desperation, she prayed to the stove god. She promised to show gratitude and respect from then on. After that, she was suddenly cured.

This seems to indicate that the stove god is real and not simply a superstition. But if that's true, one can't help but ask why a god would attend to our kitchens and, again, how it's possible to daily supervise this enormous number of minor deities.

Ultimately, I'm attracted to the view offered by one scholar regarding kitchen gods.

He said that if you set up a shrine, you will inevitably attract a god. Daily prayer and sacrifices will keep the god with you. Conversely, if you stop these actions, your god will leave.

Therefore, there's no need for a head spirit to recruit or hand out assignments. The joining of gods to people is simpler than that. It is one of the simplest things.

There seems to be one central principle that underlies all reality, but the best way to understand it is through its many manifestations.

—Cheng Yi (1033–1107)

RED IN DARKNESS

Some trees are not trees.
This is clearly indicated by an incident that occurred at a school in Tingzhou, Fujian.

A row of trees lay in front of the examination hall. The two tallest were ancient cedars that dated back to the Tang dynasty. Their broad and thick branches stretched so far out over the hall that they could be seen from every window.

I was serving as the school's superintendent at the time of the incident. Right after I was hired, I was told about the old cedars.

Being of very advanced age, they were said to have developed souls. One of the administrative staff even suggested that I bow to them, as if they were important officials, so as not to cause any offense.

However, I didn't do this. I wasn't sure the trees were anything more than trees. And even if they did harbor souls, I didn't feel like they would care if I bowed or not—especially since there was no established protocol when it came to such situations. It seemed to me that it was best to just let them be.

One night though I was walking across the examination hall deck in the moonlight when I felt something watching me.

I looked up to see two human figures dressed in red robes floating in the mist swirling around the treetops. Both solemnly bowed and then started to fade away. I immediately shouted for my assistant to hurry and bear witness to the phantoms. He made it out just in time to glimpse the figures before they vanished completely.

The next day, I made the bow that I had neglected when I first arrived. To make up for my earlier neglect, I also had the following poem written on the examination hall gate:

> *Certain things appear only when the darkness is deep.*
> *Some of these things nod respectfully.*
> *Some of these things wear red.*
> *In this, am I not speaking of you?*

THE SHADOW OF THE OLD CITY

The place where my family lives is called Jingcheng. It is an old city that has existed ever since the Han dynasty. It is so old that it really is several cities. Remnants of built-over neighborhoods and temples lie here and there: a half-standing wall, an alley that trails off.

The physical traces are disconcerting, like suddenly glimpsing a young person in an old person's face. But even more disconcerting are the spiritual remnants of the city's previous incarnations. Sometimes at dawn, when looking through the clearing mists, I am startled to see the old city walls, suddenly risen again along with their statues and watchtowers, before it all abruptly dissolves into empty air before my very eyes.

I am far from the only one to have witnessed such specters. Sightings of this nature are recorded in many historical archives. However, none of the commentators have a trustworthy explanation for how such a thing can be.

I myself think that the phenomenon likely has to do with the spiritual essence of a place remaining behind even while its material form crumbles.

While such an essence might originate in the mind of an architect and subsequently find form through his hands and the mud—it is not a static creation but a living thing. It thickens and develops in buildings and walls just as the hun and po souls inside a human being gather strength and complexity as the human grows.

It is no surprise then that a good-sized town like Jingcheng, one whose beginnings stretch far back, haunts itself. A thousand years of ripening stones cannot help but leave a shadow when they fall or to develop some rudimentary form of will or mind.

Some people might object to my comparison of cities and humans—of building essence and human soul. My only reply is that the comparison is even more fitting than I have so far explained.

People begin simple—hungry children with elementary personalities. But as they mature, they ingest a steady diet of new experiences and acquired skills and become sophisticated and clever. Their ideas magnify and gain floors. Their creative powers manifest the Tao. Consequently, their hun and po flourish.

Cities too begin simple.

A street. A single store.

But then their ideas also become more elaborate over time, and their alleyways fill with memories and secrets. As they expand block by block, and add windows and doors and festivals and traditions, as they are destroyed and rebuilt, forgotten and reinvented, they burn into the deepest layers of reality.

Thus, just as it takes far more than a day for a city to mature, it takes far more than a day for its spiritual essence to disperse—even if its bones are gone. The phantom cities glimpsed by myself and others, which manage to temporarily conjure themselves out of thin air, are most likely the dense essence of old sites. They are the structural counterpart to the ghostly essence that sometimes lingers after the death of a body and that can, in the right circumstances, retain enough vitality to manifest an approximation of the human form. Just as only some ghosts are visible, and then only visible to some people, so it is with phantom cities.

THE FIELDS IN WHICH WE WANDER

Dreams are mysterious, as they are vehicles for both the base fantasies of the animal po soul and the divine insights of the spiritual hun soul. Mysterious too is the nature of the relationship between dreams and the waking world.

Some people even claim to visit each other in dreams. My older brother Qinghu found this notion ridiculous when he was alive. He argued that one's dreams concern only oneself—just as one's thoughts are available only to oneself. He even wrote a poem that mocks the legend that the King of Chu would romantically tryst with the goddess of Mount Wu in his dreams.

I am not aware of it when you dream of me.
Nor when I dream of you is this something you can see.
Thus the King of Chu met only his own inventions in his dreams.
Besides, goddesses have better things to do than kings.

While it was admirable of Qinghu to guard the goddess's reputation, several people I know believably swear that they have in fact witnessed someone else's dream.

For example, my servant Li Xing says that he was out

walking late one night when he saw his neighbor's young wife wandering in the moonlight through a date grove.

At first, he did not think this unusual. Villagers often made a quick sweep of their garden plots when it grew dark in order to deter thieves. He figured that's what the young woman was doing and that her husband and parents-in-law would join her momentarily. Not wanting to seem like he was flirting, Xing continued his walk without calling out.

However, a little while later he again saw the woman— now heading far west into a remote field of sorghum reeds. This *was* unusual behavior since she was alone. Suspicious and curious, Li Xing followed her.

Abruptly, the young woman halted at a stream. She stood in front of the trickling water for several minutes, as if stopped at a rock wall. Then, instead of attempting to cross, she turned left and followed the stream until in the middle of a marsh. The terrain here was so difficult that she changed course again, eventually wading into a bean field, where she wandered aimlessly in a nonsensical zig-zag, occasionally tripping over a plant.

Frightened that she would break a limb if she kept falling, Li Xing revealed himself.

"Are you all right?" he said. "It's Li Xing. I saw you and was worried. This patch of land is riddled with sinkholes and quicksand."

At Li Xing's voice, the woman turned, revealing a blank, wide-staring face. But she didn't explain why she was out in the dead of night. Nor did she move closer to Li Xing. Instead, she said in an unshelled tone, "I'm lost. Do you know where my home is?" and then promptly vanished in front of his eyes.

Terrified, Li Xing dashed away. He would have kept running until he reached his front door except for one thing. When he arrived back in the village and passed the young woman's house, he saw her sitting outside with her mother, making yarn.

Astonished, Li Xing asked the woman how long she'd been sitting there and learned that she and her mother had been there most of the day. The young woman then related some further details that were as shocking as her double's disappearance in the field.

She said that earlier she was so exhausted that she fell asleep. Almost immediately, she began dreaming that she was walking through the cultivated land outside the village.

Everything felt very strange and hollow in this dream, and she wanted nothing more than to get back home. But she had no idea what direction to go in. Not knowing what else to do, she began to wander around, hoping to stumble onto a familiar path.

She crossed a sorghum field, followed a stream, got lost in a marsh, and lost in a bean field too. She was starting to panic when she heard a voice. It was Li Xing, or at least a dream version of him—standing close to her. It was the sound of his voice in her dream that woke her.

How is it that the young woman's dream and Li Xing's experience in the waking world could coincide? There is a clue in what the young woman told Li Xing about her extreme tiredness.

Sleeps that occur from extreme physical exhaustion are deeper than other sorts. They can be so deep that they are like a coma. And just as in the case of comas, the conscious mind sometimes unclenches its grip on the higher hun soul, freeing it to travel. It should be noted that the hun's departure differs from those cases in which the lower po soul leaves the body. In the latter case, one encounters an apparition that is little more than a cloud of vestigial animal energies, a collective devoid of higher, human faculties. The spirit that Li Xing encountered by contrast was a wandering hun soul, and thus it was capable of speech and thought.

* * *

The intermingling of the woman's dream and Li Xing's reality suggests that some of the people and places we come across while awake may be part of someone's dream.

There are indeed other accounts of such experiences in the imperial archives. One case is described in Feng Menglong's *Tales to Awaken the World*. This account details how a man named Dugu Xiashu encountered a phantom double of his wife while journeying far from his village. Afraid that his wife was dead and that he had seen her ghost, the man undertook the long trip home. There, he discovered that his wife was very much alive. However, she told him that she had dreamed of him and provided details that exactly matched his encounter with her double.

RULAI'S GREAT REVERSAL

When he was a child, my nephew Rulai was a model child: elegant in looks, compassionate, sincere, joyful, startlingly brilliant, and devoted to his studies. Of my many nephews and nieces, he was my favorite, and I loved him dearly.

So when Rulai married Lady Wang, I thought the union would be happy. Maybe it was at first. But then Lady Wang gave birth to their son Shuyan, and Rulai lost his mind.

After Shuyan's delivery, Rulai behavior changed dramatically—shifting toward bouts of vacancy and odd and sometimes filthy habits. It was as if Shuyan's birth had somehow drained him of qi and intelligence, and his son's waxing was his waning.

Henceforth, Rulai had to be reminded to shave the stubble off his tonsured head and to clean his face. In the summers, he'd wear thick, lined winter clothing without sweating. In the winters, no matter how cold, he would shrug into a flimsy, summer shirt and nothing else, and stagger around the fields and alleys without shivering.

His indifference to his own body was so complete that it didn't even bother to get sick anymore.

This is not to say Rulai was completely senseless. He still responded to directions. If informed it was breakfast time, he would sit and eat slack-jawed until told to stop. He had secret pleasures as well.

One was visiting the day market. He'd shove money, oblivious to the exact amount, at vendors and snatch an armful of sweet buns. Hunched over in the street, he would gobble one while chucking the rest to the children who learned to follow him.

Sometimes, he wouldn't even finish the pastry he was eating but would toss its remains in the street like a gnawed bone.

My family managed to adjust to this odd behavior, but when Rulai began to disappear for days at a time, it was too much. Unlike his other behavior, this new activity inevitably sent us into a panic, worried that he had been murdered or had fallen into a ravine.

But just as we would begin to fear the worst, he'd suddenly return home and act as if he'd not been gone at all.

One morning, two days into one such disappearance, while we were in the midst of rushing in and out of the house to share news and clues of our searches for Rulai, a neighbor dashed over to tell us that something man-shaped had been glimpsed haunting the willow woods. Sure that it was Rulai, we hurried to the forest.

We didn't have to look hard. We saw him from the road—sitting beneath a willow tree. We called out. When he didn't respond, we weren't surprised—not at first—because that was how Rulai was.

Then we drew closer. While the figure was indeed Rulai, he was very much dead.

It is hard to connect the boy I loved to the dead man I found beneath a willow tree. I think about Rulai often, trying to solve the puzzle of him.

Why did he have to die beneath the tree like that?

What was going on in his mind in his last moments? Did he feel lost?

Or had his diligent studies secretly led to enlightenment some time back, an enlightenment that his son's birth gave him permission to pursue and that we mistook for madness?

And was there a date set for his death—one that was fated to be honored regardless of his mental state, regardless of whether he was happy or sad, freed or enslaved, ready or not?

There is one final detail that I have not shared.

While Rulai was afflicted, I went to live in Fujian for a long stretch of time to serve in a post there. When I went back home to visit, Rulai rushed up to me and bowed in a ritualistic manner like one would bow to an official. Upon standing again, he said in an intimate and loving way: "Dear uncle, it's hard, isn't it? Sometimes, it feels like too much."

"What can I do?" I replied, surprised at his directness. "This is what life is, isn't it?"

Rulai seemed to drift away then, to disappear into one of his vacancies, but suddenly the sharpness returned to his eyes. "Do you truly think you're meant to suffer like this, uncle?"

Rulai walked away before I could think of an answer to give him. That was the last lucid thing he ever said.

When I think back now, Rulai seemed like he was trying to communicate something very important that day, something too large and profound for me to comprehend at the time. To this day, I'm not fully sure what he meant. He must have meant something though.

THE VISITORS

East of Xian County is a village known as Double Spire, and on the outskirts of this village is a Buddhist monastery.

The monastery is deserted now except for weeds, rubble, and whatever wild birds might visit. But it was once inhabited by two elderly monks who lived together like brothers and was frequented by many worshippers during the day when its front gates were open.

One evening, several of these worshippers saw two old travelling Taoist monks come through the gates and march up to the cell that the Buddhist monks shared. The Taoists knocked and asked for shelter for the night.

As later reported by a witness, the two Buddhists were initially put off by the Taoists' request since the two religions are rivals. However, one of the Taoists said: "Are our two religions so different? We all practice renunciation of worldly things, and the cultivation of spiritual gifts and compassion. Aren't we sincere? Being sincere, do not our hearts naturally open to one another?"

Impressed by the argument, the Buddhists invited the two

Taoists inside. A little while later, the Buddhists were seen locking the front gates of the monastery for the night.

While ordinarily opened at dawn, the next day the gates remained locked.

Worshippers gathered outside and started to gossip about what might be wrong. One shouted to the monks over the monastery wall to ask if they were all right, but no one answered back. Eventually, someone jumped the gate and forced open the door of the monks' cell, which was locked from the inside.

The monks' belongings were there, including a large amount of gold that the Taoists had been carrying in their packs. But as for the men themselves, they were quite gone.

Since there was no sign of an emergency or a planned trip, and since the door was still locked, the absence of the monks made no sense. Extremely worried, a few of the bystanders rushed to report the goings-on to the local authorities.

Soon after that, Li Qianlong, the district magistrate, came to make a personal assessment of the case.

It was around this time that a young shepherd stumbled upon what looked like a dead body in an old well ten li south of the village. The magistrate and several police officers mounted their horses and galloped over to the site—with the shepherd boy in the lead. The dead body turned out to be *four* dead bodies, stacked like fish, and these stacked bodies turned out to be the missing monks. Though dead, they didn't have a single mark on them: no laceration, no abrasion, not even a bruise.

"I have no idea what happened here," said Li Qianzhong. "A theft? But nothing is missing.

"A rape? Given the advanced age of the victims, that's doubtful.

"A personal disagreement gone wrong? Improbable given we're dealing with men who are strangers to one another.

"And none of these scenarios can explain a murder without an injury or a defensive wound. Yet, here these men are far from where they were left behind locked doors. And here we are with several unanswered questions.

"Why did these men die together? How did their bodies get transported to a well so far away? How did their bodies leave a windowless room still locked from the inside?

"All of this is beyond the limits of reason. Ultimately, one must conclude this was not a natural occurrence. Rather, it was supernatural. And while the legal system can hold humans accountable for crimes, it cannot hold supernatural forces accountable. Therefore, there is nothing more I can do here."

After saying this, Li Qianzhong rode away to write up his assessment for his superiors, rendering in writing what he had spoken aloud. They carefully reviewed the facts and agreed with his opinion. The case was closed.

The investigator and magistrate Ming Sheng of Yingshan, a man of great wisdom and vast experience, eventually heard about the case. He said this about it:

"This incident came to my attention when I first moved to Xian. Once I heard about it, I couldn't get it out of my mind. For years, I've generated hypotheses and imagined scenarios, but nothing fits.

"It is one of those happenings that is best explained by being classified as 'the unexplainable.' If instead of treating it this way, you try to prove yourself by forcing a rational explanation on it, this explanation can't help but be full of holes and reflect poorly on your integrity and judgment."

While some criticized Li Qianzhong as thick-headed for not supplying a rational explanation, I fully support his assessment. It is as much an error to offer a natural explanation for a supernatural phenomenon where it does not fit as it is to do the opposite.

THE RAT IN MY FRIEND'S ROOM

My colleague Li Qingzi told me this:
"One night while sleeping in a friend's spare room, I was awakened near dawn by thuds and hissing. Frightened, I sat up and peered into the room. Through the dimness, I could make out two rats—a larger one in ferocious pursuit of a smaller one.

"Hurtling from one side of the room to the other, the rats were a blur of yowls and tails. Amazed, I watched them leap and roll over each other like juggling balls—wildly slamming against cups, dishes, and then a heating lamp, and causing it all to crash to the floor.

"Suddenly, the smaller rat dove into a crevice in the wall just large enough to wiggle through. In response, the bigger rat screeched angrily, shot in the air, plummeted to the floor, sprung up again as if bounced, fell a second time, then slumped, sagged, and moved no more.

"Blood dribbled from its eyes, nose, and mouth, and seeped through its matted fur. Stunned, I tried hard to make sense of what I'd just witnessed. When I could not, I called for help.

"Almost immediately, a servant arrived at my doorway.

The fat, white candle clenched in his hand illuminated the mess on my floor. 'Has anything like this ever happened before?' I asked.

"Shocked, he indicated it had not. Not only that, but he said that he had never heard of anything similar and had no idea what could have caused the rats to behave so. At first, I had no idea either. But as he was tidying up, I noticed that a small dish had fallen to the floor and spilled red aphrodisiac pills. Several were visibly gnawed.

"What had transpired was clear then. The larger rat had eaten the drug. It had flooded him with lust, prompting him to pursue the smaller rat, which had frantically dodged the larger one until it found an escape. Its escape though meant that the dark energies boiling in the large rat no longer could be discharged. And so it had exploded from the inside out.

"Right as I deduced this, my friend appeared and asked what the commotion coming from my room was about. After I explained everything to him, he burst out laughing. But he then frowned and looked serious. 'You know,' he said, 'those pills are more powerful than they look. Maybe they're not a very wise medication for an old man like me.' After saying this, he threw the pills away."

* * *

In his decision to dispose of the pills, Li Qingzi's friend was wise because the rats were a warning. I have seen many such cases. Men, especially older ones, fear the loss of heat and so dabble in herbs, chemicals, and other means to unnaturally fan their flames. Such a fear is not one that just belongs to the unsophisticated or the unaccomplished. Even great poets like Han Yu are known to become addicted to sulfuric solutions despite their loftier and more sublime thoughts, and to tempt imbalance and destruction by overdosing.

THE SETTING OF A CLOCK

Objects and people sometimes demonstrate knowledge that seems impossible for them to possess. So it was with my third daughter who died in the summer of 1790 when she was ten.

The day before her death, my daughter was at her most violently ill and thrashed around in delirium.

It was obvious to everyone that her small body could not endure much more. I was away at the time though, having been ordered to oversee the midsummer rites at the Shrine of Fangze in the capital. I had no idea how long this would take. However, there was a lot to be done, and it looked like I would not be able to see my child a final time.

But then suddenly in her bedroom far from me, my daughter regained lucidity, shocking those who had gathered around her.

"Today is too early," she said aloud. Her voice was clear and coherent—that of a perfectly healthy person, not a child who'd just roused from a state of unconsciousness. "I will wait until the chen shi hour[1] tomorrow to leave this life. Father will be back by then, and I can say goodbye."

My daughter was asked how she knew when she was

going to pass and at what hour I would return. But the question came too late. Her eyes had closed again. And she was as senseless as before.

I finished my duties at the Shrine of Fangze and hurried home that next morning. I arrived just in time to see my child's last breaths. There was a Western-style clock mounted in her room. As I stood there gazing at her going still for good, the clock chimed eight times—although not set to do so.

Such oddities are as much a part of our world as everyday occurrences. They are probably among the most important things.

---

1. The "chen shi hour" is a period of time between seven and nine in the morning.

ROOF WALKER

Li Youdan told me about an eerie thing that occurred in the town of Dongguang. Late one night, at the hour when everyone is sleeping or about to, every dog in Dongguang broke out howling and carrying on, their combined bray echoing down the dark streets and washing through the courtyards like a flood of shadows.

Alarmed, villagers threw open doors and windows. They discovered that there was something outside—a kind of man. A strange one. He was strolling along the tiled rooftops, every so often leaping the gap between one residence and another in one great stride.

As he walked, the man's long hair billowed against the white funeral robes he was wearing, and a large sack swung in one of his hands. From the sack came a sound like a sky full of ducks and geese.

During the man's walk, it was noted that he would pause for a few moments on this roof or that. No one thought anything of it at the time, given how bizarre everything was. But the next day, ducks and geese tumbled from those roofs where the stranger had paused the night before.

Since he was initially thought an unknown god, the birds

were assumed divine gifts and cooked by those families "lucky" enough to have received them. While they tasted as delicious as birds obtained in the more usual way and did not cause poisoning, the families that got the birds suffered dramatic and sudden deaths within a year.

It was too late, Li Youdan told me, when the people realized that the roof walker was of the evil sort.

One of the families that received birds that night was none other than my wife's family. It was just as Li Youdan narrated. Within a year of eating the dropped birds, one of them died—Master Ma Gengchang, my wife's uncle and a respected magistrate who practiced in Jingni.

That someone dies is not unusual. The number of deaths since ancient times is as uncountable as grains of sand. So, why then did the coming deaths in Dongguang warrant the signs of that strange night?

What factor decided which families would receive the birds?

And why did the signs take the shape of birds dropped from roofs? What did this in particular signify?

The language of ghosts and deities is full of elusive symbols. It is therefore at best only partially understood. I have written down here the events as they occurred. As for what they mean, I leave that to the reader.

JADE CHICKEN

A Fujian woman adored the taste of cats so much that she invented a special way to prepare them.

Key to her method was a long soak in a tub of boiling limewater. After just a day's immersion, a cat's hair would fall out, and its blood would thicken and concentrate in its organs, leaving behind a newborn-smooth body and meat orders of magnitude tastier than even virgin chicken.

It was so white, silky, and delicious that it was like edible jade.

For the most part, this woman was like everyone else. But when it came to satisfying her appetite, she was relentless.

She devoted entire days to experimenting with ways to kill cats, and the first thing she did every morning was to set out nets and mechanical traps to catch a fresh one.

Once caught, she would swap it out for a lime-soaked cat that went straight into her stove. Thus, every night she could sit with a plate of cat meat and eat to her stomach's content.

She would have probably ended every evening exactly this way until old age had she not contracted a deadly illness while still quite young. The disease attacked suddenly, stranding the woman in her bed.

There she writhed in terrible pain, making cat-like sounds —meows then yowls then shrieks—for close to two weeks before she finally expired.

* * *

This incident was shared with me by my daughter's husband, Yinwen. The cat woman was his father's neighbor so Yinwen's knowledge comes first-hand.

Later, Yinwen told me a second story too: this one about a young man that he knew who, although hailing from a highly respected family in Jingzhou, was held in low regard.

This young man was one of those kinds of people with lightless eyes, the sort who never smiles unless someone of a superior social status looks their way. Like the Fujian woman, he was single-minded in his pursuit of pleasure and since a child had amused himself through terrorizing cats and dogs. Even after he reached adulthood, he would run them down, hooting and hollering.

Once he caught one, he would twist its feet, one by one, until they snapped and flopped, and then he'd laugh wildly while the animal screamed in pain. When the young man later became a father, his offspring were all born with malformed feet.

* * *

And there is what happened to my servant, Wang Fa. Fa had a talent for firearms, and he got whatever he aimed at—no matter how small or from how far he shot. Birds were his favorite target. He routinely brought down 40 or 50 of their tiny bodies a day with his musket.

Wang Fa had a son, a charming boy named Jining Zhou.

Jining Zhou was happy and healthy until the age of twelve when he was suddenly afflicted with ulcers.

Red and swollen like burns from hot pokers, the ulcers wept pus and looked exactly like the wounds on the birds' bodies after Wang Fa shot them.

The resemblance was so exact that inside each sore lay a round, iron pellet. No one knew how this could be. It was as if Jining Zhou's body had suddenly become the body of all the birds his father shot.

When Jining Zhou died, so too did Fa's family line.

* * *

Needless killing creates bad karma. Therefore, many schools of thought practice fasting or restrain eating in other ways—such as rules about how an animal is killed or which ones can be eaten.

Some emperors, for example, have maintained the niu jie (牛戒), the beef taboo, out of respect for the hard work that cows do on farms. Doctors don't recommend beef either since it is thought to disrupt the body's internal balance. They put similar prohibitions on eating some other animals. Likewise, many intellectuals refuse to kill dogs or pigs because of their high intelligence. Even Confucians avoid needless killing and extend compassion to animals.

Such measures are both wise and kind. However, some taboos against eating animals seem confused or half-hearted.

For instance, while several Buddhist sects avoid eating animal flesh altogether, others only forbid it on certain occasions. One such sect has a fasting day dedicated to Guanyin, and one dedicated to Cundi Bodhisattva, and claims just fasting on these days is enough to make Buddha happy.

I asked a Buddhist monk that belongs to this sect how

Buddha could not care about the suffering and killing that occurs on non-fasting days.

He responded that not all days are equal. Some are holier and injustices committed on those days are more serious. The fasting periods of his order were chosen to fall on holy days.

What about vegetables and fruits? I asked him. Why are they allowed on fasting days? Why isn't killing them linked to accumulating bad karma? They are born, grow, and die—just like humans. Or is there something about the flesh of animals that makes it special?

The Buddhist monk had no answer to any of this.

* * *

What kinds of creatures are we? Just because we want a piece of meat, we take a life. Just because we want a bowl of soup, we kill the child of another being.

In exchange for a good taste in our mouth that will last seconds, we take endless years from another animal, causing them to suffer fear, pain, and sadness.

These questions are not odd to ask. Centuries ago, the famous poet Su Shi asked them too—as have others.

We all must eat of course. But we should find a way to do this compassionately. And our efforts should be more thoughtful than a short fast here and there. Such half measures foster evil while making people feel like they're accomplishing great good.

THE REPEATER

Upon his dismissal from a government post in the Shandong province, my father's former classmate Dai Suitang became our family tutor. Sometimes after lessons, he would tell us stories about his father—a famous inventor who could have easily occupied the top scientific posts in the kingdom except for one thing. He despised Westerners and could not stay out of arguments with them.

Eventually, Dai Suitang's father even picked a fight with his superior at the Imperial Astronomical Observatory—the Jesuit Ferdinand Verbiest. Verbiest was the chief astronomer and weapons-maker for the emperor at the time, and so it was no surprise to anyone that Dai Saitang's father was swiftly demoted to a low-level post in Liaoning, a province so remote and frigid that it allowed little opportunity to debate Westerners.

One day, while Dai Suitang's nephew Bingying was visiting, Dai Suitang told us a new story. It was about how as a boy he'd walked in on his father tinkering with a very special invention.

The gleaming something looked like a musical instrument to him—perhaps a pipa or other kind of lute. But when he asked his father about it, his father said, "It's a gun," and showed Dai Suitang how the device's organs fit together.

The "gun" was quite ingenious. Its explosive powder and ammunition were packed into its rear compartment, which swung in and out via a wheeled mechanism. Near this compartment was a seamlessly interlocked firing system involving pins and convex and concave parts. When the gun's trigger was pulled, it caused a bullet and explosive powder to drop into the gun's spine, and a piece of flint to be struck by a beak-like pin. This ignited the powder. Its resulting detonation then spat out a bullet at high velocity. Unlike other guns which were capable of only firing a single bullet before needing to be reloaded, this abomination was capable of repeating 28 times in a row. The resulting hail of ammunition was a nightmarish curtain of death.

After certain refinements of design and test firings, Dai Suitang's father was satisfied with his invention, and he wrapped it, intending to present it to the military authorities the next day.

But that night he had a dream. In it, an immortal scolded him thus:

"The Divine Ruler of the Heavens is devoted to life. This thing you have made though is life's enemy. Consequently, if you press ahead with your plan of delivering it to the emperor's armies, Heaven will turn against you and your family line will be extinguished—as surely as if you all were standing in front of the weapon rather than behind it."

When the immortal finished speaking, Dai Suitang's father awoke. Frightened, he swore that he would never let the secret of his invention out into the world.

Dai Suitang went silent at this point in his story and turned to his nephew Bingying. "Didn't my father store his device at your house, Bingying? Do you think you could run and get it? I'd like to show it to Ji Yun."

Looking pained, Bingying made no move to rise. "I'm sorry, uncle, but it's gone. While I was away, training for the Department of Revenue, my brother's son stole it and sold it. I have no idea who he sold it to or where it is now."

Dai Suitang's nephew might have been telling the truth. It is also possible though that he had become unnaturally attached to the gun and did not want to risk it being taken away. Regardless, that Dai Suitang's father built such an extraordinary device inspires awe, even as the fact that it's loose in the world inspires fear.

A NOTE ON CONJURED SPIRITS

The world is full of hustlers of fake magic. But the art of planchette divination is the real thing. Spirits really do take control of a medium's hand and guide it as it scrawls characters in a table of sand. I say this because not only have I examined the matter closely, but I also have served as a medium myself.

This said, such divination is not a straightforward matter.

Besides the fact that there are those who fake being possessed by a spirit and simply write what they want to write, there are trickier issues.

First, spirits aren't always what they pretend to be any more than people. Some declare themselves gods when they are clearly not.

Others claim to be ghosts of this or that famous person, although they remain ignorant of the details of the person's deeds—such as what essays or poems they wrote while living. When called out for such discrepancies, these alleged ghosts claim to suffer from dim memories of their mortal lives. Given how they profess to clearly remember other things, this is less than convincing. One therefore can't help but wonder what is really going on, or what these spirits actually are.

A second thing of great interest about these entities is that human beings act as instruments for their communication in ways more significant than simply lending a hand or a voice.

In fact, the spirits' communication is profoundly filtered and affected by the peculiarities of our personalities: our intelligence, our sense of humor, our senses—just as a container affects the taste of wine or individual incarnations express the soul differently in each cycle of reincarnation.

Say, for example, that a person channeling spirits is a gifted calligrapher.

In that case, the letters shaped in the sand will be well-formed and beautiful.

Or, say the person channeling has poetic gifts.

The spirit will then also show itself to be talented at rhyme, the creation of images, and the selection of words.

If the person lacks either quality, so will the spirit—even while their predictions and insights are later proven true and thus the spirit a genuine manifestation.

For instance, when I am the medium for spirit writing, the communication is poetic and elegant. But the handwriting leaves much to be desired. For my cousin Tanju, the opposite is true.

A writer, no matter how gifted, needs a pen to write a single word.

A candle must be lit before it yields light.

And spirits can do nothing, *say* nothing, on their own. They require a human agent.

Yes, it is true that our ancestors tossed twigs and dried-out turtle shells in the dirt to peer through time. But such dim things had no magic on their own. It was only when they were touched by human hands and brushed by human intent that power flared in them.

REVENGER

My maternal uncle, An Jieran told me this:
"Every day, people mysteriously disappear or die in surprising or unexpected ways. Some may be the work of vengeful ghosts.

"Many such examples are recorded in books. As well, I have heard about occurrences straight from people's mouths.

"In May of 1763, however, I witnessed a case with my own eyes, when I was returning to the village of Cui from Geng Jia Temple in Yanshan.

"The man, who was wearing a grass hat and linen shirt, looked to be in his fifties. He must have been travelling somewhere because he had a donkey with him, loaded with luggage. The donkey was tied to a willow tree on the edge of the river, and the man was resting against this same tree. Following their example, I also tethered my horse and sat down for a rest.

"Suddenly, this man jumped up and started waving his hands around as if batting something away. As he did, he kept repeating variations of these words: 'You're right. A life for a life. But please make it quick. Stop hurting me.'

"For a long time, the man jerked and winced and cried out

until his words slurred and his voice became unrecognizable and inhuman.

"It was then that he abruptly turned around, ran straight for the river, and jumped in. The muddy water instantly closed over him, and he did not come back up.

"There were more than ten people that day who witnessed the man's death with me. We all put our palms together, recited some mantras, and prayed for his soul.

"I don't know exactly why the spirit sought revenge, but it must have involved horrific violence of some kind. 'A life for a life' was what the man himself said."

It is the nature of all that exists to acquire consciousness and for this consciousness to deepen in ever-increasing degrees. Even an old rag gains its own mind after a while.

—Yu Zhengxie (1775–1840)

BENEATH A GREEN COAT

This is a story about an event that transpired at the country estate of my grandfather—as told to me by my mother.

One summer, something began to dance violently in front of the family compound late at night, bewildering all who lived there.

While it was clear the "something" was dancing, it was not clear what the something was. It danced in the shadows. And whenever anyone ran toward it for a closer look, it ran off.

Finally, one evening when the moonlight was streaming down, the household got a good look at the thing from the windows of the main house. However, that glimpse did little to unravel its mystery. From a headless, turtle-shaped torso that glinted silver beneath a green brocade coat, four spindly limbs emerged. These approximated arms and legs but culminated in lumps rather than fingers and toes.

No one had ever seen such a thing.

Several days later, Ziheng—my mother's uncle—assigned several of his tallest and stoutest servants, armed with knives, clubs, and ropes, to crouch outside of the front gate in the bushes and await the creature's arrival.

Soon, the creature made its nightly appearance and started in on its dance.

Immediately, the group of men leapt.

It took off at a surprising speed though, flashed through the compound front gate, and up to the top of an outside staircase where it hid in the shadows.

A lamp was shone on the shadows to confront the creature. But there was no creature there.

Instead, the lamp's light shone on something leaning against the back wall near the staircase, something wrapped in green silk. The fabric was unwrapped. Beneath it was a tiny silver boat with four wheels.

The boat was identified as a large toy from years before, when the family's fortunes were greater and they could afford as many expensive toys as the children wanted. The dancing fiend's green coat was the silk cloth the boat was wrapped in, and its limbs must have bubbled up from the wheels.

There was no part of the boat that could serve as a head. That was why it lacked one.

An old servant woman later said, "That toy disappeared while I was still a young girl. I remember because all the servants my age were beaten for the crime of stealing the toys of our master's children. I thought it had just been lost, but I guess someone stole it and hid it in this room. And here it stayed, lost and forgotten, until after a long time it became the creature we saw. Perhaps anything that's forgotten by those that once cherished it can become demonic."

Shortly after this, the toy was melted into more than thirty taels of silver.

*　*　*

Some people find such transformations hard to accept. But Confucius—as recorded in Gan Bao's *Soushen Ji*—taught that animals and such things as grass and trees can change into human-like creatures once they reach a certain age.

Why shouldn't they?

After all, everything is made of the same five elements, and it is quite common for substances to take on new natures with age, such as rice aging into wine.

And once you think of a monster as a collection of changed and aged elements, why be scared? Such creatures are probably no more dangerous than those things from which they sprouted.

THE SHARD AND THE HUNTER

My acquaintance Wang Fanghu told me about a Mengyin County hunter named Liu who decided to visit his cousin in another village.

Right before Liu left, a mutual friend asked him if he'd heard the rumor about his cousin's haunting.

When he saw that Liu had no idea what he was talking about, the man said that he'd heard reports about a strange entity glimpsed during the night at this cousin's place and how some people had been knocked off their feet by something sharp and hard like a piece of iron or a stone.

Not easily frightened, Liu took this information in stride, and told the man that he would bring his hunting equipment —including his favorite bird gun.

"Let it show its face," Liu said, "or what it has that passes for one. We'll see if bullets can hurt it."

A few nights later, Liu was reading next to a lamp in one of the three empty studio rooms in the rear of the house. He looked up and saw the entity peeking at him from around the corner of the room opposite his.

The thing resembled a small human. But there was something unfinished about it. Its eyes and eyebrows were too far apart and didn't line up. And its nose and mouth ran together as if disfigured by a fire.

Keeping his eyes fixed on the creature, Liu slowly slid his hand toward the gun under his chair. He hoped to shoot the creature before it was aware that Liu was looking, but it noticed him and flashed behind the curtained doorway of the room and into its shadows before Liu could shoot.

Its retreat was momentary, however.

Minutes later, its inhuman fingers curled around the door frame and part of its face peered out as before.

Liu again tried to line his gun up for a shot. Again, the creature jumped back into the room.

Soon it was apparent that Liu and the creature had each other trapped. The creature didn't want to risk being shot while fleeing the room. Liu didn't want to rush the creature and risk being attacked.

But then the creature made a gesture with its tongue so vulgar that Liu couldn't help but angrily fire off a round, even though he knew the shot would be sloppy.

Sure enough, the bullet shattered the door frame but missed the creature—illustrating the wisdom of the old saying that in a confrontation between two military forces, the one that moves first will not achieve victory.

Liu did learn something though. The creature was scared of the gun. This implied that it could be harmed by one.

The next night, Liu hid behind the window panels in the room in which the creature had appeared.

It was a long wait, but his patience was awarded a little after night fell. There was a disturbance in the air, and the creature slowly began to take form—a shadow putting on flesh.

As soon as it looked solid enough, Liu fired his gun.

The creature fell to the ground with a sound like shattering pottery.

Liu examined the area where the creature dropped and

found a broken jar. On one of the shards was a child's scrawled attempt to draw a human face—the features clumsily off-kilter exactly as the entity's had been.

Art, it would appear, even that of a child, cannot be made without investing it with life force. Thus, it sometimes invades our dreams or haunts our house, and occasionally someone might see something they've drawn walking along a lonely country road at night.

PLAYMATES

There were five slightly older children that I used to play games with, up until I was around the age of three. They wore matching multicolored outfits and gold bracelets, had very bright eyes, and would chase me around the yard—joking, teasing, and shouting, "Little brother, little brother."

We liked each other a great deal and played all the time. I always assumed that they must be the children of neighbors or their relatives.

But a little past my third birthday, they suddenly quit coming over.

Upset, I asked my father what happened to my playmates and described them in detail. After I finished speaking, he was silent for a long time then said this:

"Before your mother, I had another wife. She was your mother's older sister. As soon as we married, we began trying to have children. When this proved difficult, she grew desperate and had the nuns at the Buddhist temple make her shrine dolls. They were made from clay, had painted faces, and were wrapped in multicolored thread. There were five in total.

"Such dolls are very powerful. If you treat them like real children, they can make your womb fruitful. So your aunt named each of the shrine dolls as if it were a real child. She slept with them, talked to them, and even nursed them. When she died, they had become so real to us that we dug graves for them in the empty field behind the house.

"Later, I regretted acting so sentimentally. Figures that have been stamped with human features and treated in a human way can become unpredictable and dangerous.

"But when I went looking for the burial sites, I couldn't find them anywhere nor any other sign of the dolls. I think the dolls were your mysterious playmates."

* * *

The first wife of my father touched my life in a second way as well. Every year, on the day that she died, we would burn sacrifices for her and say prayers.

One year after the rituals were done, my actual mother fell deeply asleep and dreamed that my aunt angrily shoved her awake. "Is this how you act a mother?" she scolded. "Letting your son mess about with knives?"

This dream was so real that my mother woke up in a panic and sat bolt upright. And the first thing that she saw as she looked wildly about was me trying to pry my father's long knife out of its sheath.

Some argue that the annual rituals for the dead are empty gestures. I know from experience that this is not the case.

WHAT THINGS BECOME

My late grandmother, Madame Cao told a story about Cao Huachun, the infamous Ming dynasty royal eunuch.

For his burial, the eunuch's family dressed him lavishly, including a jade belt cinched around his waist. A few years after his funeral, a cream-colored snake with a slightly darker and unusual segmented pattern was frequently seen lurking around his tomb—as if it had a nest nearby.

Eventually, the eunuch's tomb and gravesite were severely damaged by a flood that laid waste to that part of the country, and he needed to be reburied. When his shattered coffin was picked from him and the dirt brushed away, except for natural decay the eunuch was found to be the same as when he was entombed. His jewelry, wine and grain jars, and funerary replicas were still with him.

But one thing was missing—the jade belt.

Those who had seen the snake realized then that its pattern was exactly like that of the missing belt.

One can't help but wonder if a snake's soul found a way to make the jade belt into a body through some mystical process of transmutation or if the jade found a way to become a snake. Whatever the case, things constantly change into other things. This is a matter that invokes both awe and sadness.

YEREN STONES

While I was exiled to army service in Urumqi, I often interviewed prisoners—both to collect information important to the emperor's military concerns and tales relevant to my project of recording the strange.

In this way, I happened to interview a criminal named Gang Chaorong. He told me about a merchant who had journeyed to Tibet a few years before to sell goods. This merchant was accompanied by a second merchant and two donkeys loaded with merchandise.

The journey went badly.

First, the small band got lost in the middle of an icy, Himalayan mountain range.

Then, as they were desperately seeking a familiar landmark, they saw a dozen figures leap down from a rock shelf in the distance.

Terrified, the merchants were sure that they were about to be robbed and killed. But as they trembled and waited to fight for their lives, the bipedal figures drew closer, and the merchants saw to their shock that they were not bandits.

The figures were not even human.

Between two and three meters tall, the towering creatures

that approached the merchants were covered with dark hair streaked with yellow and hazel brown. And while their faces verged on being human, they weren't quite there.

The same could be said of their speech—if that's what it was. While it contained some nonsensical sounds that were human-like, others were more like sharp grunts and hoots made by an animal.

Frightened by the creatures' appearance, the merchants threw themselves to the earth, covered their heads with their arms, and bawled and pleaded as if about to be torn into pieces. But instead of attacking, the humanoids burst into animalish guffaws. After gently picking up the men as if they were no more than children's toys, they forcibly marched them and the donkeys up and over hills and rocks until arriving at an open, flat space.

This appeared to be a frequent gathering place for the creatures. Because once there, they pushed one donkey into a hole and cut up the other.

After cooking the donkey meat on a kindled fire, the creatures foisted some on the two men as if they were guests. Exhausted, hungry, and relieved they were not apparently bound for the fire themselves—the men happily ate. As they did, the creatures also gobbled the meat, while chatting with each other in a bizarre tongue and casting sharp looks at the men. When full, the creatures patted their swollen abdomens and broke out in sharp, high-pitched and horsey sounds like some kind of weird, celebratory song.

A little while later, a few of the creatures picked up the men and carried them off at an incredible pace, as quickly as monkeys can swing or birds can fly while carrying something —up and down wooded slopes and valleys—until they reached a well-travelled road that was familiar to the merchants.

There, the creatures dropped the men to their feet and gave each a melon-sized stone before flashing back into the forests.

The stones turned out to be turquoise of a particularly high quality. Upon reaching their village, the men sold these stones for far more than what they had lost.

I can't identify the species that the merchants encountered. However, it's clear that the creatures weren't supernatural—neither mountain divinities nor demons. Rather, they seemed to have been a race of wild human beings that keep themselves hidden among the remote mountains and desolate gorges.

Those who find the supernatural world too strange to believe simply have not looked closely enough at the natural world. It is equally strange.

REMEMBERING THOSE WHOSE NAMES ARE FORGOTTEN

1. Sister Hui

The nun, Sister Hui, was very mysterious. No one knew her family or if she had one. No one knew whether she'd been raised rich or poor, educated or uneducated, in a village or in the capital city. "Hui" might not even have been her given name. It could have been only a religious name or nickname. And I had no clue if 慧 was the correct character for her name.

The first time I saw Sister Hui, I was at my grandparents' house in the village of Sweet Water Well. From the beginning, she impressed me.

It is not wholly uncommon for religious people to have a reputation for greed or bad manners or breaking holy rules when they don't think anyone is looking. Sister Hui was not that sort.

She strictly followed the rules laid out by her order, as well as those that arose from her own sense of decency. She refused, for example, to eat animals. This included candy and cakes made with animal fats. The one meal a day that she allowed herself consisted of a few vegetables or fruits.

Similarly, she wore no fur or animal hides. She even rejected silk, which some argued as a permissible fabric. She told us that you had to murder a thousand worms just to make a single foot of silk. You could not wholly escape participation in the cycle of life and death, of course. But Sister Hui felt that you could, with effort, dramatically minimize the suffering you inflicted.

Some Buddhists use their religion as an excuse to scrounge for alms. Sister Hui did not. She gave rather than took and always tried to give things of quality. For example, she regularly made offerings of wheat-gluten loaves to the Buddha. This, in and of itself, was not unusual. What was unusual was to make these loaves yourself rather than buying them at the market. This is what Sister Hui did.

"Those market bakers use their dirty feet to knead the dough," Sister Hui said. "Would Buddha be gladdened by such an offering? I knead loaves by hand."

One day a handmaid who worked for my grandparents visited the temple to make an offering of a roll of fine cloth. When she presented it to Sister Hui, Sister Hui examined the cloth for several minutes and frowned.

"This won't do," Sister Hui said. "An offering's value lies in the spirit in which it's given and the purity of the gift. Not in the gift's monetary worth. This cloth is not yours to give. It was stolen. Its theft, moreover, caused several young servant girls to be beaten. How could it possibly be a fitting gift for the Knower of Worlds?"

Deeply shaken by Sister Hui's response, the maid confessed all.

She said, "There were so many bundles of cloth in that house that I didn't think anyone would notice one missing. When I found out that the other girls were beaten because of it, I hated myself. I thought that if I made an offering, the Buddha might forgive me."

Sister Hui pushed the cloth back toward the maid. "What would be ideal is for the Buddha to use divine power to correct your wrong. What would be more ideal is for you to act on Buddha's behalf and take this action yourself. Put the cloth back. This will restore the girls' good reputations and your peace of mind."

This story was passed on to me by one of Sister Hui's disciples. Years later, when Sister Hui was around eighty, she visited me at my home on her way to Tanzhe Temple to oversee the initiation of a young novitiate. In the course of our conversation, I asked her about the handmaid and the cloth. She shook her head. "That's a good story," she said, "with a fine point. But it was made up by those scoundrel disciples of mine. Not a word is true."

We chatted for a few more minutes, then Sister Hui said she had to hurry off. Before she did, she asked me to do some calligraphy for her—of fine enough quality that it could be used to make a plaque for her temple.

I agreed and asked her to wait for me while I went to work on the piece in my studio.

Once I was in my studio, I remembered some other tasks that needed to be speedily completed. So I asked my assistant Zhao Chunjian to do the calligraphy and sign my name to it.

I thought no one would notice the difference since Zhao Chunjian was quite talented and a good mimic too. However, when presented with the calligraphy, Sister Hui immediately recognized that the handwriting was not mine.

"I'm sorry," she said, pressing her palms together. "But I can't put this on the temple. The calligraphy is very beautiful, but the handwriting is not yours. Please, if it's not too much trouble, let the one who actually did the calligraphy sign his handiwork with his name. This way, Buddha will not be presented with lies."

When Sister Hui said this, it struck me that her reaction

showed a spirit similar to the one illustrated by the story that her disciples had made up. This meant that there was something true in that false story after all. This, in turn, means that some false stories are truer than others.

The chance meeting with Sister Hui happened many years ago, and I haven't seen her since. When she recently came to mind, I asked some people from Sweet Water Well about her. No one knew who I was talking about.

Her name, whether given or made-up, has been forgotten, as has she.

But my story about her remains, and the original story told by her disciples is probably still making the rounds too—even if her name has been swapped for another, and even if she's been turned from a nun into a monk in that story.

2. Third Master

There is a monk who lives in Jingcheng. He is the third disciple of the abbot of Tianqi Temple.

Because he's the third disciple and highly respected, over time he has become known simply as "Third Master," and his real name has been forgotten.

Many of the abbot's disciples are indecent. They spend their days trying to raise funds—not for charity but so that they can live luxuriously.

Third Master is different.

He isn't full of fake smiles and charming, insincere words like the monks who try to wheedle favors out of temple guests.

He isn't arrogant like the monks whose job it is to chant the rituals.

Instead, Third Master is disciplined and avoids any extravagance that might weaken his will. Even if he's assigned a mission that requires him to travel thousands of li, he'll walk rather than take a horse. Once, my late brother Qinghu ran into him on the road and could not, no matter how hard he tried, get Third Master to climb onto his carriage.

In keeping with the spirit of the sutras, Third Master doesn't distinguish between the rich and the poor, or the politically powerful and the politically weak. When a bureaucrat visits the temple, he receives no special treatment or blessings —even if he donates generously. When the villagers come, Third Master is just as polite to them as he is to the high and mighty and bows to them just as low—even if they donate nothing.

While Third Master is in every way a master, he is not concerned with power or authority, and he teaches as much by his absence as by his presence. Occasionally, he even becomes invisible.

For example, there's a room in which he meditates. Temple visitors sometimes wander into the room and do not see him—although they sense that there's something holy about the room.

A window's value lies in its transparency and in what one can see through it. So, too, a true master's.

This is not to say that Third Master doesn't attract others. He does. But he does so not because he has a superior air, not because he's learned to tell excellent jokes or say profound things, but because he's reduced himself and gotten rid of anything phony or artificial.

Therefore, he has freed himself of all obstructions to his ability to relate to others.

The Taoists and the Buddhists teach that perfection lies in decreasing and simplifying, not in increasing and complicating. It is no surprise then that while many people remark that Third Master's character is very good, they have difficulty saying why. If you ask them what it is about him that strikes them as noble, they shake their heads.

When I was younger, this puzzled me so much that I once

asked my father about it. "Why do people think Third Master is so advanced yet can offer no proof of his superiority?"

My father replied, "Do you really think one has to be able to fly on sticks or float in a wooden cup across the river, like the immortals in the old tales did, to prove they're enlightened? If so, then you grossly misunderstand what it means to be enlightened."

The Third Master passed away recently. So perhaps his real name is still remembered by some, unlike Sister Hui's. I could probably question the students from his hometown and find out his name.

THE SECRET OF THE WHOLE DESIGN

During the Song dynasty, a fearsome weapon was invented—a gigantic crossbow known alternatively as "Heaven's Bow" and "The Great Defeater." This instrument was so massive that it could not be cocked by hand but had to be set by foot. And an arrow fired from it could pierce iron armor like paper from three hundred paces away.

Because of its power, the bow was a key weapon for the Song armies in their battles against the invading Jin people, who were perpetually trying to seize Song territory.

Song soldiers were severely punished if they abandoned it on a battlefield. In those cases in which defeat was imminent, the soldiers were instructed to shatter the Great Defeater into unrecognizable parts to prevent the enemy from copying it.

These orders were well thought-out. But eventually, Kublai Khan, the king of the Mongols, managed to obtain the design. The weapon proved crucial to his victory over both the Jin and the Song.

Kublai Khan was also cautious about sharing the weapon's design. And by the time that the Ming dynasty replaced the rule of the Mongols, the secret to making the Great Defeater was lost except for a few partial sketches in the *Yongle Encyclopedia*.

The *Yongle* sketches were less than helpful.

From the beginning of its invention, great care had been taken to never illustrate more than a single part of the Great Defeater on a single page so that one needed a great many pages from different sources to assemble the whole contraption.

It was impossible, therefore, based on the information in the *Yongle Encyclopedia*, to understand measurements, how the Great Defeater's nail-less male and female parts interlocked— or to comprehend where wood became bronze and how to construct and place the trigger mechanism or the gears.

Even after I and my colleague and friend, Zou Nianqiao, spent half a week trying to build one, we wound up with nothing more than a pile of mysterious parts whose joining seemed a logical impossibility.

Finally, I suggested to Nianqiao that we make copies of the sketches to pass onto some Westerners to study. They had a good reputation for machine making.

Nianqiao liked my idea. However, when I informed my late teacher Liu Wenzheng about my intentions, he dismissed it.

"Westerners are not a transparent and straight-talking people," he said. "Full of secrets and stratagems, they tell half stories. Take, for example, their method for calculating special square roots. They learned this from us. But if one of us, unschooled in this method, asked them to teach it, their teaching would be partial, and they would keep key parts of the formula to themselves.

"Perhaps this is a wise course of action. Perhaps not. Regardless, if we do as you suggest then it's quite possible that, yes, the Westerners will figure out how to make the weapon. But it's equally plausible that they will pretend like they cannot make it and keep the secret for themselves.

"Therefore, we should leave the *Yongle Encyclopedia* at Hanlin Academy where it's stored and not send copies out all over the world.

"If we wait patiently, one day in the future a Hanlin scholar will review the drawings and suddenly grasp the secret of the whole design. Some people have such an ability—to grasp the shape of the whole on the basis of a few parts."

Since Liu Wenzheng was known for his sage advice and had a great deal of practical experience dealing with Westerners, Nianqiao and I preserved the sketches for others to use later.

We felt confident, thanks to Liu Wenzheng's words, that when the right information reached the right person, the secret of the whole design would reveal itself.

HOUSES AT NIGHT AND OF THE MIND

A s for those beings known as fox spirits, we cannot know for sure whether their human forms are real or illusions created by magic. All we can know is that they are beautiful and getting involved with them leads to disaster.

In the case of ghosts, we know more.

They are made out of the remnants of the vital life force left behind when a human dies.

Because they are a remainder, a *less than*, whatever power a ghost has cannot be greater than that of a living person. This includes the power to conjure objects or animals from thin air, to transmute the tiny into the large, or to turn the repulsive into the seductive.

Yet, I have studied hundreds of reports of ghostly encounters, and personally heard just as many—several from direct witnesses. Among them are descriptions of lavish homes and extravagant courtyards into which human guests are invited and entertained only to find such dwellings suddenly changed into coffins and tombs.

And there are many records of encounters with ghosts who died horribly. By hanging, by drowning, by tiger, by burning, or by rape. These ghosts are, however, beautiful when they present themselves and quite charming.

Based on such testimony, it seems that when a person becomes a ghost they acquire incredible, new abilities. It only seems that way though. Because there is a far more likely explanation: people have these powers all along. Upon death, they realize this and learn to use their abilities.

Once, while I was taking a carriage to Liangzhou in Gansu province, the driver pointed at a mountain we were about to travel over.

"I've slept here before," he said. "When I was in the army and helping escort supply wagons north. We stopped here for the night, lit a fire, and gazed up. The mountain's side was illuminated with the flickering of hundreds of lights—from the lamps of mudbrick dwellings built into the slope. Even from where we were, we could clearly see the tiny, shadowed figures of the inhabitants moving inside the homes. The next day we had to travel upward through the area where we had seen the houses the night before. I was looking forward to it because I hoped to find a market. But there were no houses. Not a one. Where we had seen homes, there were now old graves because that whole side of the mountain was a cemetery."

This driver's experience points out something else about ghostly powers. They're not exercised solely for the sake of the living. Even when they think they are alone, ghosts may use their abilities to bring themselves solace through conjuring homes and other things with which they were familiar when they were alive.

The ancient ones may have considered such matters.

This is possibly why they promoted burying miniature wooden houses and clay horses with the dead, and the burning of papier-mâché beds and donkeys, along with other funerary replicas.

THE RED SECT

1.

There are many false magicians in the kingdom, as well as individuals who convince themselves that they have powers when they do not. However, I know a religious sect that has actual supernatural abilities—the red sect of Tibetan Buddhism.

There are two major types of Tibetan Buddhists: the yellow and the red. The yellow sect's adherents, led by the Dalai Lama, have the support of the emperor and are devoted to purifying their conduct and teaching the ways of karma and nonattachment. In spirit, they are similar to Chan Buddhists. The red sect, who the yellow sect openly calls out as heretics and witches, are quite different. They pursue power and are concerned with magic—often of the black kind.

One should not think ill of Tibetan Buddhism because of the red sect. In truth, they are false Buddhists, adherents of an ancient religious order that passes itself off as a Buddhist.

In fact, this order is explicitly condemned by the Buddhist scriptures. Through my own research, I've traced them back to individual sorcerers active in the Western regions during the Han dynasty. These sorcerers entertained the public with fire and sword swallowing in exchange for money while in private honing a far darker craft.

2.

Despite its ancient pedigree, the red sect is as active today as ever, and there are many witnesses to their feats.

Liu Baozhu, Director of the Bureau for Managing Barbarians, said that he once accidentally insulted a red lama during a stay in Tibet. Not long afterwards, a local tipped him off that the lama was going to magically attack while Baozhu was travelling on a nearby mountainside.

Taking the local seriously, Baozhu disguised himself and hid in the back of his travelling party while sending his litter, now occupied by a dummy, ahead.

Sure enough, a little into the trip, one of the horses went crazy and attacked the litter-bearers, as well as the litter itself —dashing it to pieces with its sharp hooves. If Baozhu had been in the litter, he would have been grievously injured.

This account comes straight from Liu Baozhu's mouth.

My friend Jiang Xinyu shared a second account that also testifies to the red sect's power. It concerns a man who travelled two thousand li away from his home for an extended time to conduct business.

One day, this man went to a party on a pleasure barge and found himself mesmerized by the party's hostesses.

They were all extraordinarily beautiful and entertained the crowd with an unusually graceful confidence—plying guests with liquor, singing songs, and dancing skillfully.

But one of the hostesses, clad in a dress as red as a poppy, particularly drew the man's attention. She looked exactly like his wife back home. The similarity was so remarkable that he could barely resist calling out.

The man approached the hostess, expecting the similarity to dissolve. But instead, it became even more exact the closer he came—down to a wine-colored mole on the woman's right wrist.

His wife had the same mark. It too was the size of a millet seed.

Nevertheless, the hostess's eyes glided right past the man as if he were a piece of furniture. And she remained oblivious to him as she tuned the strings of her pipa and pushed up the sleeves of her dress so that they didn't droop in her wine as she gulped. But it was the way she laughed that convinced him that she wasn't his wife. Her voice was completely different. Nor did she mask her laugh with her hand—as his wife would have so as not to bare the naked pink inside of her mouth.

Although now convinced that the hostess wasn't his spouse, still the man was so unsettled that he left the party to pack and wrap up his business so that he could travel home and check on everything.

Before he managed to set out, a messenger arrived with a letter—the date of which indicated that it had been sent six months before. Halfway through reading, the man cried out. The letter disclosed that his wife had died months earlier.

The man returned home and took care of the kind of things one does after the death of a family member, and he made the visits that one makes.

The man's deep sadness was visible to everyone he met. But his close friends noticed that he seemed haunted by more than grief. When they interrogated him, he told them about the strange woman. He couldn't shake the feeling that the woman he'd met was a type of ghost, but one shockingly different in personality from his wife.

His friends insisted that this couldn't be the case. The similarity had to be a coincidence. Ghosts weren't known to hire themselves out as party hostesses. And nothing else that he told them fit what they knew about ghosts—if such things were even real.

However, several months later, the man heard about a stranger who had moved to a village near the Jiangsu and Jiejiang provinces and rented a house. Strangely secretive, the stranger didn't introduce himself to neighbors. He attended no public gatherings. And he refused all dinner invitations, instead staying locked up in his house, alongside a large collection of concubines and servants.

There was one exception to the stranger's isolation.

Every so often, he would visit a matchmaker to sell off a concubine. This ignited gossip that he was a trader of women. But since he didn't make trouble for his neighbors, they left him alone.

One day, not too long after he'd moved to the village, the stranger was seen rushing to the river. There, he hired a boat to take him to the Buddhist monastery on Tianmu Mountain. According to witnesses at the monastery, as soon as the stranger hit shore, he asked a novitiate to deliver a donation and a request for a protection ritual to the head monk.

The head monk refused the request, finding the stranger's request suspiciously vague about why he wanted the ritual. Unable to change the head monk's mind, the stranger started back home. On his way, an odd storm stirred up and lightning ended his life.

Later, one of the stranger's servants confessed that he was not a servant. Not exactly.

He was rather a disciple of the dark arts that his master practiced. One of these arts was a technique that the stranger had learned from a red sect lama.

This lama could, through special incantations, suck in the

spirit from the netherworld and blow it through the dead lips of a young woman's corpse, reanimating it. The body's new resident would then swear to do the lama's bidding in exchange for inhabiting the body.

This technique was the source of the stranger's steady stream of "concubines." However, eventually the spirits that safeguard human beings passed a death sentence upon him for profaning life. Soon thereafter, a dream warned him that death was coming for him. This is why he sought the protection ritual and did not explain his reasons.

My friend Jiang Xinyu told me that when the man from the pleasure barge heard this story, he concluded that his wife's body had fallen prey to the stranger or a man like him.

Maybe. I'm not sure about this. What I am sure about is that members of the red sect have no qualms about profaning corpses. Liu Baozhu himself has heard similar reports. They are so widespread that the yellow sect went to the trouble of making a general public declaration that this practice is evil and thus forbidden.

3.

I would be more skeptical of tales about the red sect's black magic if I did not have my own to tell. But I do.

One day in Urumqi, a horse got loose, and a soldier suggested we hire a nearby red sect lama to get him back. Upon arriving at the camp, the lama asked for a stool. This, he planted in the dust and circled around it, chanting words and waving his hands. Suddenly, the stool moved, although no one was touching it—first spinning wildly around like the mechanical arm used to lower a heavy container in a well and then, after it fell over, flopping and bucking its way through the dust at an extremely fast pace—as if intent on reaching a chosen destination.

"Let's follow," the lama said to the soldier who owned the horse. In a very short time, they found the missing horse trapped in a gully.

HOW TO SPEAK A SPELL

My friend Yan Yudun has a tenant farmer whose last name is Sun. This Sun is very good at shooting birds. Out of one hundred times he shoots, not a single time does he miss his target.

One day, I saw a golden oriole and asked Sun to demonstrate his skill.

Sun asked, "Do you want it alive or dead?"

I replied: "What do you mean? A bullet's so fast that you can't control it. Especially from this distance. The bird is a dot no larger than your bullet. You'll be lucky to hit it, much less have the bullet follow specific instructions."

Sun said: "If you want it dead, I'll directly shoot the bird. If you want it alive, I'll shoot near it to spook it first. Then when it takes off, I will shoot its wing."

"If this is so, please leave it alive," I said.

Sun raised his gun, fired once—the bird panicked upward —fired again—it fell, its wing clipped.

That's how accurate Sun is. At least most of the time. Because there is another person I know with a rare talent too— a talent for spells.

Specifically, this person, a Buddhist, knows how to cast a life-preserving spell.

The Buddhist talked Sun into letting him demonstrate the effect of the spell on Sun's shooting. He said, "If I recite the spell three times, you will miss every shot out of one hundred shots."

Skeptical, Sun couldn't resist the challenge.

And sure enough, the result of the spell was just as the man predicted. To Sun and everyone else's astonishment, nothing living that Sun shot at was hit.

However, neither Sun's ability nor the Buddhist's is what surprises me the most. What is difficult for me to accept is the language of the Buddhist's spell.

One would expect the words of a life-preserving spell to be elegant and refined like poetry. Or to be wise and subtle like philosophy. The spell had none of these traits.

When Sun shared its exact wording, I was shocked at its ridiculousness and childish simplicity. It sounded like a mockery of a spell, a shoddy fake created by a bad pretender.

How could such doggerel have the power to shape reality? I asked myself.

Yet, the truth is this: all the prevention spells I've encountered since, at least those that work, use ridiculous language.

There seems to be something about the willingness to accept the absurd, the childish, and the nonsensical by those that create these spells that contributes to their power.

CIRCUMSTANCES IN COURT

Qian Wenmin, the proctor who oversaw my municipal examination, firmly believed that neither natural disasters nor good luck is random. Rather, they are the products of a divine system of punishments and rewards—one upon which the human justice system is modelled.

It is true that many things that humans have built are copies of divine architectures and that one may understand something of divinity by closely examining natural phenomena.

Nevertheless, one should be careful in making claims about how the divine world works and one should be skeptical of those who make such claims.

Say, for example, that you receive orders to demote and indict an official.

Looking over the order, you have an impression of a blameless, even exemplary, individual when it comes to character and the performance of professional duties. Here, he has no fault.

His only crime is this: his house faces an inauspicious direction, and its construction began on an unlucky day.

These are the offenses for which he is to be charged a fine and banished.

While there is no human system so ridiculous as to set fines this way, according to some this is how the divine system works.

Is this just? Or are such punishments so unfair and irrational that they insult the wisdom of the divine order?

Or say there's another man who is recommended to you as a candidate for promotion.

You're given his records to review, and you see that this man is depraved in almost every way that one can be—completely lacking in the qualities that make for a respectable official.

But his house faces a good direction. And it was built on a lucky day. These factors determine that he will be promoted.

Should such an outcome be accepted? And if one disapproves of such reasoning, is it possible that the spirits themselves smile on such cause and effect?

I say, "No."

Such a notion of justice is too foolish for a human system much less a divine order. This is why, unlike many of my friends, I don't hire feng shui masters when building or arranging my household.

However, I do not wholly disbelieve the claims of those who practice feng shui either. Nor do I deny that their system stems from some genuine insights and truths. Locations do of course influence one's emotions and one's fate. This is especially so in the case of haunted houses. I'm personally acquainted with two such houses that illustrate this point.

The first house is adjacent to the Temple for Those That Don't Have Anyone.

It was once occupied by no less a person than Governor Cao Xuemin himself. But he lived there for a very short time because on the same night that he moved in, two servants died, and he decided to move promptly back out. In total, counting General Cao Xuemin's servants, I've visited this house five different times to offer my sympathies after a sudden and strange death.

The second house lies off Fenfang Liuli Avenue.

A teacher named Shao Dasheng moved in there for a short time. He was a practical and fearless man. And although he saw many unsettling things occur in the residence—even during the brightest times of day—he shrugged them off and went about his business.

Not for long though.

Because just like the governor's servants, he died suddenly and mysteriously. Counting his death, I have had to visit this house seven times to extend my sympathies.

My former teacher Liu Wenzheng remarked that *The Book of Classical History* explores predictions based on the interconnection between one's fate and geographical formations and that *The Book of Rites* devotes long passages to discussing the effects of certain days and celestial bodies. It would be irrational to think wise people throughout history have devoted significant time to writing on and practicing divination if it was entirely without merit.

Ultimately, one can admit a richer interconnection between all things than our mortal courts allow, while also admitting that many of those who urge us to acknowledge this interconnection nevertheless grossly misunderstand it.

A MESSENGER RIDES FROM ONE CAMP TO ANOTHER

1.

The Taoist philosopher Liezi includes in his chronicles a story that illustrates the impossibility of fully differentiating between the dream and material realms. It suggests that perhaps the most useful way of understanding these two realms is to consider them as neighboring villages with no sure borders.

Liezi's story begins with a man in a forest.

The man was collecting firewood when he heard the bleating of an injured deer.

Thinking how good deer meat would taste, the man found the deer and beat it to death with a rock. He then buried it under branches while he ran home for a horse and rope.

Upon his return, the man couldn't remember where he buried the deer. Finally, he concluded that there was no deer and that he had dreamed it.

A few hours later, the man stopped at a tavern. He told some acquaintances about his dream. A second man at a neighboring table overheard the whole thing. He used the clues in the first man's story to find the deer and took it to his own home.

When the second man staggered into his house, bloody and breathing hard, his wife was frightened.

"I'm fine," the man said and told her about the deer. "A stranger dreamed it. In a tavern where I was resting. He described the place where he buried it so well that I recognized it. So on a whim, I went to look for it. The deer was exactly where the stranger dreamed it."

His wife gave the man a thoughtful look. "You say a stranger dreamed the deer. But I wonder if the truth is that you dreamed the stranger. And so it was your dream that came true and not his."

The man thought about this until he felt too dizzy to continue. "Well, I have the deer now, don't I? So ultimately who cares whether the clues were in my dream or in another man's?"

Meanwhile, the first man did actually have a dream about the deer he had lost. He dreamed the second man found it and dragged it home. The dream was so vivid that it woke him. Once dawn lit the sky, the first man used the details from his dream as clues to find the second man's house.

When he learned that the second man had dug up the deer for himself, the first man demanded it back. They argued and fought for a long time before agreeing to let a judge settle the matter.

The judge listened incredulously to their story then put his head down in silence for a while. When he looked up again, he said, "There's no precedent for this so let us carefully consider the details."

He pointed at the first man. "You," he said. "You originally found the deer. However, you then decided that it did not exist. Now, you've changed your mind again."

The judge turned to the second man. "In your case, you

originally thought the deer was another man's dream. Later, you concluded it was a real deer. As for your wife, she maintains it was originally your dream and not the other man's."

Now addressing both men, the judge continued, "This is all very confusing. But there is a way through this confusion. Regardless of whether the deer is somebody's dream or somebody's lucky discovery in the material world, there's still only one deer. Therefore, you two can settle the matter by cutting the one deer in half."

Eventually, the emperor himself heard about this extraordinary case and discussed it with his chief advisor.

The advisor commented: "It is hard for mere mortals like us to always discern what is a dream and what is not. The case we have just discussed may have actually unfolded in the world, or it might be someone's dream that became a popular tale. In either case, it's obvious that the judge's decision was wise."

2.

Something happened while I was exiled in Urumqi that bears some resemblance to Liezi's story.

I was assigned to inspect a military camp on the western front and worked closely with an officer named Liang to review the camp's details.

Late on my first night in the camp, a runner, sent by an official in a town not too far away, rushed up and thrust a sealed document toward me.

I found that it contained information that needed to be passed onto the capital immediately. In other words, I needed a mounted messenger.

Usually, I wouldn't task an officer with messenger duty, but the camp was nearly empty that night because most of the soldiers were out on maneuvers. Thus, Liang was the only man in camp with a horse. So I shook him awake and ordered him to carry the message until he found a substitute who could carry it the rest of the way.

After riding hard for a dozen li, Liang found such a substitute. He then rode back to camp and went to sleep again.

When I woke Liang the next morning, he grasped my arm.

"I had the strangest dream, and you were in it," he said. "You asked me to rush a document to a messenger who could take it all the way to the capital. Because of the urgency, I rode my horse hard. It was a very realistic dream. My hindquarters and legs even feel sore this morning. Isn't that incredible?"

"All of this actually happened," I corrected Liang. "Your dream was not a dream at all."

When I said this, Liang's servants, who had been getting his clothes ready for him while we spoke, burst out laughing. However, Liang's confusion didn't amuse me. It unnerved me, and I recalled Liezi's story.

Later, I wrote a poem about the incident:

A horse is whipped so that it jumps,
from dream to waking then back again.
Our lives leap like this too.
Our past is felt but also forgotten.

Childhood incidents feel like dreams.
The remembered becomes the imagined.
And both get buried in the forest under brush.
Who knows which deer are real?

3.

Officer Liang mistook reality for a dream. There are also those who mistake a dream for reality. My cousin Cichen is acquainted with one such event that occurred in Jinghai County.

A man there went to bed one night and fell asleep while his wife stayed up in a room on the far side of the house—weaving cloth. The man dreamed that he was trying to fall asleep when suddenly his wife cried out right before he saw several huge men dragging her past their bedroom.

The dream was so vivid and realistic that it startled the man awake. He leapt from his bed, grabbed a cudgel, and rushed outside in pursuit of the kidnappers.

He caught up to them—or thought he did. They had a shrieking woman pinned to the ground and were trying to rape her. Enraged, the man charged them, cursing and swinging his stick until the howling kidnappers fled.

The man bent to help the woman he thought to be his wife and was shocked to find out that she was instead a woman from a neighboring village.

Confused, he escorted the woman home and dazedly returned to his own home. His wife was there, safely weaving away, just as she was when he fell asleep.

The astonished man realized that his wife's abduction had been a dream that nevertheless somehow bled into the reality of an actual abduction. His dream had been used as a divine tool by powers beyond to help the woman.

Everything that exists is formed from qi, that sacred ether that is not matter itself yet condenses into the things of the material world—just as vapor in the air condenses into water on the ground before again melting into the sky.

In this way, the forms of the animals that we see originate in the heaven realm. As the spiritual seeds of these animals grow and unfold in our realm, they take in qi through their breath. As they become old, they give qi back the same way. Plants are similar. The seeds of their being come from the shadows of the earth, not the sky. Yet just like animals, their growth depends on taking in qi. This they do through leaf and root—inhaling and exhaling in rhythm with the seasons and the infinite transformations of yin into yang into one another. Thus, they bloom.

Upon its birth, a living thing takes in qi day after day—through skin, through eyes, through mouth and ear. One day, it reaches its full maturity. After that, qi seeps from it, quicker than it can take it in, so that eventually it becomes dry and not wet, shriveled and not plump. When qi is inside a thing and accumulating, it is of the category "spirit." When qi is leaving a thing to return to its origin and decreasing, it is of the category "ghost."

—Zhang Zai (1020–1077)

WHAT QI BECOMES

1.

Although rare, it's not unknown for ghosts to kill people. In keeping with the mysteriousness of the realms beyond the material world, many times their reasons aren't evident. But sometimes they clearly murder to feed off the spirits of the living. Ni Yujiang told me that he once heard Shi Liangsheng offer an explanation for this:

"A ghost is made from the vital qi that's left behind after a body dies. With time, such qi will naturally disperse. However, by feeding on the vital qi of the living, ghosts can delay their disappearance from our world. Female ghosts generally seduce human beings to draw out their qi. Male ghosts generally kill people to draw out their qi. This is the difference between draining blood from an animal over time or hacking it into meat straight away."

2.

One day, Liu Tingsheng told me and my teacher Bao

Jingting a story about five travelling students who were studying for their official exams.

The students got caught in a vicious summer thunderstorm and sheltered for the night in an abandoned temple. Exhausted from travelling, they quickly fell asleep on the floor of one of the rooms. All except for one student, who stayed awake to serve a rotation as a guard in case bandits were about.

Suddenly, gusts of cold wind shot inside the room, and the temperature plummeted.

Before the bulging eyes of the guard, mists with the vague shapes of people drifted inside, settled over one of his sleeping companions, and began to suck out gossamer threads of qi from his pores.

The guard shouted at his companions to wake them, but his cry was cut short. Almost as soon as his mouth opened, one of the sentient mists broke against him, and he felt too weak to use his voice or move his tongue.

Thus paralyzed, the guard watched as the ghosts finished draining the first sleeping student—leaving him husk-dry and dead—and then moved onto the second and the third.

The ghosts were just about to start feeding on the fourth student when an unfamiliar, old man ran into the room shouting.

"Stop!" he said to the ghosts. "These gentlemen are fated to pass their exams and become officials one day. Therefore, the divinities of Heaven forbid their coming to harm."

The old man's cry powerfully affected the ghosts. Not only did they stop, but they fled the room too.

The stranger disappeared right after the ghosts, causing the two survivors to wonder who he was—a former temple monk or a ghost of some kind himself? As for the students, the one who acted as guard went on to become the principal of a local Confucian school, while the other student became a teacher at this same school.

When Liu Tingsheng finished his story, Bao Jingting burst out laughing.

"Well," he said. "For most of my life, I've personally looked down on scholarly sorts, as well as government officials. So I'm slightly surprised that such positions would carry significance for a ghost."

That is Bao Jinting's opinion, and there is merit to it. But who knows? One could also read the situation not as a fabrication invented by vain scholars but as an actual case that illustrates Shi Liangsheng's theories.

A SPELL FOR DICE

A spell is recorded in the *Youyang Zazu* that allows one to control dice. The words of the spell are these:

"Yi Di Mi Di, Mi Jie Luo Di."

If you say these words 100,000 times, by the end of your recitation you will have gained the power to control up to six dice. These you can turn and toss as you like, and their result will turn out as you will it every time.

100,000 times is a lot of times to recite something. But I know several people who have tried this spell, and it worked perfectly for some.

Some.

The spell didn't work for everyone. I've thought a great deal about why and have decided that there is even more to a spell than knowing the right words and reciting it the right number of times.

This "even more" is a matter of purity of intent.

Purity of intent is the most important factor. If you have it, you can even cure an illness simply by chanting a single word associated with the appropriate medicine, such as "donkey," rather than administering the medicine itself.

What is purity of intent?

To possess it means that your will and spirit focus on a single purpose so that you can see it and only it.

It means that you think and feel as if what you want to accomplish is already true.

If you do these things, the qi of what you imagine will vibrate so that it resonates in sync with divine energies, and the thing or event will move from the realm of the imaginary to the realm of the true.

If however, you feel like you are simply experimenting and waiting to see what happens after chanting a spell, there will be no change in the vibration of qi, and nothing will happen.

Purity of intent is the power source of all spells. The dice charm is one example.

HORSE IN SNOW

A Lord Guan temple was given a horse by a local business owner as an offering to Lord Guan. Since a horse is an unusual offering to make, the temple's attendants did not know what to do with him. So they built a stable for him to sleep in at night and let him wander around the grounds and eat grass during the day.

Soon, the horse began to disappear for long periods of time, strongly preferring the woods and the fields to the temple property. However, twice each month he returned to visit.

On the first and on the fifteenth, the exact days when the temple's worship rituals took place, he would come back before dawn and stand outside of the temple—so still that he looked like a statue.

The place he stood was always the exact same spot—differing not even by an inch. And he always got the day right, regardless of whether the month had 30 days or 31 days.

When the worship rituals were done, he would disappear again until the next ritual day, weeks later.

When this phenomenon first came to my attention, I suspected the Taoist priests of leading the horse to the temple early in the day and then making up a wild tale about his devotion to impress villagers.

However, on the lunar ritual day of February the first in 1770, I made it a point to arrive at the temple in the early hours of the morning when no one else was around. I was standing there when suddenly I saw the horse walking slowly up to the temple—all alone on a gravel road beneath the falling snow. With its ears hanging, it calmly marched up to its customary spot and took up its position.

There was absolutely no one else beneath the falling snow.

It was only I, the horse, and Lord Guan.

This is marvelous.

THE MARKED PEARS

My great-uncle Chen Deyin had a cat who was always stealing food. Because the maid hit or kicked the cat whenever she caught it stealing, an intense hatred grew between them.

One day, my great-uncle's family went out to visit relatives and left the maid in charge. As soon as they were gone, she locked the doors and lay down for a long nap. When she woke up hours later, she found some pears that had been placed on the table to ripen were missing.

These were not ordinary pears, but a special variety both expensive and difficult to acquire. The maid was in a panic as she looked for them everywhere that she could think of—inside and outside the house, once then twice.

The whole time the cat stared at her with unblinking severity—as if taking pleasure in her predicament.

When the family returned, my great-aunt noticed the pears were gone and angrily accused the maid.

The frightened maid swore she did not eat them. But since the front door was locked, her denial held no weight. She was beaten until she couldn't stand and sent outside to think upon her crime.

Later that evening, my great-uncle sifted the cold ashes in the stove to ready it for a new fire. While doing so, his stick struck a lump and then, after feeling around the cold ashes, found several more. The lumps turned out to be the pears.

After washing the pears, my uncle saw that they were covered with marks made by cat teeth and cat claws.

"It was the cat. It had to be," my uncle declared, "although the creature has never shown interest in fruit before today. It seems that intelligence just like anger may be awoken in creatures unfairly treated, and the maid's treatment must have awoken the cat's intelligence. The cat used this intelligence to frame her."

The maid was invited back inside and told about the cat's trick. Immediately, she grabbed a stick, but my great-aunt seized her arm.

"Haven't you learned anything? Even if I let you kill the cat, don't you think its spirit would get its revenge? If its actions were harsh this time and its intelligence troubling, what do you think would happen when it returned from the grave? What else might you find in the ashes?"

The maid considered my aunt's words and ceased to hit the cat. Consequently, its temperament became more peaceful around her.

A THING DONE IN A MOMENT

A rash of tiger attacks plagued Jingde County while my cousin Ji Zhonghan was magistrate there. The attacks were so bloody, brutal, and continual that the residents were sure that a pack was behind the violence until the evidence of hairs and tracks determined that, no, a single animal was responsible.

After that, the county's hunters tried to trap the clever beast or kill it with an assortment of weapons. Most could not find it, or at least claimed they couldn't, and the few that did get close were maimed or massacred. Finally, a group of citizens demanded that my cousin hire the services of the Tangs, the famous tiger-hunting family from Huizhou.

He agreed and dispatched a servant with the high fee that the Tangs charged. A few days later, the servant returned with the news that the Tangs had agreed to take on the task and that two of their best men would arrive soon.

The Tang family specialty began during the Ming dynasty when a tiger killed a Tang man shortly before the birth of his son. The distraught mother swore revenge and found the best hunters in her province to train her son to kill tigers. She swore to him that if he did not devote his life to doing so then she would disown him. This same vow had been made by the son and his wife to their children and so on until the Tangs became what they were.

The residents waited with great anticipation for the Tang hunters. They were eager to be free of their fear but also curious about what kind of men that generations of such single-minded breeding produced. They conjured images of black-bearded brutes, thick-bodied like hunters in old paintings, massive hands wrapped around guns designed for big game.

Then the actual tiger hunters turned up, and everyone's hearts fell.

No thick bones.

No black beards.

No guns.

What their money had bought was an old man with a white beard, a bad cough, and a short-handled axe, and a vacant-looking youth, of around sixteen or seventeen years, with arms barely thicker than bamboo.

* * *

My cousin reddened when he saw the pair, and he was stiff and silent as they announced their identities.

But despite his near certainty that the Tangs were playing a practical joke, he decided to treat the "hunters" seriously until he saw what they could do and called out for food and drink.

The old man, discerning my cousin's skepticism, waved away the offer.

"Hold off," he said. "There's nothing yet to celebrate. Feasting can wait until we see to this tiger of yours."

A guide escorted the ungainly pair to where the tiger had been last seen—a steaming valley at the bottom of a steep path near the county border. At the top of the path, the guide halted. "This is far as I go."

Laughing, the old man patted the guide's arm. "What?" he said. "You don't trust us to protect you?" He then motioned the distracted-looking boy to his side, and the pair descended into the valley.

Near the bottom, the old man stopped the boy. "The beast must be sleeping," he said. "Call it."

Hunched over, the boy thrust up his chin, spread his mouth wide, and let loose from his scrawny body a startling imitation of a tiger's roar.

One roar.

Two.

The boy did not have to make a third because halfway through the second, the tiger bounded out.

Roaring itself, with eyes and teeth flashing, and moving forward so fast that it seemed thrown in anger, the tiger headed straight for the old man. It seemed certain that the tiger would tear him into blood and guts. But just as the tiger leapt, the old man ducked and rolled onto his back, his axe held tightly in one hand as he gracefully dodged the massive paws.

When the tiger landed, blood and ichor dumped from its belly, and it crashed to the ground dead. The guide realized that just as the tiger sailed over, the old man and his tiny axe had sliced it open from throat to tail.

The celebration that night was wild with applause and cheers. Toward the end of the meal, someone asked the odd hunters how they managed to accomplish killing a tiger so quickly.

The old man stopped eating and said, "I did not kill the tiger just like that. It might have appeared to take just a moment. But my part took me a lifetime to learn. First, I had to spend ten years strengthening the arm that held the axe so that a man could swing from my arm without unsteadying it, then another ten years to hone my eyes so that they could track the fall of individual raindrops and resist blinking even if tickled with a feather."

* * *

My cousin's account of the two men and the tiger bears witness to the truth of the philosopher Zhuangzi's observation that innate talent counts for little in life. Intelligent, strong, and gifted people are born all the time whose attributes never bear fruit or who never contribute anything to the world. It is not innate talent but practice that nurtures the superhuman. It is fidelity and dedication that enables the impossible.

Once I saw the scholar Shi Sibiao write a long line of poetry in the dark with his brush. His fine writing style was no different in the dark than it was in the light—which is more than can be said for most people.

Even more impressively, I was told that Li Wenke, former Vice Head of the Department of Penalties and Justice, can repeatedly write the same character on a hundred separate pieces of very thin paper with such precision that each character is exactly the same—with no deviation of any stroke. He does this so perfectly that when he stacks the pieces of paper and holds the stack up to the sun, the light shines through and makes it seem as if a single character is floating in mid-air.

The only trick in all these cases is humility and faith enough to devote yourself to one small thing. How accomplished one could be if one modestly focused on just one thing and never left off until the performance was perfect. This is how the mundane becomes the divine.

WATER AND THE OBJECTS WITHIN

In southern Cangzhou, there's a temple built on the bank where the river curves. During a spring flood, it was severely damaged. Two stone lions guarding it tumbled into the river along with part of the bank.

When this occurred, the temple's monks didn't have sufficient funds to repair the temple, but several years later they did. As part of their rebuilding efforts, they searched the river for the lions.

Over a dozen volunteers dived in the water near the temple, but no one could find the beasts. It was decided the current must have carried them forward a long way. So the volunteers took some boats out and dredged the river with long iron poles. Although they searched downstream for over ten li, they found nothing more substantial than big rocks.

During dinner one evening, the temple monks were talking about the volunteers' failure.

A visiting scholar who was teaching a class to young children in one of the temple rooms during the day burst out in laughter. "Of course, you had no luck," he said. "Your theory that the current carried the two lions forward assumes that stone behaves like wood. But wood floats while stone sinks.

The nature of these two substances is completely different. Unlike wood, which would have moved far downstream, the stone lions must have sunk in the sand of the river bottom. You were right to initially search near the temple, but you should have dug deeper."

Several people agreed with the scholar's theory. But one person did not. He was a veteran of the emperor's navy, and he knew the ways of water and things that moved in it well.

The veteran said to the scholar:

"You're right that we should consider the principles underlying the nature of things. But just because one thinks one understands the principles involved in a situation doesn't mean that one does.

"You talked about the principles of stone, the principles of wood, and you talked too about the principles of water. But you talked about them without considering how these principles interacted with each other in this particular situation—probably because of a lack of practical experience.

"Heavy stone doesn't just sink where it sits when water and sand are involved, at least not in cases like this.

"To be more precise, when water slams against the back of a large stone object in a forward-moving stream, its force can't move the stone.

"Consequently, the water is pushed to the bottom of the stone object and slowly washes sand and gravel out from beneath it.

"In this way, a depression is created, and the heavy stone object falls backwards—over and over as the process repeats—until the stone object has moved backwards a considerable distance."

The monks decided to follow the navy man's advice. Just as he predicted, the two lions were discovered a couple of li upstream.

This incident points out that while some people claim that

their ideas are superior because they have considered deep principles, this is not necessarily so.

Based on one's prejudices when observing a situation, including those that come from one's life experience, one can easily miss important factors.

Even if one does consider all principles involved, one must also correctly consider their interaction. One can know one thing and not another.

However, we assume too often that because we know one thing, we therefore know everything.

Since ancient times, writers of conventional histories have testified to the existence of those who history would otherwise forget. While zhiguai explore the strange, there is no reason they can't also preserve records of individuals who deserve to be remembered.

—Ji Yun, Locust Tree Notes

THAT WHICH REMAINS

During my uncle Zhonghan's tenure as an official in the Anhui province, a local farmer was planting crops one day when his digging implement uncovered a coffin with a corpse inside.

Time had reduced it to gummy soil and splinters with one notable exception. Amidst this decay sat a fresh-looking human heart, gleaming fat and red.

Frightened by the heart's preternatural state, the farmer dashed to the river and hurled it far out into the water. He then returned to the digging site.

Minutes later, he found a long, flat gravestone near the decayed coffin that was inscribed with writing. He brushed away the dirt to render the characters legible.

What was written there was so disturbing that he put the stone back and fled the area, vowing to never return.

Eventually, my uncle Zhonghan heard about the incident and let it be known that he wanted to see the stone.

The farmer and his neighbors panicked when they heard this. It was bad luck to mess with old graves. This was why the farmer had gotten rid of the heart.

So to avoid any more involvement with the burial site, they

shattered the gravestone into pieces and tossed them into the river too.

As an added precaution, the farmer then went around telling everyone that he had invented the whole story.

A busy man, my uncle soon forgot about the case. But after he retired, he came across a rubbing someone had made of the gravestone. He learned then that not only was the farmer's original account true but also the story behind the heart.

The rubbing read thus:

Daughter, your pale jade is blemished.
Not by you, but by others,
By wrongs done.

Near water, you died.
Afterwards, I put your body
At the bottom of this mountain.

In this life,
I failed you.
I could not even clear your name.

But I swear to you this:
I cover your tomb now
Not just with dirt.

I cover your tomb with a promise.
The centuries will not forget the injustice
Done to you.

I pray this to the spirits:
If you were at fault,
Let your heart rot.

If the only wrong was that done by others:
Let your heart never die.
Let it testify to the truth that they did not.

My nephew Zhaoxian, who told me about this incident, and I agreed that the father's message indicated his daughter was unjustly accused of some crime and died as a result—whether through suicide or murder.

The grief-stricken father, unable to accept this, used her grave tablet to protest and accuse. Subsequently, sympathetic spiritual forces abetted his cause and allowed the daughter's heart to remain fresh to vouch for her good character.

While the father's efforts are praiseworthy, unfortunately the note on the tablet was undated and signed with his writing pseudonym, "A Miner of Stones and Gems," rather than his real name. And no relatives could be traced through inquiries or historical records. Consequently, the girl's identity has been lost to time.

The architects of the wrongs done to her shall never be named. Her name will never be cleared. And, sadly, the full circumstances behind her tragedy can therefore never be fully comprehended.

All we can do is try to imagine.

WOMEN WITHOUT NAMES

History is filled with women of fierce character and extraordinary integrity. Many of their stories have been forgotten or destroyed. But some have survived. One involves a case that my granduncle Yuntai told my father about.

Toward the end of Ming dynasty, when upheavals and riots were everywhere, and people were fleeing the cities to escape their chaos, a married couple was travelling on a desolate stretch of road when a bandit saw them.

Even from a distance, the bandit's practiced eye observed that a money belt was tied around the husband's waist and tucked beneath his shirt. So, without the least bit of hesitation, he unsheathed his knife and ran toward the couple.

The couple saw the bandit coming. The husband reacted by abandoning their belongings and sprinting away. The wife stood her ground.

When the bandit reached the woman, she launched herself at him, grabbing him around the middle and refusing to let go.

The bandit stabbed her and did not stop until blood streamed from her guttering body. Still, she did not let go—not until the moment she died.

It is a shame that I do not know this woman's name.

* * *

Here's another story about a fierce woman, this one told by my father's granduncle, Zhenfan.

At the end of Ming dynasty, the five provinces near Hebei suffered famine. It was so bad that people slaughtered each other for food and restaurants openly sold human meat. Even government officials, wary of setting off a rebellion, didn't interfere.

Visitors to the five provinces were rarely prepared for the horrors they would encounter. One day, a visitor from a region near Dezhou and Jingzhou stopped at a restaurant to have lunch and was horrified to see a naked, young woman there—gagged, bound in rope, and laid across a cutting board to await the butcher's cuts.

The terror visible on the woman's face was so great that the man could not bear it, and he rushed up to the butcher to offer him twice what he had paid for the woman to secure her release.

The butcher agreed to the sale. But as the man was helping the woman out of her ropes, his hand touched her breast. And since he saw her as a bought thing, he did not apologize or try to correct his mistake.

In response, the woman angrily said: "I am grateful to you for saving me. For that, I would have dedicated my whole life to you as your servant and taken on any job no matter how hard. But I can see that you would want more than this. You are not trying to buy my freedom but trying to buy me. This, I will not allow. The reason that I was sold to the butcher in the first place is that I refused to marry the husband my family chose after the man I loved died."

After saying this, the woman took her clothes back off and threw them on the floor. Hunched naked over to the cutting board, she shut her eyes.

The butcher did not kill her right away. Angry at her willfulness, he cut a piece of flesh from her thigh without first slitting her throat. For a long time, she screamed and cried out. But her sounds were never ones of regret.

It's a shame that I do not know this woman's name either.

ROAD GHOST

My younger brother's former nanny, whose family name was Man, fell ill one summer. And she had word sent to her daughter Lijie who lived in a neighboring village.

It was not safe in that part of the country for women to walk alone at night, but Lijie's husband was away on business when she received the message. So she decided to set off alone for her mother's house.

When Lijie left her farm, the light was already turning tea-colored. By the time she reached the tiny road that led to her mother's village, it was pitch black and the darkness was full of the snuffling of night animals. The sounds were unsettling, but she walked briskly through the empty countryside and did not feel overly anxious—not until she heard footfalls from behind, moving quickly as if someone was trying to close the distance between them.

Heart pounding, Lijie sped up. When the person did too, she knew she was in trouble.

The closest habitation was miles away so no one could hear Lijie if she screamed. But rather than her mind becoming undone with panic, it became unusually clear and a quiet determination to reach her mother's side filled her.

Just as she felt this conviction, a curve in the road put her out of sight of her stalker. She took advantage of this moment to sprint behind a poplar tree next to an old grave.

Once in position, Lijie stripped off her jewelry, roughed up her hair, and tied her robe's silken belt around her neck like a hanging rope. After that, she bulged out her eyes, cocked her head limply to one side, stuck out her tongue, and leaned against the tree—the spitting image of a hanged woman's ghost.

All this time, the stranger had hurried closer.

One step, two, three, four, and just like that, he was on the road next to Lijie, looking wildly around.

Suddenly, his gaze found her.

So still that her figure half-blended into the tree and the shadows, Lijie felt the stranger studying her vague outline, trying to decide if she was real or a trick of his mind. She saved him additional effort by gurgling deep in her throat and stepping into the moonlight, where she motioned him to come closer.

The response of Lijie's pursuer was simple and direct. He made a broken sound and fell to the ground in a faint. Immediately, Lijie dashed away. She did not stop running until she reached her mother's house, where she pounded loudly on the door and burst inside, barely recognizable in her terror.

After Lijie told her story, several outraged family members voiced their desire to see the stalker beaten until he couldn't stand, and servants were sent off to find the criminal. But there was also laughter at Lijie's creative defense—including her own now that she was safe.

Although the culprit wasn't found that night, the next day word arrived about a strange incident in Lijie's village during the early morning hours. Previously sound of mind, a neighbor's son suffered a fit that led to his wandering the streets in a disordered state and babbling about an evil ghost.

After he was led home, this young man took to his bed. Periodically, he would shout out that the ghost had followed him and even now was hungrily ogling him.

Over the ensuing months, doctors and monks treated the man, but nothing eased his frightened mania. His senses never returned. For the rest of his life, he would regularly break down into sobs or cry out at unexpected moments, as if being touched by invisible hands.

How does one interpret a case of this nature?

Perhaps the illusions of our mind can be as lethal as real dangers.

Or perhaps sometimes spirits take advantage of a weakened mental or physical state to attack a person.

It could be too that divine forces decided to punish the man in such a way that he might comprehend what he made Lijie suffer.

THE SWAP

1.

Chang Tai, a supervisor for the Department of Revenue, employed a maid who was married to another servant. Although in her early twenties and perfectly healthy, one day she suddenly had a fit and collapsed to the floor unconscious. By that night, she was dead.

The next morning, Chang Tai tasked a few servants with rolling the woman's cold body from her bed into a coffin. Just as they were about to touch her, the body twitched.

The twitching increased in intensity and degree until the "dead" woman was actively flexing and flopping her arms and legs, as if loosening and warming them. Finally, her eyes popped open, and she pulled herself up in bed, shocking those gathered around.

"What is this place? Who are you all?" she cried out, as if she'd never seen the room or the people in it before.

Over the next few days, while signs of outward physical illness disappeared—no dizziness, no fatigue, no seizures—the woman's inner nature proved dramatically altered. It was as if the person who'd left was not the one who returned. The maid now moved and talked like a man, had no understanding of women's clothing, how to do her hair, or how to decorate her cheeks and lips with color. And she acted as if her husband was a stranger.

When asked what was wrong, she offered an answer for her changes that astonished everyone.

She was not actually *her*, she explained. Rather, *he* was an upper-class man who'd died around the same time as the previous owner of the body he now occupied.

Upon the man's death, like so many before him, this man travelled to the underworld realm. But unlike so many others, when he arrived he was told that it was not yet his time and that he must return to the material plane.

However, there was a catch.

He was not being sent back to his own body. Instead, because of the cruelty and contempt he'd shown toward women and servants during his life, he would be reanimated in the body of someone recently deceased who was both. And so this man had awakened in Chang Tai's home in a body not his own.

Of course, the alleged "man" was asked to provide details to verify his wild story. He declined and said that if he verified his identity, it would also verify the immoral conduct that had brought him to occupy his present body and consequently bring shame on his family name.

Thus, the servant woman's story was rejected by most as a fabrication. Even so, she continued to act as if it were true and for a long time refused to have marital relations with her husband, only eventually giving in because the law forced her. Each time afterwards, she would sob uncontrollably until dawn broke the next day.

Other strange behavior continued as well. She was often seen talking to herself as if she were someone else and was once heard complaining, "An education in the Classics for twenty years, a high-level government career for another thirty, and my fate is this: humiliation by marital servitude for the rest of my life."

The woman's husband reported too that she said odd things in her sleep. One time, she said, "The worst thing is the loss of the fortune I worked so hard to amass. I have access to none of it. It is for the pleasure of my greedy children and their children alone."

When the husband shook the woman awake and repeated her words, she said she had no idea what he was on about.

After a while, Chang Tai, thinking talk about ghosts foolish and dangerous, forbid gossip about the woman's situation. But its reality remained nevertheless. Roughly three years from the time she reanimated, the woman died from sorrow and loneliness—her true name known by none but herself.

2.

Wang Lanquan, a Vice Head of the Department of Penalties and Justice, shared the particulars of an incident similar to that which occurred in Chang Tai's home.

According to him, Governor Hu Wenbo had a younger brother, and this brother had a wife, Mistress Hu. She died briefly and after she was resuscitated, she no longer recognized family members. What's more, she angrily rebuffed her husband's affections and insisted that she was the dead daughter of a family with the surname Chen.

Mistress Hu even provided details specific enough for this line of Chens to be tracked down. Upon meeting them, she identified every single member of the family by sight and supplied information about them that only a true daughter would know.

Afterwards, she asked for permission to return to her old

family, but everyone concerned argued that this was impractical.

Eventually, a mirror was forced upon Mistress Hu, and she realized it was impossible to resume her previous life. Begrudgingly, she agreed to stay where she was.

A third account, preserved in *The History of The Ming Dynasty: The Volumes of the Five Elements*, is reminiscent of Mistress Hu's situation and that of Chang Tai's servant as well.

It concerns a woman who had been dead for three years taking up residence in the recent corpse of another person, one Yuan Matou.

The case is interesting not only for its details about body swapping but also because of the way the legal authorities during that period dealt with this case. They concluded that when determining identity one must give precedence to the nature of the body rather than the soul. They arrived at this determination not because it was inherently more just, but because it was more practical.

Only the physical could provide the type of evidence with which courts were comfortable. If, conversely, they had ruled in favor of giving precedence to the soul, illegal and immoral conduct could be blamed on evil entities and influences. This would make it difficult to accurately distribute fault.

PEONIES

As a young girl, my mother was visiting her aunt, Lady Cao, one summer in Wuqing County when a strange thing occurred.

A tall wooden pillar at the estate sprouted two peonies just above eye level. One peony had blue-green petals and the petals of the other were a light plum. Both were vividly colored and shot through with gold. They were extremely beautiful.

But what truly amazed everyone was that the flowers had impossibly managed to sprout from solid wood. This was taken as an omen of good luck.

However, within a week the flowers withered and shed their petals.

A plant so tough that it sprouted in solid wood should then die just like that made no sense to my mother nor anyone else. What was even stranger than their accelerated decline was the stems that the flowers left behind. They were at their roots indistinguishable in color, texture, and grain from the wood of the pillar—as if they were a continuation of the wood rather than independent plants.

My grandfather Zhang Xuefeng thought the whole situation unnatural. Agitated, he complained it gave him a bad feeling and said, "The invisible world keeps its distance from ours as a matter of law and design. The only exception to this occurs right before personal disasters. At such times, a family's ancestors occasionally press the gods to send a warning to their family. Events that violate the laws of nature should therefore be regarded the same as a stranger knocking on your door late at night. Thus, these strange flowers do not bode well."

My grandfather turned out to be correct. Shortly after the peonies' death, the Caos were visited by a string of disasters.

THE REALNESS OF PAINTINGS AND DEMONS

Sometimes, the appearance of things when you are watching them is very different from when you are not.

Take the case of a painting brought to my attention by Huo Yangzhong.

Entitled *A Xian Nü Fairy Makes a Deer Her Steed*, it is signed by the famous Zhao Zhongmu. While this signature might be a forgery, the painting is nevertheless striking—so much so that the family who bought it hung it in a place of honor on their wall.

Soon afterwards, the family began to receive reports from passersby that sometimes, when the house was empty, the figure of the xian nü would step out of the painting and walk along the wall.

There, it was indistinguishable from other shadows except for two things.

One, it moved eerily and bonelessly as if alive.

Two, it remained tinted with the colors of the painting.

After hearing the reports of the passersby, one morning the household head tied a cord to the bottom roller of the painting and pretended to leave the house. In reality, he hid inside. And as soon as the xian nü figure flitted from the painting to the wall, he yanked the cord.

This sent the painting crashing to the floor, where it rolled back into a scroll—so quickly that the figure was left stranded on the wall like an insect caught between cupped hands.

At first, the colors of the figure's skin and clothing were just as they were in the painting. But as the day wore on, they faded. After around twelve hours, they had faded so much that no trace of the xian nü remained—not even a stain.

My early thoughts on cases like these are that there was no actual painting spirit involved.

How could there be? I reasoned.

The entities that the paintings depicted were representations of things, not the things themselves, and so they lacked the internal vital qi required to generate a soul that might then enable the generation of a physical body.

This is not to say that I did not think any actual spirits were involved. I did. But I thought they must simply be regular demons who had assumed the shape of characters from paintings to cause confusion and wreak havoc.

However, my thinking on this subject evolved when I had the opportunity to read Zhang Hua's *Notes and Reflections on Things in the World*. Therein, Zhang Hua shares an account about the occult capture of a painting demon in the Yellow Flower Temple during the Northern Wei dynasty.

Yuan Zhao, the man who captured the demon, found a way to interrogate it. And he said to the demon, "You should not have material essence since you are merely a product of the imagination—a thing of paint not divine qi. How is it then that you appear before me? How is it that you have life?"

The demon replied, "You make too sharp a distinction between both ideas and spirits, and living things and art. Human lives in fact are like paintings undertaken by the subjects of the paintings—subjects who only emerge fully into existence through the act of painting themselves. Just as human beings struggle to become authentic and real, artists struggle to reveal the deeply real. If they manage to do so, through words or paint, their work attracts spiritual energies. These imbue it with enough life to manifest. This is how I came to be. A crucial stroke was added. Consciousness sparked. Body followed."

The demon's explanation in this case is worth thinking about.

MISTRESS CHEN'S DEVOTION

After my grandfather's first wife Mistress Chen died young, he married Mistress Zhang. The wedding day was long, and during a break in the activities, Mistress Zhang retreated to her bedroom to rest. While she was relaxing, a young woman slipped through the draped entryway that led to the room and sat by her side.

Mistress Zhang was surprised at the company. But she assumed that the young woman was a family member whose face she had not yet memorized—this despite the young woman's striking appearance.

A blouse of a rare golden yellow hue. A milky green skirt. And the whole ensemble brought to a strong conclusion by a reddish-black cape.

As well, this young woman had the superior air of someone who is used to having their orders followed. This was evident when, without even bothering to introduce herself, she launched into a description of the family's affairs and its various members. She held nothing back. While her analysis was brutal, it was also honest, thorough, and useful information to have to run the household.

Before Mistress Zhang could thank the woman, a servant

brought in a pot of tea, and she seized that moment to say her goodbyes.

A few days after the excitement of the wedding died down, Mistress Zhang asked about the young woman since she hadn't seen her since. She described her face, her mannerisms, and her distinct clothing. The clothing did the trick. Immediately, the outfit was recognized. It was the same outfit that Mistress Chen had been wearing when she was put into her coffin.

History is full of stories about the dead who get involved in the lives of the living. In Mistress Chen's case, maybe she was so worried about Mistress Zhang's ability to run the household that she temporarily delayed moving on to the nether realms to deliver her information. Certainly, this is possible since Mistress Zhang did not see Mistress Chen again.

However, it is notable that those in our family who are descended from Mistress Chen are those that have done remarkably well on the imperial examinations and prospered the most.

Maybe this is due to the strength of the bloodline. But perhaps they had some help from Mistress Chen's spirit. Perhaps the dead help us in ways that we do not ordinarily perceive.

ONE EXTRA AT A WEDDING

My mother's family had a nanny with yin-yang eyes. Thus dirt roads that appeared empty to others sometimes looked crowded to her, and she observed many other unusual things.

One day, my grandmother asked this woman about the saddest ghost she'd ever seen. This is what she said:

"To protect the reputations of the people involved, I won't tell you their names. I won't give you any other personal details either. But I will tell you this. The family was a good one. And the ghost belonged to a man who died when he was around twenty-seven.

"I was close friends with the young widow. So, on the 100-day anniversary of her husband's death, she asked me to visit to cheer her up.

"We sat inside the widow's house, along with her baby boy and ill-tempered sister-in-law, and talked. No matter the topic, every so often she broke down sobbing. Each time, like a small ripple coming from a bigger one, her boy cried too. A while into my visit, I looked up and saw *him* through the window—the husband's ghost. He gazed mournfully at us from the shadows of a cluster of clove trees in the courtyard.

"The ghost kept a fair distance. Ghosts, being yin in nature, become confused when too close to the yang heat of living creatures. This is especially true of new ones. Nevertheless, he was keenly aware of the emotions of his family. Whenever his widow and the baby boy cried, he winced. Not wanting to upset my friend, I told her none of this.

"About a year later, my friend's family persuaded her to find a new husband. A matchmaker visited. I came over too to lend my support. By this time, the ghost could bear the heat of the living well enough to enter the widow's house—although he still pressed against the walls. This is where he was when he realized what was being discussed.

"The idea of the widow remarrying threw him into a frenzy. He thrashed about for a long time, as if in the jaws of something, and kept reaching for the widow. But he could no longer touch her.

"In the weeks that followed, amidst discussions of potential matches, the winnowing down to a final selection, and then subsequent preparations, the ghost remained in a state of barely-controlled panic. He took turns desperately following everyone around as if he could convince them to plead his case. His only deviation from these pitiful displays was whenever there was a snag in the matrimonial negotiations. At such times, a smile cracked his face.

"But then the traditional wedding gifts from the groom arrived. And the ghost realized that a dead man has no power to stop anything. Anguished, he fled to the shadows of the clove trees, his usual refuge, and bawled there a long time. After he was done, he came back inside. From that moment forward his sad eyes refused to leave his wife.

"On the night before the wedding, the widow rushed around, wrapping up this to take and throwing away that. The ghost paced wildly along the wrap-around porch outside as if rhyming her busy movements, which he watched through the open doors and windows with great alarm. Even when the widow went to bed, he kept up his spectral pacing—except for those times when he slumped against the porch columns in a defeated way, or when he heard a sharp cough or some other noise come from the widow's room. This prompted him to rush in that direction until he realized that she was not trying to communicate.

"It was hard to see the spirit suffer so, but his selfish clinging angered me too. When I was sure that the widow was asleep, I whispered to the air: 'Begone! It's time to let her go.'

"But he stayed.

"The next morning, the groom—carrying a torch to light the early morning darkness for the wedding party—arrived. The whole group, now including the bride's family and myself, marched toward the groom's residence for the ceremony.

"The ghost should have stayed behind, but the stubborn thing did not. It struggled after us, step by step, although it must have been painful to brave the brightening day and bear the wounding proximity of the living.

"Soon, we reached the groom's home. That was nearly the end of the ghost's journey.

"The groom had nailed a magical sigil, depicting two armored door guards, to the front doorway. The thought-forms the sigil conjured, invisible to everyone except the ghost and myself, blocked his path so that he could not trespass. However, the ghost must have begged so pitifully that he convinced the guardians to let him inside. Because a little while later, I saw him slip into the garden. He chose a shady spot to stand and watch the ceremony and the banquet afterwards.

"During the ceremony and the banquet, the ghost stayed as still as a stone, at least until the evening had grown so late that the newlyweds retreated—amidst laughter, applause, and scattered jokes—to the special matrimonial bed.

"This is when the ghost acted up again. Lewdly, it positioned itself outside the bedroom window, its face ugly with weeping, as if it had decided to watch the new couple become each other's mates—from start to finish. But maybe it thought it could paralyze them with its gaze, thus preventing the marriage's consummation. Or maybe it even thought my friend might change her mind at the last moment.

"Whatever the case, the sigil guardians appeared and chased it off.

"After that night, the new bride did not return to her old residence. Her little boy though stayed there with her sister-in-law so that the newlyweds could have time alone. This was hard on her son. Every day, he cried for his mother. Knowing he was fond of me, my friend asked me to go to her old house and spend time with him.

"As I played with the boy, I observed the dead husband's ghost. It was much diminished—more a disturbance in the air than a man. Numbly, it drifted, misting hands sliding over the places its wife had touched. The only time it seemed to come alive was whenever the little boy periodically broke down into tears to plead for his mother. Then the ghost would lurch toward him as if to offer comfort.

"Eventually, the aunt grew irritated with the little boy's crying. The next time he shrieked for his mother, just as the ghost moved in his direction, she slapped the boy.

"This was too much for the ghost—to see its son hurting but be unable to console him, to see the sister-in-law attack the boy but be unable to stop her. And so it broke down into a violent fit.

"Shaking.

"Clacking its teeth.

"Beating wildly at its chest and face.

"Unable to bear the sight of such pain, I made excuses and left.

"I never returned to that house. I have no idea what became of the ghost. However later, I told my friend everything. She clenched her teeth to keep from crying and fell into a despondent state.

"Not long after that, the story of her husband's misery made its way to another widow who was thinking of remarrying. The story changed her mind."

* * *

It's commonly assumed that the bonds of love dissolve upon death. This is not true. The connection remains. So too do the feelings of the dead. How could anyone not be moved when considering what they suffer? As for what we owe the dead, I think we know deep in our hearts what decisions and rites must be made in each individual case. And our natures will guide us in this—just as they determine how compassionately or treacherously we deal with the living.

Of course, some Confucians argue the dead feel nothing and that ghosts aren't real. They dismiss the existence of spirits because deluded or dishonest people say untrue things.

I am not that sort of Confucian. After all, every good law that exists was either delivered by a spiritual entity or articulated by a spiritual influence inside us. And it is just as lazy and foolish to believe nothing one hears about ghosts as it is to believe everything. Personally, I believe ghosts are real enough to hurt us and for us to hurt them.

Besides, in the final analysis, I find that the nanny's story contains more wisdom and heart than what its naysayers can offer.

THE SECOND TRICK

Sometimes, it's hard to tell whether one's truly witnessing magic or simply a clever trick that's less dependent on supernatural power than fast hands and the art of distraction.

Take the shaman who visited my grandfather Xuefeng one afternoon when I was a boy. A little into his visit, this shaman pushed a nearly full cup of liquor to the center of the table and clapped a hand over it. Instantly, the cup sank.

I leaned forward to inspect the cup. The trick seemed to be exactly what it looked like. The cup had dematerialized and sank into the table so that its mouth now lay flat with the table's surface, making a kind of little pool inside the table.

Even more striking, when my hands fumbled beneath the table trying to find the cup, I felt nothing. Somehow, someway, a portion of it had rematerialized inside the table, while the rest had gone somewhere else entirely.

When I stood back up, the shaman put his right hand beneath the table. He neatly caught the cup.

Once more, it was whole.

I rubbed the top of the table where I had seen the cup's mouth. It was smooth and flat like before.

Though I could not fathom how the trick was done, it was

still conceivable that I had been fooled through clever camouflage. However, all doubts I had were undone by the shaman's next trick. He picked up a big bowl of sliced raw fish and tossed it into the air, where it promptly disappeared.

"Where did the bowl of fish go?" I asked.

The shaman said, "It's very close. Close enough that you can go get it. To be more exact, it is in your studio room—in the middle drawer of the cabinet where your paintings and calligraphy are stored."

My grandfather and I did not see how the shaman could be telling the truth since the door to the studio was kept locked because of the precious art and heirlooms inside. But we unlocked the room anyway and inspected the cabinet.

Seeing the cabinet up close made the shaman's claim doubly ridiculous. For the fish to be there, not only would it have to have teleported, but the four-inch high fish bowl would need to have shrunk in order to fit into the cabinet's two-inch high drawer. But then we noticed the container that previously held the fish was now atop the cabinet—filled with yellow, Buddha's hand fruits instead of pink, sliced fish.

I pulled out the middle drawer.

There it was. Just as the shaman had said. The missing fish was now occupying a smaller container.

Unlike the first trick with the cup, I could not easily dismiss this one. There were too many difficulties for it to be a clever stunt, from the locked studio door to the impossibility of making a bowl disappear midair. What I had initially taken as a shaman's deception was more mysterious and unsettling.

There are times when things that seem theoretically absurd nevertheless happen. The mind recoils then because it embarrasses us to stand by something that looks ridiculous. But the superior intelligence adapts itself to the world and searches the strange for new principles and new applications of known principles.

Now, it is widely known that fox and mountain spirits and other entities not bound by material form make off with people's belongings via teleportation and that they show a talent for turning the immaterial into the material and vice versa. It is commonly accepted too that magic and shamans can exorcise, communicate with, and bend the will of spiritual entities.

If such creatures could be captured then surely they could be trained to do one's bidding. If they can steal *from* people, they can steal *for* people.

In this way, the supernatural may reveal itself to be simply another order of nature. And nature may prove to be far vaster than our current categories allow.

A SPEAKER FOR THE DEAD AND THE DISCARNATE

When I was a boy, I visited my Aunt Lu in Cangzhou and met a wily, old woman named Hao. Hao claimed she could channel fox spirits and through them provide a person with a detailed map of their fate.

Hao was bossy and rude. But her fans were many. After all, she could describe the most hidden parts of your life—details of which even close neighbors weren't aware.

What people didn't know, however, was that this information wasn't spirit-derived. Hao obtained it through a network of spies that reached out to servants who were more than happy to gossip about their abusive employers in return for money or a favor—or just out of spite.

Hao's information allowed her to fabricate accurate predictions and also gave her a way to explain away incorrect ones. For example, she once told a pregnant woman who desperately wanted a son that she would give birth to one. When the woman gave birth to a girl instead, she confronted Hao.

"Your changed fortune was your fault," Hao scolded. "You were initially blessed with a son, just as I told you. But Heaven can snatch back gifts as easily as grant them. You blame me? I think not. The person you should look at is yourself. A few months ago, your parents gave you a package of twenty pastries. Instead of giving them all to your husband's parents, you shirked your filial duty and gave them only six, while you gobbled the rest. The result? Heaven was displeased, and what you put in your belly changed what was in your womb."

At the end of Hao's speech, the shamed woman admitted that, yes, it was true. In this way, Hao convinced nearly every one of her power. But one afternoon, this all changed.

Hao began to do a reading for some clients. As usual, she lit incense sticks so that the pungent smoke filled the air and suggested the fluttering of spirits, one of which she would pretend to allow to possess her. But before she could launch into her routine, her head snapped back and her body went violently stiff.

Then a deep, hollow voice was heard in the room. It seemed to come from the direction of Hao's face but sounded nothing like her, nor any voice she could manufacture.

"Hear me, fools who would know what is not yours to be known," said the voice.

"I'm not the fraud you came to hear but a true spirit. Though this wretch has convinced you that she regularly speaks on our behalf, this is false.

"Do you really think that spirits have nothing better to do than gossip about your days? If so, answer me this: do you chatter about what so and so beetle is doing in such and such's house?

"Do you concern yourself with a stranger's petty drama in a village a thousand li from you?

"Of course not. Yet, you have allowed this old cheat to sully our names for far too long. In doing so, she has led you away from the path of true wisdom. Now, since she has made herself rich by telling you your own secrets, I think it fitting that I now tell you hers so that you know I am what I say I am."

The voice then proceeded to spill Hao's secrets, including the names of her spies. Afterwards, it left Hao's body and she woke up in extreme confusion—as if struggling to emerge from a deep cacoon of sleep—while angry clients clamored around her, charging her with fraud.

Before the day was done, Hao packed up and fled for parts unknown. No one heard anything about her after that.

THE FUTURE IN THE PAST

I have thought a great deal about the mechanics involved in predicting the future, the different elements that contribute to our fate, and about the relative influences of divine decree, karma, and one's self-cultivation. Yet predestination remains a twisty matter.

Two accounts strikingly illustrate this.

The first was passed on to me by my maternal uncle, An Wuzhan. It involves an incident in Liufu County.

A housebuilder there visited a fortuneteller to find out if he would be lucky in love. This fortuneteller was the type who liked to make themselves feel superior by fooling others. So, after he studied the builder's palms and facial features, and obtained his birthplace and time, he decided to ignore all this information and play a trick instead.

"You're going to find love," said the fortuneteller. "But only after a few dark turns. In fact, that you came to see me on this exact day is the first step toward fulfilling your destiny.

"You see, a certain Mr. Jia lives in a large town about a hundred li to the southwest. Soon, he's going to die and leave behind a young wife. After his death, this wife will become yours. At least she will if you hurry to the town to allow this fate to unfold."

Excited by this news, the builder rode briskly to the town that the fortuneteller described and rented a room at an inn. He then went around asking if anyone knew Jia.

The builder simply wanted to catch an early glimpse of the woman fated to be his wife. But, as luck would have it, the first person he encountered *was* Jia—at least a married man whose name happened to be the same one that the fortuneteller had made up on the spot.

"Why are you looking for Jia?" asked Jia.

The builder figured that since the predicted death of the woman's husband was imminent, there was no harm in letting a stranger know about it. He told Jia everything.

This was a mistake. Convinced that the builder was planning to murder him and claim his wife—an intention clumsily masked by a phony story—Jia unsheathed his sword.

His reflexes sharpened by years of manual labor, the builder easily dodged Jia's blow and fled back to his room. There, he climbed out of the window and leapt over the back wall of the inn to hide.

In close pursuit, Jia stormed into the inn just moments after the builder and ordered the inn's owner to tell him where the builder was hiding. The owner refused. Enraged, Jia killed him.

Several people overheard the commotion and alerted the authorities. Consequently, the owner's body had barely hit the floor when armed city guards arrested Jia. Soon thereafter, he was executed.

The builder fled back to Liufu County. Since he hadn't told anyone his name or where he lived, he could not be tracked down and blamed for anything. A year or so later, a poor-looking family moved to Liufu. It consisted of a hunched old woman and two younger people: her grown son and the widowed wife of her other son.

Within a few months, the old woman died. The living son then forced the widow to find a matchmaker to help her secure a new husband whose engagement gift would pay for the funeral.

The first potential spouse that the matchmaker approached was the builder. After speaking with the woman and brother-in-law, he agreed to the match. While the builder and the woman did not delve too deeply into each other's past before the wedding, they did so afterwards. It was then that the builder was shocked to discover that his new wife was none other than the widow of Jia.

What sense can one make of a coincidence like this?

If the fortuneteller hadn't decided to play his joke, the builder would have never gone to the village and set off a chain of incidents that ended in Jia's death and the widow's move to Liufu, where she eventually married the builder.

All these things did not so much lead to an end as they were drawn to one already decided. In some profound way, the future was working backwards to determine the past even as the past was working forward to determine the future.

* * *

A second event of a similar nature unfolded in the Western Xisi District in the capital. A man there set up a street stall from which he told fortunes, and he began every day by casting his own fortune using the *I Ching*. One morning, his fortune was this: he would die from a calamity in two days.

Though the prediction indicated by the hexagrams was clear, how exactly the man's doom would come about was not. Therefore, on the day that his death was predicted, the man locked himself inside his home. He felt safe and confident that his knowledge of the prediction had saved his life. Then the earthquake began. Within minutes, his house collapsed, and the man was crushed to death.

This man would not have died had he not read the prediction of his death. Such cause and effect demonstrate that the future is not just seen but rather is also created in the seeing of it. This complicates the world considerably and grants even jokes eerie power.

SPIRITS IN THE BELLY

1.

There are three incidents that I know of that involve spirits talking in someone's belly.

The first occurred when a Li Yishan from Yunnan attended a private Taoist spirit-writing event. There, a medium allowed herself to be possessed by two fox spirits who wrote out messages in a table of sand to answer questions from the audience.

The fox spirits identified themselves as sisters. Both took a liking to Li Yishan—so much so that when he left the event that day, they left with him, having taken up residence in his belly.

From that point on, Li Yishan was often seen walking around town talking animatedly with the sisters: sometimes angrily, sometimes happily, but always talking. Even when the Taoist exorcist Master Zhengyi conducted a ritual to chase the sisters out, it had no effect.

Eventually, Li Yishan's condition deteriorated. He was plagued by coughing and seizures. The sisters felt no pity for him though, and they stayed where they were until the day he died. Before he passed, I had the opportunity to observe his condition firsthand at Hanlin Academy. Thus, I am quite sure about the particulars of his situation.

2.

A second case involving spirits in the belly was reported to me by Jin Tingtao, a trustworthy acquaintance who works for the Department of Personnel. He told me about two salt transportation supervisors—Shi and Zhang—who rented a room at an inn in the middle of nowhere while on assignment.

Shortly after Shi and Zhang settled in their rooms, a stranger who was also staying at the inn delivered a note through a servant that asked Shi's permission to introduce himself. Pleased by the stranger's manners, Shi assented.

Shi enjoyed his conversation with the stranger immensely, and they talked until it was near midnight. It was at this point that Shi bowed and bid the stranger good night. In saying goodnight in return, the stranger spoke as if they would see each other the next day. Thus, Shi was surprised when he learned the next morning that the stranger and his servants had vacated the premises.

At the time, Shi shrugged this off as just one of those odd things that happen. But as the day wore on, his belly started hurting. By that evening, voices began to come from it. Shi recognized two. They belonged to the stranger and the servant who delivered his note.

When the condition failed to go away on its own, Shi visited a Taoist priest. The priest managed to remove the voices through an astrological ritual, but this turned out to be temporary. A few days later, they returned for good.

My friend Jin Tingtao told me that he suspected that Shi's situation arose because he owed a debt incurred during one of his past lives. Perhaps he had cheated the stranger and his servants out of their homes in their previous incarnations and the possession was a settling of this debt.

This is a wild theory, but it is not wholly inconceivable. Many people are born owing their lives to others because of debts acquired during previous lives. Such debts must always be settled one way or another.

3.

The final case of spirits-in-the-belly that I'll relate was passed along to me by the official Shen Yunjiao. It concerns a nun who lived in Pinghu.

Some years back, this nun's belly swelled enormously one month. Upon medical inspection, she was found to be inhabited not by a child but by spirit. When others pressed their ears against her armpits, they could even faintly hear the spirit's voice.

This possession was lucky for the nun though because the possessing entity provided information about the future, information that proved so accurate that the nun was able to charge handsomely to share it.

Eventually, it was disclosed that the spirit had also entered the nun's body because of debt. However, unlike Shi's situation, the spirit entered her body to *pay* a debt from their previous lives—not to collect one. This echoes the details of a similar story recorded in Sun Guangxian's collection of anecdotes, *Northern Dreams*, making one think that such cases may be less rare than they first appear.

Collectively, these three anecdotes illustrate that although all human beings are filled with multiple voices, some are harmful while others are helpful. Therefore, one should be careful when deciding which to heed.

To understand the interconnectedness and interpenetration of all things, one should envision a lion and its hair.

The lion with all its hairs is a unity.

It is a single lion.

However, each hair of the lion is a distinct particularity as well — different from other hairs on the same lion. In this way, wholeness and distinctness depend upon one another. If there was no whole lion, there would be no individual hairs. If there were no individual hairs, then the whole lion would not be expressed.

Unity allows for particularity. Particularity expresses unity.

Understanding this, one understands too that the particular lion is in its way a hair of something else. Thinking on such matters one begins to comprehend the infinite.

—Fazang (643–712), Master Teacher of the Flower Garland School of Buddhism

THE SHAO YONG METHOD

1.

To understand a part is to understand the whole. And to understand the beginning is to foretell the ending. Thus, feats of precognition are no more surprising than surmising that a man is hiding in the tall grass because one sees the top of his head. Accurate predictions simply require one to be born with a talent for accurate perception or to develop such talent through meditation.

One person who had a gift for reading signs was the military commander Li Xuan. A quiet man from the Gansu province, Li Xuan was a brilliant strategist who routinely made accurate predictions of all kinds—from the martial to the romantic—using the Shao Yong method of divination called "observing plum blossoms." This method treats waking phenomena as dreams to be deciphered.

Once while travelling with General Wen, the emperor's Head of Diplomacy, on a diplomatic expedition through the Western borderlands, Li Xuan ducked outside his tent to find billows of black smoke rising up and the stench of burning plants. As he was pondering what might have happened, a messenger caught his attention and led him to General Wen's tent.

General Wen explained to Li Xuan that a soldier had accidentally set the dry, autumn grass near the camp's front gate ablaze. Thankfully, some other soldiers had quickly stomped out the flames and saved the tents. But to report a near-tragedy was not why General Wen called for Li Xuan. The reason was to find out if the fire was a sign of something more.

"So," said General Wen. "Does it signify?"

"It does," Li Xuan replied. "It predicts that in a couple of days, you'll send the emperor an emergency secret message."

General Wen asked Li Xuan how he knew this.

Li Xuan gestured toward the burnt grass.

"Smoke rising in the sky like a bird is almost always a message. Furthermore, I was told that the fire that generated this smoke spread swiftly—like a quickly opened hand. This foretells urgency. That the grass was entirely burnt away signifies the message will be secret too because all secret messages are burned. Finally, see how the smoke has risen as high into the sky as it can and still be visible? And how it now bobs about there in a great black cloud without stringing apart? This tells me that the message will be one made to the highest office possible, that of the throne."

"That's well explained," said General Wen. "But I have nothing urgent or secret to report."

"Not now," Li Xuan said. "But you will. In fact, that you don't know yet what you'll report is also signified. The fire was set unintentionally, without premeditation. You'll learn the information that you'll convey in the same manner."

Although at the time Li Xuan's ideas seemed to be more of a reaching than a reading, a few days later General Wen received sudden news that required him to pass it on to the emperor secretly and quickly.

2.

A common question about augury is whether a sign for one person, say a dead bird at a door stoop or a tree felled by a spring storm, would be read the same way for different people.

The answer, at least in terms of the Shao Yong method, is no.

How a sign is read depends on who it's read for and under what circumstances. A sign does not exist apart from its larger context. And this context must be fully considered before an interpretation is made—just as one looks at a whole poem before thinking about the meaning of an image within.

For example, one of Li Xuan's methods for making a prediction was to ask a client to randomly pick an object. One time, a Hanlin Academy scholar and his friend visited Li Xuan, and both requested a reading. Li Xuan did the Hanlin scholar's reading first and asked him to pick an object. The scholar chose Li Xuan's bronze pipe, which was lying on a nearby stone.

Li Xuan said, "The pipe is lit and still generates smoke. But it does this weakly, and the smoke refuses to rise in the air. Instead, it lingers around the bowl of the pipe, tracing the rim like a finger. Smoke of this nature requires a strong puff to move higher. This tells me that your post is neither among the lowest nor among the highest."

"True," said the scholar, "But I already know this. And it's not hard to guess. Let me ask you something I don't know. Will I please my superiors well enough to hold onto my post for a long time?"

Li Xuan studied the pipe again. "I'll be blunt," he said when finished. "The answer is no. While the pipe is still faintly lit, almost all the tobacco has burnt away. This means that soon the pipe will go out, and there will just be ashes."

Despite the revelation's negative nature, since it was something the Hanlin scholar didn't know and so impressed him, he eagerly asked another question. "How long will I live?"

"Well," Li Xuan said, "the pipe is bronze. That's good. Bronze is more durable than wood. But a pipe is not meant to last a hundred years. So you'll live to be old, yes. But you will not live to be among the oldest."

After receiving the news, the scholar left the tent. This allowed his friend to take his turn. He picked up the pipe too. He was curious whether his choice of object would mean his reading would be similar to his companion's.

It wasn't.

This time Li Xuan said, "There is no discernible fire or heat in the pipe now. Not even that of the smoldering kind. This tells me that you have occupied a position with lots of responsibility, but little actual power or opportunities for advancement. My reading begins with this point.

"But other clues allow me to refine it further. For instance, the pipe was laid down right before you chose it. This tells me that not only was your position a poor one but also that you were recently fired from it.

"However, your picking up the pipe again signifies that someone helped you acquire another position soon thereafter. Finally, at this very moment, I find myself desiring tobacco. Thus, I will light this pipe again quite soon. This indicates that in the near future your recently acquired position will offer significantly greater rewards."

Li Xuan's statements about the pasts of both men were accurate. His predictions about their futures proved accurate as well. Therefore, we see that the reading of signs involves not just recognition of the interconnection between all things but also of the interconnection between all times—so that past, present, and future glitter like different facets of the same gem.

THE BLOOM

My former teacher Li Youdan told me about a person who was serving as a sub-prefect in Guizhou Province when the Miao people launched their rebellion against the government.

I don't remember this sub-prefect's first name, but his family name was Bi. He was in charge of transporting military food supplies until bandits killed him.

Long before his life ended so tragically, this Bi was assigned to explore and map the region where the Miao people lived.

One afternoon, the chief of the Miao people—who did not yet hate the emperor—hosted a banquet for Bi. During it, two special, lidded cups were sat in front of the two men.

The chief lifted his cup, pried off the lid, and stood up to show Bi what was inside: a centipede-like worm slowly turning and twisting.

The chief's translator explained that the worm was called an "orchid worm" because it appeared around the same time that a very rare orchid plant briefly blossomed, and because it fed on the pistil and stamen located in the narrow throat of each flower.

Since the orchid was its sole source of food, the worms died when the blossoms fell—either while inside burrows under rocks and old logs near the orchid plants or inside the orchids themselves.

"Luckily," the chief's translator said to Bi, "right now it is the orchids' blooming season. So the chief was able to have two of the worms captured—one for him and one to honor you."

As soon as the translator explained the cups, the chief guided Bi in lifting the lid of each one, sprinkling salt inside, and replacing the lid.

A few minutes later, the two men reopened their cups to gaze at the liquid into which the worms had melted. The substance was green, bright, and shiny like pottery glaze, and smelled strongly of orchids.

Bi later told Li Youdan that he and the chief used the orchid-worm liquid in a manner similar to how vinegar is used. But the substance was nothing like vinegar or anything else with which he was familiar. The taste of its fragrance filled one's mouth, pleasantly unfolding between the teeth and blossoming into one's cheeks—so that everything tasted of flowers and continued to do so even after half a day's time.

This story has stayed with me since Li Youdan shared it. I wish I found out what kind of worm was put in the cup.

ON THE DOUBLE NATURE OF WRITTEN CHARACTERS AND SPIRITS

Written characters are halfway between the categories of spiritual and physical things. Because of their dual nature, they can be used to control nature spirits through written spells and can even physically mark them.

The ninth-century scholar Duan Chengshi, for example, relates a story in his *Youyang Zazu* about Prime Minister Guo Yuanzhen.

One night, Guo Yuanzhen was resting in his hut on a desolated mountainside when a humanoid entity with an enormous, round, albino face and a very broad forehead materialized next to him. Instead of running away, Guo Yuanzhen snatched up his writing brush and in a flurry of quick strokes scribbled the following spell on the startled fiend's head.

Years of waving swords, yet the soldiers rust.
Even the horses they ride must gallop into dust.

In response, the startled spirit cried out angrily and promptly vanished.

Guo Yuanzhen thought that was the end of the encounter. However, a few days later, he was hiking in a densely forested area when he came across a massive white fungus growing from an ancient tree. His lines of poetry were written around the cap of this fungus.

Duan Chengshi's story is similar to others I've read or heard. Collectively, they suggest that the spirits of things do not necessarily correspond to their physical bodies. Consequently, the spirits of humans very likely do not always look human, and spirits that *do* look human may be something else entirely.

PAPER HORSES, WOODEN HOUSES

In the olden days, the deceased were buried with miniature replicas of everyday objects—tiny houses, clay servants, foil money, and statues of horses and carriages. The moderns gave up burial, opting instead to make their replicas out of paper and burn them, thus releasing their spiritual essence to the netherworld.

These practices vary slightly. But both try to ensure that the spirits of the dead are not stranded in the next world with nothing but their names. The poet Meng Yunqing, however, saw these customs as wasted effort. He argued in a poem that objects are not needed by the dead—whether buried or burnt.

The dead require no things from us.
No houses or horses, just our love.

Those who share Meng Yunqing's view see funerary objects as simply tools to help the living cope with grief, and not as helpful to the dead. I, however, have no choice but to side with those who came before Meng Yunqing. For I witnessed proof of their theory in the case of my eldest son Ruji.

When Ruji's long illness reached the point where it was

obvious that he would soon die, my granddaughter made a paper horse and had a servant burn it. Not long afterwards, Ruji jolted briefly back into consciousness.

"Daughter," he said, "my soul made it out of the gate, but I did not know what way to go from there. Then I heard a noise in the mist, and it partially cleared to reveal the form of our old servant Wang Liansheng.

He had a horse with him and indicated for me to mount it. I did. However, the horse refused to budge. When we examined it, we discovered that its rear leg was injured."

When Ruji finished speaking, the servant who had burned the paper horse cried out: "It's my fault. Forgive me. Before I lit the horse, I accidentally ripped its rear leg. I did not think it would matter."

* * *

Then there's the case of my maternal uncle's wife, Mistress Chang.

On her deathbed, witnesses heard her complain: "I just saw my new house in the netherworld, and it won't do at all. From far away, it looked elegant and carefully made. But up close you can see that the eastern wall is rotten and falling apart. How can I live in such a place?" Afterwards, when the coffin that had been built for Mistress Chang was examined, a small moldy hole was found on its eastern side.

Such matters prevent me from siding with Meng Yunqing. Perhaps burning a thing releases its spiritual essence to accompany the human essence. Or perhaps the thoughtful burying of an object activates an occult principle of correspondence that ensures the things of this world are mirrored in the next one. Whatever the explanation should prove to be, the result is significant.

While these materials have been collected in pursuit of truth, I cannot guarantee they are all free of fabrication or distortion since they come from eyes not my own.

But this is not a problem unique to strange tales. Even in the case of orthodox histories, we are given different versions of the same event by credible historians.

As for my work, I have recorded faithfully those materials that came into my purview—historical record and eyewitness account alike.

I have no doubt that some exaggerate or misremember.

Nevertheless, I am confident my work contains ample truth to shine light on the way of spirits. Certainly, there is enough to guide those who would follow me. That alone makes me satisfied.

—Gan Bao (fl. 315), Historian of the Strange, *Soushen Ji*

A QING DYNASTY NEAR-DEATH EXPERIENCE

At Hanlin Academy, I worked alongside a clerk named Yi Shi. One day, I and another co-worker, Bo Xizhai, saw Yi Shi without his shirt and were shocked to see that his body was disfigured by scars. We asked him what happened.

"War," Yi Shi explained.

Yi Shi went on to tell us that he had been involved in the Battle of Yili years earlier. The fighting there was bloody and savage, and a full quarter of his regiment was destroyed. He himself was stabbed by spears over seven times, and his injuries put him into a coma so deep that his fellow soldiers left him for dead.

"But I didn't die," Yi Shi said. "Two days later, I revived, found an orphaned horse wandering around, and rode until I found the remnants of my regiment."

When Bo Xizhai and I expressed amazement at Yi Shi's tale, he told us that he hadn't even revealed the most incredible part.

"It began while I was bleeding on the ground," he said. "There was no pain. I felt very weak though and couldn't keep my eyes open. Almost as soon as they shut, my spirit rustled loose from my body, and the next thing I knew I was standing unwounded in the middle of a howling wind of dust and sand so thick I could not see anything through it—not even my own body. It was then that I realized I was dead.

"This knowledge filled me with incredible loneliness. But my sorrow was even greater: sorrow over the hardship my family would suffer because I was not there—especially my son who was just a child.

"My sorrow grew, hollowing me, until I didn't feel like a man anymore but like a dried-up husk, a leaf—weightless, trembling and flapping, on the verge of being scattered apart into dust and eternity. Then suddenly something heavy and determined took shape inside me: a refusal to yield. I was not ready to die. I would not abandon my fellow soldiers or my family.

"As soon as these thoughts passed through my mind, I had weight again. About the same time, I saw a hillside looming in the distance and swarming with our enemies. Knowing now that I was more than my old body, I willed myself to become a new shape: fiendish, tall, deadly, and as unshakable as an iron pillar. I took a quick step toward the hill. That was when I awoke back in my wounded body on the battlefield, curled up in a pool of blood. After staggering to my feet, I called the orphaned horse to me and rode off to join the rest of my regiment."

Bo Xizhai and I were quiet for a long time at the end of Yi Shi's story. Then Bo Xizhai drew in a breath, and slowly let it back out. He said to Yi Shi, "While warriors and martyrs accept death every day, normal people are terrified to even think of it. But your account changes the meaning of everything. Not just of death and war but of life too."

A QUESTION PUT TO THE OFFICE OF GHOSTS AND YIN REALM MATTERS

The afterlife realm is said to work the same for the newly arriving dead as any major city in the living world works for newly arriving residents.

For example, the dead must jot their names and other personal information down in the official records.

That's the claim. But while I've heard this more than once, I find it puzzling.

Consider this: The world is a sphere with a circumference of at least 90,000 li, and a diameter of 30,000 li. This is a huge expanse of territory, and the number of towns, cities, villages, and indeed entire countries and empires within it must be mind-bogglingly large.

Therefore, the total population of the living in the entire world must easily exceed our country's population by a hundred times, and the population of the dead must exceed our country's population by at least the same multiple.

Given this, why do visitors to the afterlife realm report only seeing Chinese ghosts and not foreign ones?

Is it the case that every territory's afterlife realm is supervised by that territory's deities and run according to that territory's customs?

Are these territories divided up as neatly as we divide up nations here in the mortal realm?

I put these questions to Supervisor Gu Demao in the Office of Ghosts and Yin Realm Matters because he collects accounts about encounters with the afterlife realm.

Alas, he had no idea.

A similar conundrum presents itself when considering the existence of immortals. There are dozens, if not hundreds, of immortals recorded in ancient accounts.

But not one ancient immortal has been encountered today. The only immortals that people report meeting are all newly made. Did ancient immortals simply transform into lustrous bodies of light and evaporate as Wei Boyang the Taoist alchemist was said to have done?

I asked the celebrated Taoist sage, Lou Jintan, about this. He walked away without providing an answer.

THE SCROLL OF GHOSTS AND FIENDS

The celebrated painter Luo Pin credits his work to an unusual ability: the ability to perceive ghosts—even during the day. When I asked him to explain his gift, he said this:

"Wherever you'll find people, you'll find ghosts, and they differ in temperament and appearance just like people. That said, I most often encounter two main types. The first is dangerous. Their human lives ended bloodily. They glide through abandoned buildings and forgotten roads. This sort will try to attack or possess you. At the very least, they'll attempt to turn your thoughts to depression and suicide. They are the sort that most frequently occur in tales.

"But there are common, average ghosts too—just like there are common, average people—not too happy, not too sad, not in a rush to get anywhere. Harmless, these make up the greatest number.

"In the mornings, when the sun is high and bright, and yang energy is at its most intense, I see them clumped against the shade of courtyard walls and orchards—or huddled under the shade of a roof. There they stay until the sun begins its descent, marking the increase of yin energy for the night and the waning of the yang. Becoming stronger then, they stir and wander around.

"They go through walls like we go through doors but refuse to use doors themselves because direct contact with the yang energy of a human being causes pain.

"On the other hand, I've never seen these ghosts far away from humans either. The human world draws them, and they huddle around stoves to inhale the aroma of spiced meat and rice. But then one also finds them around latrines. Their attraction is more mysterious in this case. Maybe because latrines stink of the human, but yet have few humans around them at any given time? Or perhaps excrement by its nature is the yin energy left over after the yang aspect of food and drink has been extracted for nourishment and so provides ready sustenance for ghosts?"

This is Master Luo's account of the otherworldly creatures that his gift allows him to observe. I'll be blunt. When I heard it, I teased him that it was fabricated to attract buyers for his work. Although our shared belief in the spiritual world was a bond we shared, several of the creatures he described seemed too comical to exist. For example, he painted a being that had an enormously swollen head with human features and a shriveled body, from which trailed fetal limbs. I thought to myself, how can such an absurd thing be real?

But then I recalled my father telling me about a friend from Yaojing who went to bed with his window open one summer night. He wasn't quite settled yet when an enormous face filled the ten-foot-wide window space, impossibly large for any natural creature. Although terrified, my father's friend snatched up a sword hanging on the wall and jabbed one of the creature's bulging eyes.

Howling, the creature immediately dematerialized. A hysterical servant then ran up to the window and called out to my father's friend. He had witnessed the whole thing—not just the creature's vestigial body, which matched Luo Pin's painting in its details—but he had also beheld its original ascent from a specific point in the ground. Excited about the prospect of discovering the secret of the being's origins, my father's friend and his servant dug a hole, the depth of which was about double a man's height. They found nothing but glittering dirt, roots, and worms.

While the double testimony of my father's friend and his servant verifies that such creatures are real in some sense, I wish I understood more about them and that special ability that allows one to see them.

It is clear that there is a difference between the imaginative faculty which leads one to dream nonsense and paint or write unreal things and the imaginative faculty that enables one to come up with practical inventions and ideas, grasp the underlying principles of phenomena, and perceive things that other people can't. Yet, the two are quite difficult to distinguish at times. It would be useful to have an expert in these matters to consult.

EVERY BODY IS A WORD; EVERY WORD IS A FUTURE

1.

One year before she died, my concubine Dawn Jewel was mesmerized one night by the sight of long shadows splayed across her pillow.

Cast by bobbing oleanders outside her bedroom window, the shadows were enigmatic and beautiful, and they filled her with a fierce desire to write a poem. After grabbing her writing materials, she did. This is what she wrote:

> *The moon-lit flowers outside*
> *are also unbroken shadows inside:*
> *dancing and swaying on my bed.*
> *Except for two.*

> *Decapitated by the window curtain,*
> *the heads of these flowers drift alone,*
> *while their bodies lay upon my bed.*
> *Connected to nothing—*
> *No, not anymore.*

The poem proved to be one of Dawn Jewel's favorites. But she did not have long to enjoy it. A year later, she died. She did not die alone. Shortly after she passed, her eighteen-year-old maid, Yu Tai, succumbed to illness also.

It is not hard to see that the poem Dawn Jewel wrote a year earlier foretold this double death. The broken shadows of the two flowers in the poem were the figures of Dawn Jewel and her maid.

Such a thing makes one wonder about what other revelations are hidden in what we write and say.

2.

That signs of various sorts occur before the events they foretell is incontestable. But the processes underlying this phenomenon remain varied.

In some cases, the operation of signs is as simple a matter as a soft glow stirring in the clouds before dawn, or a wooden structure feeling damp to the touch before a storm.

However, the mechanism may also be more mysterious. It might involve the activation of deeper parts of oneself by an art like poetry.

I have had the opportunity to observe this in action more than most because from the time I was four years old until now, I have made it a habit to write every day. In doing this, I have noticed that frequently poetry will drift into sorcery.

For example, a story or image or phrase that begins in the lines of a poem may end up concluding or repeating in the real world—just as the real world finds itself captured and explained in the lines of a poem.

Here is one example:

In 1792, I decided that it would be an amusing diversion to write an elegy for myself. Thinking the finished product witty, I showed it to some colleagues, saying: "If Tao Qian can compose his own obituary poem, there's no reason I can't too. So I have. Listen."

A storm of official forms and protocol.
The rough waves of howling documents.
Alas, I am a lonely gull struggling to fly over this government sea.
Which is to say others' histories are holes through which I worm.
Alas, these are the only adventures owned by me.

"I don't know," said my friend Liu Shi-An. "It's good. But this poem does not sound like you and your wild life. Nor does it accurately reflect your job. If the poem is about anybody here, it fits the life of Editor Lu the best."

Three days after Liu Shi-An said this, we were brought news of Editor Lu's death.

Are not those who refuse to acknowledge a connection where one is obvious as bad as those who imagine a connection where there is none?

3.

One can see the close relationship between poetry and prophecy in the small day-to-day matters of life that involve only one person's affairs just as well as one can see it through the prediction of great events that affect an entire nation.

For instance, in 1770, a Hanlin Academy scholar under me used the planchette to ask the spirits about his future.

As is common for spirits, they spoke in poetry—or rather poetry proved to be the best medium for translating the communication of spirits.

After deciphering the characters that the planchette stick had made in the sand while his hands were guided by the spirits, the scholar read the following poem:

A happy wind snatches a bamboo cane from a man's hand.
The whirling of peach and plum blossoms fills another's eyes.
But then the soft crash of two butterflies chasing a scent.
They cleared the walled gate, yes, but not each other.

When my underling first read the poem, its lines made no sense to him. But a little while later he was told that he would soon be promoted to a magistrate post in remote, rural Heyang County.

Both the location of his post and his duties were extremely similar to those of the renowned Jin dynasty writer and politician, Pan Yue, and so Pan Yue leapt immediately to his mind. More significantly so too did a famous anecdote about Pan Yue planting plum and peach trees across Heyang County. Thus, the second line of the spirit poem proved prophetic.

The events foretold by the second line then led to the first line coming true when several of the scholar's friends turned up at his gate one night to celebrate the news of his promotion.

The gatekeeper, who was lame in one leg, shuffled to the gate with the help of a cane to let the jubilant visitors inside. On his way, he became so excited by the guest's celebratory noise that he couldn't resist shouting out himself: "Today is the day of transformation!"

He accompanied his shout with a happy hop. It was this hop that upset his balance and sent him tumbling down the stairs that led to the gate—so violently that he shattered the shin bone of his previously good leg and bloodily fulfilled the fate foretold by the first line of the spirit poem.

The gatekeeper's injury caused a big commotion in front of the gate. A commotion as big occurred a couple of days later—just as the first strokes of dawn light brushed the sky. This time the scholar was directly involved, as well as two of his servants and their families.

At first, the reason for the commotion wasn't clear. But the outcome was. With much shouting and cursing, the scholar threw his two servants and their families out of his compound.

Everyone was curious about what happened, and the rumors boiled wildly for days. However, none were particularly convincing—at least not until my wife Mistress Ma was given crucial details by her seamstress, who was also employed by the scholar.

It turned out that because the gatekeeper post was a relatively higher one—well-paid, well-respected, and less grueling than other positions—several members of the household set their eyes on it.

More specifically, the two servants who had been thrown out along with their families, had talked to a third servant, who they thought was a disinterested friend, about how to get the recently opened position.

This third man, however, wanted the post for himself.

So, he craftily advised the other two servants to send their wives to seduce the scholar with food and sex under the cover of darkness. The third man supplied explicit instructions about both the timing of the women's visit and the path they should take.

In this way, the women found themselves fumbling through the dark at the same time, their arms loaded with tea and cakes. When they inevitably ran into each other, they dropped what they were carrying and began loudly quarreling. This woke up the scholar.

The scholar angrily questioned the women. When he discovered their plot, he fired the two servants and made the final two lines of the poem come true:

But then the soft crash of two butterflies chasing a scent.
They cleared the walled gate, yes, but not each other.

4.

The reader may be interested to know that the immorality of the third man in the anecdote above eventually led to his downfall.

This happened a little bit after it became obvious that the original gatekeeper had healed well enough that he would not have to surrender his position.

Unwilling to accept this, the third man buddied up to the gatekeeper and offered to treat him to a night at a brothel, knowing full well that the scholar disapproved of them.

He planned to report the gatekeeper to the scholar while the gatekeeper was occupied. But the gatekeeper was smart enough to figure out the scheme and promptly reported it to the scholar instead. Thus, the third man was dismissed.

The layered plots revealed in the anecdote above are clear examples of the need to consider that we may be considered prey by some, even as we are considering preying on others, and that perhaps we are being secretly watched even as we are secretly watching others.

This is the same message conveyed by the parable of the cicada, the mantis, and the yellow oriole. The cicada is unaware that a hungry mantis waits on the branch above, and the mantis likewise is unaware that a hungry yellow oriole sits on the branch above, while the yellow oriole is unaware that a hunter's arrow is aimed at its head from the palace window.

What better image could there be for our fraught place in this world? It is equally applicable to both the relationship between human beings and between human beings and spirits.

DIFFERENT MAPS OF THE SAME PLACES

Poetry is filled with references to fantastic places—such as the Three Divine Peninsulas and the Ten Mysterious Islands in the Eastern Ocean. But are these real places?

I have studied Japanese maps and talked to explorers and traders from across Korea and Japan. There is not a single report of anyone seeing the Three Divine Peninsulas or the Ten Mysterious Islands for themselves. Nor is there a report of anyone catching a glimpse from afar of the silver palaces that are said to gleam from their storied soil.

The Five Shining Cities and Twelve Towers of Awe in the Kunlun Mountains offer additional examples of likely fabrication.

The elevated land that the ancient texts say these architectural wonders are built upon is widely colonized by farmers these days. It has also been combed through by treasure-seekers and miners. Yet no one has found any trace of the Jade Pool, the Floating Garden, the Tree of Precious Beads, or the Field of the Red Reishi of Immortality—all of which are claimed by the poets to be important landmarks at these sites. Instead, one finds rocky earth, shrubs, and small, unremarkable lakes.

Of course, sometimes someone will encounter a place that appears in the poets' stories, such as The Drowning Sea.

Even then problems arise. For example, the Drowning Sea is calm most of the time, and its waters are safe unless there's a storm.

The nature of Crashing Thunder Monastery has likewise been exaggerated. In ancient texts, it is portrayed as a city of otherworldly architecture, one containing artwork so profound that just a glimpse can trigger convulsions and enlightenment. One reads of ornately carved bannisters, terraced pools, and stunning gardens.

As opposed to many other fantastic places though, the details of Crashing Thunder Monastery's case can be checked since specific details are given about its location.

Not many years ago, some of our troops stumbled onto coordinates that matched those in the ancient writing. Sure enough, they found a monastery—one identified as "Crashing Thunder Monastery" on over a dozen artifacts.

The monastery was interesting in many respects.

It was quite large, with over 600 cells and innumerable dome-shaped shrines. The shrines were filled with small statues of Buddhas and Bodhisattvas inscribed with scripture written in ancient Sanskrit. The troops also encountered several bands of Muslim nomads. They had taken up residence in the monastery's abandoned buildings.

However, there was almost no resemblance to the magnificent descriptions of Crashing Thunder Monastery offered by the poets.

I could go on.

There is also, for instance, the copper city of the Muslims. The people in the East claim it lies in the West, and the people of the West claim that it lies in the East.

And there is the Jesuit Ferdinand Verbiest's "Map of the World." The map is filled with drawings of fantastic creatures and bizarre plants, as well as illustrations of "The Seven Architectural Wonders." This too is most likely the product of a fevered imagination.

My ultimate point is this: of those places mentioned by poets and mystics, most are fabricated or exaggerated. Thus, one is tempted to hold any geographical claim made by a poet or a mystic in great suspicion. I certainly did for a long time. But then one day I discussed this matter with the Hanlin librarian, Zhou Shuchang. He said the following, which made me see the matter in a different light:

"Perhaps, it takes a person who has cultivated their spiritual nature to see the divinity in the world. A person who's not a Buddhist might have trouble seeing the Buddhist's world, just like someone who's not a musician might not hear a piece of music the way a musician hears it.

"Therefore, you cannot decide whether something exists or doesn't exist by relying on common opinion and common ways of seeing things.

"For example, I once talked to a Taoist who's also been to the Kunlun Mountains. What he described to me was no different than the descriptions of marvels and wonders that occurred in the ancient Taoist texts."

PART II

FABLES AND PHILOSOPHIES

Although fictions are products of the imagination, nevertheless sometimes they are proven quite true.

—Ye Shishou (1752–1823)

YELLOW LEAF

Early autumn in Jiahe County is beautiful. The air is warm and cool, the trees blaze with vibrant colors, and there is a lake in the area that is a lovely place to visit. These charms brought Wang Kunxia, a Taoist priest of my acquaintance, to hike there one morning and stray from the popular path to explore the far side of the lake.

A few hours into Kunxia's walk, the woods gave way to a bamboo grove and then to the remnants of an orchard and an abandoned mansion. Excited, he exhausted himself exploring his discovery and decided to take a nap in the mansion's overgrown garden.

Except Kunxia didn't quite fall asleep.

When one sleeps in the usual way, one's spirit is no longer bound to fixed forms or the laws of time and space. Then, imagination and reality, and dreams and spiritual experiences, freely mingle. Sleeping and waking are thus distinct ways of being.

But sometimes a person will get stuck between realms. This is what happened to Kunxia. He was limited by the laws of the physical world and still tethered to his physical body. Yet, he could perceive the spirit world. So it was that his spirit looked up from his resting physical form to see a ghost—dressed in old-fashioned powder-blue robes—bowing with his hands intertwined in front of Kunxia.

When the ghost saw that Kunxia saw him, he smiled. "Welcome," he said. "It has been years since I had a visitor, and decades since anyone has actually slept here. I am delighted to find you. Which is to say, please don't fear me."

Kunxia relaxed at the man's words, although he was sure the man was a ghost, and asked him where he was from.

"My family name is Zhang," the ghost said. "Originally, I come from Leiyang, but I moved here during the Yuan dynasty. When I died, I decided to stay rather than returning home because this land and I are well suited to one another. We've been a good match for a long time—long enough for the lake to grow larger then smaller again, and for the garden to have over a dozen different owners, then none, and finally to be forgotten by all."

"Isn't it rare for someone to remain a ghost for so long?" asked Kunxia. "I thought most spirits move on to be reborn."

The ghost nodded. "True. Many spirits feel out of sorts if they remain this near the earthly plane without occupying matter themselves. This is not my sentiment though. Whether dead or alive, one remains oneself. A living person can see mountains, rivers, forests, the moon, and other sights. So too can a ghost. A living person can lay on a hillside at night to be clarified by the immensity of the stars and then write a poem. So too a ghost. Therefore, in no way is a ghost inferior. Indeed, there are many secluded places in the mortal realm too isolated or dangerous, too deep or too high, for a human to venture. In these, ghosts, however, can wander and witness in the silence of the night and the dawn.

"The only things we ghosts lack is the ability to touch what we see or to keep a souvenir from our adventures. This inability disturbs those who cling to life because they can't imagine no longer being able to embrace a lover or a child, or to drink wine or eat fruit. Such a person upon entering the netherworld feels unbearably lonely and impotent—like a high official sent back to his home village after losing office.

"But there are people who have always lived in the countryside. There are people who have never held rank. There are people in the world who have remained unattached to family or friends for their whole life, people who sit silently while others chat and drink. They need no company. They are content to dig their own wells and plow their own land. They find nothing to feel sad about."

"Even if you feel that way, the cycle of death and rebirth is part of the deep design. How did you escape it?" asked Kunxia.

"By realizing the greatest secret. Everything is a choice. Whether you're talking about a ghost avoiding rebirth or a person declining a position, all of it is a choice. Once you understand this, you are free."

After the ghost finished speaking, both he and Kunxia were quiet for a time, each lost in their own thoughts. Then Kunxia said, "One who is as fond of sightseeing as you must have composed a lot of poems."

"I chant a line or two when in the mood," said the ghost. "But I seldom complete a poem. I find myself forgetting them almost as soon as I compose them. Consequently, there are only four or five poems that I've written that I can remember."

Kunxia's eyes flickered with interest, and so the ghost recited:

The fading sunlight leaves the mountain empty.
Chant this while all goes dark and vast again:
There is no inside.
There is no outside.

When the ghost finished his stanza, Kunxia cried out in admiration and implored him to recite more. Flattered, the ghost agreed. But he just managed to utter the phrase "yellow leaf" when a loud noise from the side of the lake awakened Kunxia. Sitting up, he looked at the lake and saw some fishermen yelling greetings to one another as they pulled creatures from the water.

NOT THAT MAID

There are those who we love at first but then hate bitterly. This is not uncommon. But neither is it unheard of to grow to love someone that we initially dislike. Song Qingyuan from Dezhou told me a story about a maid once employed by the Zhu family that illustrates this perfectly.

This maid, whose name was Jia, was an ugly child: sallow skin, bowl-shaped face, and with uneven teeth that seemed randomly pegged into her gums. She moved crudely and spoke the same—eyes bulging with slyness and ill-will.

But a miracle happened shortly after Jia entered womanhood. Her teeth no longer looked random but artfully placed and full of charm. Her face seemed less rice-bowl than moon, her skin turned golden, and her eyes were now kind and seemed to follow others with the sole intent of keeping them from harm—particularly Zhu.

It surprised no one that Zhu confessed a romantic interest to Jia. And when she consented to be his partner, it turned out to be the best luck he'd ever had. Intelligent and strategic, she organized the affairs of the household as neatly as beads on an abacus. Her ability gained the respect and obedience of the servants—even the sneaks, the troublemakers, and those unhappy unfortunates who seemed to dislike everyone.

To Zhu's delight, his lover's intellect proved as nimble in business matters as household ones. She directed the wholesale purchase of investment goods: vegetables, fruits, and fabrics, all of which doubled and tripled in price not long after purchase. In a few years, Zhu was much richer—materially and in terms of the harmonious bond that he and Jia shared. They had the kind of relationship that others envied.

At least it was that way until suddenly it was not.

One day, Jia grabbed Zhu's shoulders and peered into his eyes. "Do you see me?" she said in a strange voice.

"What do you mean?" Zhu asked. He then loudly said her given name followed by her nickname, as if hoping to call her back from whatever spell into which she had fallen.

"I'm neither one of those people," Jia said. "That maid of yours? That woman ran away a long time ago while still a girl and settled down in another village. Today, she is married and the mother of a young son. Temperamentally, she's changed little from the unpleasant little girl that she was. No, dear Zhu, our bond is not to be found in her childhood. Its beginning is found nine of your lifetimes ago—when you were a rich trader and employed me to watch over your accounts.

"You were a good man even then. I was not. I repaid your trust with the theft of thousands of taels of silver. Consequently, after I died I was sentenced to be reborn as a fox. Since then, I have labored over several hundred years, through meditation and the training of my heart-mind, to cultivate the Tao and evolve from a brute animal back into a being capable of honor and compassion.

"I have made progress. But to advance further, I needed to find you and make amends. Thus, when your unlovely servant made her escape, I took her place. Over the past ten years, I've done everything I could to pay you back. This past month marked the full repayment of my debt. Soon, I will quit this flesh. After my spirit leaves, this body you have held against you night after night will return to its true form—a fox.

"However, although dead and rotting, this body will have one final task. Therefore, you must order your servant Yi to bury me. Not because he will make a good job of it, but because he will disobey you. Instead of burying me, he will hang me upside down by my hind legs and drag the tip of a knife around my feet and my tail.

"Yi will then peel the skin from me, feeling much greater pleasure than expected. This is because four of his lifetimes ago, while I inhabited my fox form, I came across his dead body on the side of the road. This occurred during the days of the Great Famine, and I made a meal of his corpse. Skinning me will balance things between us and settle my last debt so that I don't have to reincarnate again."

Her confession complete, Jia made a tiny cry and slumped to the ground—a dead fox instead of a live human. Almost immediately, a tiny beautiful woman only a few inches long wiggled out of the fox's matted ear. Zhu instantly knew the figure was Jia although her features were no longer the same.

After the figure vanished into the sky, Zhu went off to find the servant Yi, but minutes into his search, he changed his mind. He could not bear the thought of his lover's corpse being brutalized. He buried Jia himself. Unfortunately, this gesture proved futile. The next morning, he went to pay his respects at Jia's grave to find it vandalized and her body gone. He learned that Yi was the grave-robber and that he had skinned the fox's corpse and sold its hide.

Yi's actions in this case illustrate that we are not absolved of past debts just because we become better people. These accounts must be settled. The wounds we inflicted upon others in our past remain even if we change.

THE FIRE THAT BURST INTO FLAMES FAR FROM WHERE IT WAS SET

Just like ordinary foxes, the shape-changers known as huli jing like to build their underground lairs in abandoned cemeteries. My friend Fa Nanye told me about one such lair that used to exist in an old cemetery a few miles outside his home village.

Over the years, villagers had spied naked women loping through the woods at night near the cemetery.

Eventually, another pack—this one of obnoxious young troublemakers—heard the rumors. One evening, just as it was turning dark, they crawled up to the fox holes with their fists full of nets and hooks. Soon they caught two foxes.

Hooting and hollering, the young men threw the animals against the ground and jabbed large needles threaded with cord into their haunches. Thus, each fox was fitted with bloody loops—the other end of which the leader of the young men wrapped around his fists.

The leader showed the captured foxes his waist knife and said, "Here are my terms. Change to your human forms and amuse us. Dance. Serve us moonshine. Do all the other things that we command. If you do well enough, we might let you live. If you refuse, we'll stab you to death right now."

Instead of changing, the foxes gazed at the men with wild eyes and carried on—moaning, snapping, and thrashing about—as if nothing more than dumb animals.

Enraged, the leader grabbed a fox by the snout and stabbed it through the throat. This broke the spirit of the remaining fox. Giving up her pretense, a trembling human voice came from her still-whole throat. "You ask me to change. But if I do, I'll be without fur or clothing. Please don't make me humiliate myself like that."

But her plea only made the young men more eager, and the leader pushed his knife beneath the fox's chin.

It was then that she finally changed to the form of a young woman. The men responded with cries of celebration and forced her to amuse them, one after the other, while holding the cord tightly in hand. Afterwards, they rested on the ground and told her to serve them moonshine.

The fox woman said she could not. It was impossible to move about with a leather loop running through her leg. Since she seemed too beat-up to flee, the young men agreed to pull out the cord. However, the instant it was gone, she sprang away and darted into the woods, too fast to follow.

It was not far from their homes when the men saw the smoke. Plumes of it billowed from their village. From that direction too came the glow of fire.

They started running. But it was too late. Each of their houses had burnt to the ground, any former occupants now standing outside in their bedclothes. The only exception was the leader of the young men. What happened to his household was much worse. Not only had his house burned to ash. So had his daughter inside.

It was then, in the midst of his grief and horror, that the

leader understood the nature of fox justice. It is a terrible and merciless rhyme.

THE STONE THAT BOUNCED

Mencius and Confucius laid great stress on the moderation of our emotions. Like leaves buffeted by the wind, unchecked they sway this way and that—depending on who or what we encounter, and thus easily lead to chaos and destruction. Therefore, even when we must punish others, we should bow to law and propriety rather than anger.

But it is hard to maintain one's calm. And for most people, it is not self-cultivation but the fear of death that keeps them in line.

Laozi agrees with this, although he further argues that the poor are less afraid of death since it is so common among them. Hence, the poor are not as constrained by the thought of death. I don't completely agree. But I do agree that when the fear of death is removed, there is nothing to hold a person back.

The following tale, which I heard as a boy, bears witness to the wisdom of Mencius, Confucius, and Laozi. It begins like this:

A wealthy family was robbed and offered a huge reward to whoever captured the thieves. Within a few months, the whole gang was caught. Since incriminating evidence was found with them, they confessed their crimes and hoped for leniency. While the court considered their case, they were kept locked up.

This could have been the end of the matter: a robbery, a reward offered, justice.

But the head of the household that had been robbed was proud. For decades, he had basked in the sense of power and safety that wealth provides, and the robbery had shaken him to his core. His anger over his newfound vulnerability led him to bribe the prison guards to torture the thieves.

This torture went beyond beatings.

Beatings are quick. The wealthy man did not want quick.

Instead, the bandits were chained up tight so that they were forced to stand tip-toed, even during the sleeping hours, and had no choice but to vacate their bladders and bowels into their clothing. Within a week, their soggy clothes were infested with maggots and beetles, and their cell reeked like a festering wound.

It was all too much, and the bandits began to yearn for death. However, the wealthy man ensured they were well fed and had no way to kill themselves.

After several hellish weeks, one morning the guards unchained and washed the thieves and dragged them before the magistrate. Although there were no charges of violence, for that wasn't the thieves' way, their robberies were so extensive that the magistrate sentenced them to death. The bandits did not contest their sentence. But they did, to everyone's surprise, announce they had more to confess.

As the full courtroom stared at them, full of curiosity, the bandits proceeded to graphically and elaborately detail how they had defiled and degraded every member of the wealthy family—pressing upon the audience in the courtroom images that would haunt them for the rest of their lives.

The bandits' goal was revenge by humiliating the wealthy

man. They achieved it. By the time they quit speaking, everyone in the courtroom gazed at him with pity and disgust.

The wealthy man understood the bandits' stratagem. And he wasted no time in denouncing their "confessions" as lies. But no one believed him once it got out that he had paid for the thieves to be tortured.

One villager summarized the consensus this way: "Such excess can only come from hatred rooted in a far more heinous violation than robbery. The bandits therefore must have been telling the truth."

In the following weeks and months, those who had long been jealous of the robbed family's power eagerly added their own details to the bandit's fabrication. Eventually, even those that doubted its truth couldn't help but see the wealthy man and his family differently. Such is the power of stories once they're told. Even if later doubted, their shadows remain.

None of this had to happen.

The bandits would not have sought revenge if the wealthy man had simply let justice take its course. They would have accepted their punishment as a fate they deserved, even if it was not desirable.

However, their illegal torture was more than they could bear. How they then reacted proves the wisdom of the saying that if one tosses a stone too forcefully, it will bounce back to wound you.

IN A COAT YOU'LL RECOGNIZE

My childhood friend Tian Baiyan relayed to me a story that Zhu Ziqing from Jinan passed onto him.

One day, someone moved to Zhu Ziqing's village that caught everybody by surprise. This was because the new resident was a voice without a body. When asked who or what it was, the voice identified itself as a fox spirit.

Indeed, it soon demonstrated a fox spirit's gift for wordplay, moving Ziqing to invite it to the parties that he held regularly—affairs locally famous for their raucous drinking games and battles of wit and poetry.

The voice accepted the invitation and was an instant hit. Its performances were unbeatable—whether it was reciting Taoist poems and trading poetry couplets, or engaging in philosophical debates about the Confucian classics. Then one night, after a successful performance, an audience member demanded that the voice show its true self.

"What I really look like?" the voice laughed. "You don't have the right kind of eyes to see such a thing. But if you want, I can show you how I sometimes appear to some people. Keep in mind though that different people see me differently. So in seeing me, you'll not so much see me as see something about yourself."

The voice's response failed to put off the audience member. Others even joined in with his entreaty. "Show us what you look like," they clamored.

"All right. All right," said the voice. "But first tell me what you think I look like."

After a short silence, a person shouted, "I see in my mind's eye silver hair and silver eyebrows like those of an old man."

As soon as the person finished his speculation, the voice indeed had a body that matched the description.

A different person declared: "A master, yes. But not like you describe. I see a Taoist master who has become one with the Way. Light streams from his whole body. The master is everything, and so he is nothing at the same time."

In response to this description, the voice's form turned into a light identical to that of which the man spoke. But not for long because another person said, "I see an immortal. She wears a hat in the shape of a star and a long coat made of feathers."

Then a fourth: "An innocent child. Soft skin. Big eyes. A large head."

A fifth: "A goddess, like the beautiful and pure mountain maidens of which Zhuangzi has written."

The voice made its appearance match every speculation until finally an older person objected. "These appearances of yours are astounding, voice. But each one is someone's fantasy and thus a refusal to show us how you truly look. *That* is what I want to see."

The voice sighed and said, "The kingdom we live in is all there is beneath the sky. It stretches wide and vast between the four seas. In it, there are many provinces with many people with many customs and rules for how to appear before others.

Yet, I have never met a single person willing to show who they really are. So why in the world do you think I would be the first one in all of history to do so?"

With that, the voice laughed and faded away.

CRAB SONG

1.

During the Song dynasty, there was a popular poem called "Crab Song." The beginning goes like this:

> *No water can wash the black spots*
> *from a crab's legs.*
> *So when autumn comes,*
> *it will surely be seen.*
> *And then in a ceremony of steam,*
> *it will receive the red crown.*

In this poem, crabs are metaphors for corrupt people, and the poem was written to indict a corrupt, Song dynasty official named Zhu Mian. While Zhu Mian's powerful connections allowed him to escape punishment in the human courts, the poet envisions the black spots on a crab's legs as symbols of the corruption in Zhu Mian's heart.

Such corruption can't be washed away.

Not by water.

Not by time.

Not by disguise.

And so this dark mark will follow Zhu Mian to the end of his days and eventually draw the attention of those divinities who serve as authorities in the spirit worlds. They will deliver to him what the human justice system did not.

Zhu Mian's punishment will not be death itself, but a special kind of suffering. This is why the crab is used as a metaphor.

While death comes to every animal that is a food source, for most it is quick. The crab's death alone is unusually vicious and slow. It is thrown alive into a cooking pot rather than killed first.

As the water heats, the crab struggles to escape—battering the sides of the pot with its claws, scrabbling, scratching—all the while growing weaker and weaker as it boils to death inside its shell.

And here is the worst part: during the long span of time in which this occurs, its fading senses detect beings around it that could help but do not, beings that find the crab so ugly and primitive and worthless that its pain means nothing to them.

Like animals, all people die too. Most quickly move on to an incarnation that is better, or at least not worse, than the life they just lived. However, the corrupt are reincarnated into lives filled with suffering. The most corrupt are reincarnated as crabs.

2.

Legend has it that the Governor Zhao Hongxie once dreamed that he entered a great hall, dimly lit and filled with former servants. When the servants saw Zhao Hongxie, they knelt and cried out for forgiveness.

"Forgiveness for what?" Zhao Hongxie said.

The servants replied: "While we were alive, your family treated us well, but we stole from you, shirked our duties, and were insolent and cruel. Nothing could be done about us. We worked together to cover up our misdeeds. And if some were found out or suspected, we let it be known that punishing us was unwise since we could sabotage the family in all kinds of ways.

"The power we had was intoxicating. But because of these sins, after our human deaths we were reincarnated as crabs. Over and over. Doomed to live a short life of fear. Doomed to be caught, thrown into a suffocating bag of piled bodies, tossed into water, boiled to death, and then have the same thing done again.

"This has happened over a dozen times since we were last human. We have sought you out because tomorrow a bag of crabs will arrive in your kitchen. We will be the crabs. Please, don't allow us to be boiled alive again. Instead, forgive our sins and take us back to the ocean. Only a person who is willing to show us the goodness that we failed to demonstrate while alive can break the cycle."

Zhao Hongxie agreed to do as asked. When he awoke, he told his kitchen staff about the dream and ordered them to take the crabs to the sea when they arrived. He also gave them money to hire Buddhist monks to perform a prayer ceremony for the crabs.

Zhao Hongxie hoped that by telling his current servants about the dream, they would learn something important from the example of those who came before. Instead, they met up outside the house and said to one another, "Zhao Hongxie is a crafty one, for sure. That crazy story of his is obviously a lie to keep us from eating our fill of crabmeat on the sly. But who's backwards enough to believe such a tale these days? And who's stupid enough to release a crab during the autumn frost when the meat is its juiciest?"

The servants decided to keep the money intended for the Buddhist monks and ate all the crabs.

Zhao Hongxie never found out about the betrayal, but the servants later bragged about it to their friends. They had no idea they were dooming themselves to the same fate as their predecessors' until it was too late. Perhaps, one day some group of servants from that household will come along and show the mercy that the others did not. And so the cycle will be broken.

THE DOGS THAT FOLLOW

Counselor Song Futang told me this story:

One day, a fox bolted past a startled cemetery caretaker who worked for a rich family in the capital's Haidian District and into a dead-end alley with a pack of braying street dogs hot on its heels.

The caretaker could tell by the fox's gory lacerations that the dogs had savaged it. He could tell too that they intended to finish it off. A soft-hearted man, he couldn't stand this thought and chased away the dogs with a piece of wood. Afterwards, he carried the near-dead fox home.

Over the next few weeks, the fox slowly healed. When it seemed to have recovered enough, the caretaker freed it in a nearby meadow.

A few days later, his door was abruptly thrown open, and in marched a beautiful young woman.

"Who are you?" he asked.

The woman bowed and said, "I'm the fox you saved. Because your kindness moved my heart, I've returned to keep you company—if you're so inclined—until the end of your days."

Although the shapeshifters known as huli jing were known

to be dangerous, the caretaker figured that this one would not be because of their history, and he happily assented to her offer.

Two months of near-constant lovemaking followed.

The caretaker had never been happier but never had his health been worse either. His weight plummeted. He suffered incessant fatigue. His bones ached.

It would have been easy for him to connect his changed state to his new lover, but he refused.

Then one night, while the couple was in bed, a strange woman began shouting from outside the house. "Aliu, you low bitch! I've found you out! Did you really think I'd let you suck this man dry in my name after he saved my life? Think again. My sisters and I have come to put an end to you."

As soon as she heard the shouting, the caretaker's lover scrambled to her feet and hurriedly dressed to make her escape. But she wasn't quick enough. Before she managed to flee the house, the stranger and her sisters stormed inside and tore her apart.

The original huli jing explained the truth of what happened, but the caretaker was too much in love with the imposter to listen. Heartbroken, he wildly launched himself at the fox sisters—sobbing, shrieking profanities, crying "murderer." When he grabbed a sword down from the wall, they gave up and left, tears streaming down the face of the huli jing he'd saved.

Over the course of the rest of his life, the caretaker told his story many times to many people. No matter how much time passed, whenever he told the story his voice would fill with hatred and grief. He never came close to admitting the truth.

THE DOGS THAT FOLLOW

Counselor Song Futang told me this story:

One day, a fox bolted past a startled cemetery caretaker who worked for a rich family in the capital's Haidian District and into a dead-end alley with a pack of braying street dogs hot on its heels.

The caretaker could tell by the fox's gory lacerations that the dogs had savaged it. He could tell too that they intended to finish it off. A soft-hearted man, he couldn't stand this thought and chased away the dogs with a piece of wood. Afterwards, he carried the near-dead fox home.

Over the next few weeks, the fox slowly healed. When it seemed to have recovered enough, the caretaker freed it in a nearby meadow.

A few days later, his door was abruptly thrown open, and in marched a beautiful young woman.

"Who are you?" he asked.

The woman bowed and said, "I'm the fox you saved. Because your kindness moved my heart, I've returned to keep you company—if you're so inclined—until the end of your days."

Although the shapeshifters known as huli jing were known

to be dangerous, the caretaker figured that this one would not be because of their history, and he happily assented to her offer.

Two months of near-constant lovemaking followed.

The caretaker had never been happier but never had his health been worse either. His weight plummeted. He suffered incessant fatigue. His bones ached.

It would have been easy for him to connect his changed state to his new lover, but he refused.

Then one night, while the couple was in bed, a strange woman began shouting from outside the house. "Aliu, you low bitch! I've found you out! Did you really think I'd let you suck this man dry in my name after he saved my life? Think again. My sisters and I have come to put an end to you."

As soon as she heard the shouting, the caretaker's lover scrambled to her feet and hurriedly dressed to make her escape. But she wasn't quick enough. Before she managed to flee the house, the stranger and her sisters stormed inside and tore her apart.

The original huli jing explained the truth of what happened, but the caretaker was too much in love with the imposter to listen. Heartbroken, he wildly launched himself at the fox sisters—sobbing, shrieking profanities, crying "murderer." When he grabbed a sword down from the wall, they gave up and left, tears streaming down the face of the huli jing he'd saved.

Over the course of the rest of his life, the caretaker told his story many times to many people. No matter how much time passed, whenever he told the story his voice would fill with hatred and grief. He never came close to admitting the truth.

ILL WINDS

Once one trains oneself to look more closely at the world, one becomes aware that water and air frequently host strange vortices connected to supernatural phenomena.

For example, Zeng Yinghua, a colleague from Shandong province, told me that he was walking with friends in a threshing field one evening when a whirlwind pitched up out of nowhere—swirling leaves and other plant debris every which way.

The wind's suddenness and ferocity startled the friends. And, peering closely, they saw that the wind was made from dozens of spirits wrestling and tugging at each other. Zeng Yinghua swears that he also faintly heard their voices debating the philosophical ideas of the School of Principles versus the ideas of the School of Universal Mind.

This tale, regardless of whether it records an actual event, reminds us that while we assume all our questions in this life will be answered in the spirit worlds, disputes of many kinds will probably continue there too.

Perhaps there is a further realm beyond the spirit worlds where all questions will be resolved.

SPRING STORMS

The spring is full of storms. Sometimes, it will rain for a week in the capital city, and this will turn all the roads leading there into mud.

The road that runs from Huang Village to Fengyi Gate is one such road. It was here one darkening afternoon that Li Xiu of Gu'an County spotted a flash of white face and dark hair ahead, while shouting at his carriage horses to pick up their pace.

At the sound of the carriage, the stranger turned. Xiu saw that he was quite young—about fifteen or sixteen. He was also quite pretty, with the glowing skin of a beautiful woman.

Imagining he saw desire for a warm ride in the boy's expression, Xiu pulled at his horses' reins and invited him into the carriage.

The boy shyly accepted Xiu's offer and sat beside him. Almost immediately, Xiu began to woo him with significant glances. When the carriage stopped at a tiny village for food, Xiu strategically treated him to snacks. While the boy wolfed down the food, Xiu boldly remarked on his good looks.

The boy played dumb throughout all these efforts, limiting his responses to blushes and demure smiles.

Then a thing happened when they were back in the carriage and again on their way.

Suddenly, the boy looked different, as if someone had made a copy of him—exact except for a few crucial details—and swapped this copy out for the genuine article without Xiu noticing until that moment.

Now that he did notice, the difference was palpable. The lips were less rosy and the cheeks less fat. The look in the boy's eyes was blunter and less shy as well.

Initially, Xiu convinced himself that the boy's changed appearance was a visual effect generated by the fading light of evening, which tended to make everything look older. But soon the differences became so obvious that they were undeniable. A distance of ten li more, and the "boy's" upper lip and chin were covered with hairs, and his hands and arms had turned lean, knotted, and muscled.

Boy no longer, the beautiful stranger had somehow become a man in his twenties. Unnerved, Xiu abandoned his romantic intentions.

By the time they reached the city, and the carriage was rattling by the West Gate of Nanyuan, the boy had become a middle-aged man: wrinkled forehead, receding hairline, rough skin, a beard massive and black.

And when they at last reached the inn where Xiu intended to stay and the carriage rattled to a stop, the stranger looked nothing like he had at the trip's start. What had been fresh and young, blossoming and tempting, was now toothless, shriveled, and gray.

The gray thing took Xiu's limp hand between its own and damply pressed. In response, Xiu's heart jumped like a fish as panic flooded his veins, disordering his mind so much that he had the odd sensation that he himself was a vulnerable young boy and the stranger an old letch. For a terrible moment, Xiu felt the horror of what he himself was.

"Thank you for your attention this whole trip," said the now old man. "I was deeply flattered by your hinted offers. But, alas, I've slept with time too long to be interested in sleeping with man anymore. Such desires have been washed away by time, along with much else."

The old man barked out a laugh and disappeared into the night.

Xiu related this encounter to his younger cousin who worked in our family's kitchen for a while. I was so struck that I researched several volumes of records to see if I could find a similar demon in any other accounts. I found no match to anything in history. His species remains mysterious.

THE GIRL WITH FLOWERS IN HER HAIR

The following is a story that was told to me by the mother of my employee, Wang Yanyou.

One Spring Festival's Eve, a peddler of rice-paper flowers started pounding and kicking on the door of a house in Qing County.

The door flung open to reveal the very unhappy face of the homeowner who demanded that the peddler explain himself.

The peddler wasted no time in loudly complaining that someone in the household had stolen flowers from him.

"Nonsense," said the owner.

The peddler insisted that he was telling the truth and went on to describe a young girl with long, wild hair that had snatched flowers from his basket without paying. He said he watched her with his own eyes flee into the house.

The homeowner wouldn't believe the peddler, and the two argued back and forth until an astonished cry from inside the house interrupted their fight.

Moments later, an old, servant woman rushed up. She informed the men that when she overheard them quarreling, she searched the house to see if a thief had crept inside. She found no thief.

"But," she said, "someone did bring flowers into the compound. Brought them and braided them into the bristles of the old broom by the toilet in the rear courtyard."

The homeowner demanded to see the broom, and the old woman brought it.

Yellow and red flowers were indeed threaded through the bristles—as if woven into a girl's hair. The peddler identified them as the ones snatched from his basket.

The impossibility of what was happening deeply unnerved everyone present so much that the homeowner ordered the servant woman to break the broom into pieces and throw it into the kitchen-stove fire.

As the broom burned, blood boiled out of its blackening wood, along with cries and shrieks that sounded human. Then it went quiet and stirred no more.

* * *

Since all things move toward assuming human form, which in turn moves toward returning to divine form, there was nothing wrong with the broom entity learning to take on human form.

But it foolishly decided to make trouble instead of quietly cultivating its energy until it could permanently take on the form of a girl.

Many people make a similar mistake when they first begin to cultivate talents. Rather than quietly work on themselves, these people are too quick to show off the little they have, or they take on risks disproportionate to the meager size of their talents and successes.

In this way, they beckon flames.

APRICOT SPIRIT

Zhu Tianmen from Yidu told me about one of his students who became an itinerant scholar after graduation and would sometimes stay at Yunju Temple.

This young scholar was the flirty sort. And during one of his stays, he noticed a beautiful youth, around fifteen years old, who also frequented the temple. One day in the courtyard, the scholar tried his luck with the boy.

The boy blushed but didn't flee. So, the scholar kept talking. Soon, he talked the boy into coming to his room.

The next morning, the scholar was basking next to the sleeping youth when suddenly his door flew open.

In walked another guest. The surprise on the stranger's face showed that he'd simply entered the wrong room by mistake. But whether the intrusion was intentional or not, the scholar had been caught in bed with a lover, and he readied himself to fire off a volley of excuses.

Amazingly though, the guest showed no sign that he saw the youth sprawled next to the scholar.

The scholar shrugged off the guest as peculiarly nonobservant. But the same thing happened half an hour later when a monk came into the room to leave the morning tea.

When at last the youth's eyes fluttered open, they found the scholar's eyes peering down.

"Why is it that no one else can see you?" the scholar asked.

"Please," said the youth, "don't be frightened. But I'm not the boy you think. Rather, I am an apricot tree spirit. Like the rest of my kind, I can choose who sees me."

"Ah," said the scholar. "That makes sense. It explains why I found you so irresistible. You bewitched me. Correct?"

"No," replied the youth. "There was no bewitching. You approached me of your own volition. Unlike evil ghosts, demons, or mountain monsters, tree spirits believe it's wrong to enchant humans."

The scholar was unhappy with this response. "Maybe you didn't bewitch me outright. But your human form attracted me, and this has turned out to be a disguise. Isn't that deception?"

"Only if you have a too limited and fixed understanding of things," said the youth. "Both humans and trees are more changeable than you allow.

"When I was a young tree, like other young trees my energy was simple and my form rigid. However, by the time a tree nears a thousand years old, it has naturally collected so much vital qi that its internal energy begins to alter its spiritual form into a human one.

"The Taoists call the spontaneous development of a human form due to accumulated qi, 'Jie Sheng Tai.' This means the formation of a human without conceiving a fetus. Such a thing is very natural and no odder than the development of a plant from a seed. That too, after all, is a dramatic alteration of form."

"These things you say are known to me," responded the scholar. "But aren't apricot spirits usually female—while you are obviously male? How can there not be trickery afoot?"

"You're mistaken," said the youth. "The outer form of tree spirits may be male or female."

The scholar remained unsatisfied with the youth's answer. "All right, that may be," he said. "But I still think you're dodging. Because you're not wholly male either, are you? You seduced me in a feminine way and behaved thus in bed."

"Who seduced who is an open question," said the youth, "but, yes, I'll admit that it's true while my external form is male, my internal principle is female. You see, a thousand years is a long time to wait. Even for a tree. And I impatiently borrowed qi from a woman to speed up my change. So I am now both male and female. Thus my case is like those human female souls who are reborn into male bodies or those male souls who are reborn into female bodies."

"Except in this case you're not quite the innocent you pretend to be," said the scholar. "Since you illicitly used your magic to siphon the qi from a human female before appearing to me, isn't it accurate to say you seduced me through magic?"

"Claim what you wish," said the youth, gathering their things to leave. "However, as long as you insist on calling me tree, or man or woman, or seducer or seducee, you will not clearly see me or yourself."

Between the scholar's questions and the apricot's explanations, there is much wisdom to ponder about both the nature of things and one's desires.

TURTLE TREASURE

My grandmother told me about a younger cousin of hers named Zhang Baonan. An important government official in the Sichuan province, he was a dutiful son and always tried to make his mother happy. Nothing made her happier than eating turtle soup.

One day at the market, Zhang Baonan's cook bought a giant turtle. He took it home, washed it, flipped it over, and chopped off its head with a cleaver. As the head rolled away, a tiny humanoid figure a few inches long wiggled out of the neck stump and raced around the table.

Shocked, the cook stumbled back and tripped, knocking himself out. Luckily, his fall—accompanied by the clatter of pans and kitchen utensils—was heard by other household staff and they ran in to help.

Back on his feet, the cook searched for the tiny figure, but it had vanished. He concluded that he imagined it. But a little later when he slit open the turtle's belly to disembowel it, he saw the tiny figure again—curled up damply in the turtle's guts as if sleeping.

Feeling braver this time, and more full of wonder than terror, the cook poked the tiny body. There was no response.

Assuming the thing was dead, the cook plucked it out and examined it closely.

Almost indistinguishable from a human being, it had a nose and lips, tiny ears, diminutive cheekbones, and miniature doll-sized hands and feet. It was even dressed like a person, although exotically so. It was wearing a daffodil-yellow hat, a cobalt jacket, a scarlet sash, and coal-black boots that rose to its knees.

The cook recognized these garments although he couldn't make sense of why the figure should be wearing them. The figure was dressed exactly like one of the Muslim people in the famous painting *Zhi Gong Tu*, which records how foreigners from different countries look.

The cook was still examining the figure when the family tutor Cen appeared. Cen was much less astonished than the cook had been. "Ah," said Cen. "So, you found a turtle treasure."

The cook asked Cen what he was talking about.

Cen said, "Turtle treasures are very rare and very desired creatures. Some people spend a lifetime killing turtles and rummaging their guts in hopes of finding one. Because if you catch one before it dies—and they die quickly once their host dies—you can cut a slit in your arm and the creature will squeeze into the wound.

"From that point forward, it will live in your body like a worm—just as it did in the turtle's. This is lucky because the creature's host gains certain abilities as a result, such as the ability to see through the earth and locate hidden treasures.

"There is a downside though. Your life will be shortened. This is because the creature consumes blood at a slightly faster rate than you produce it.

"Therefore, you should decide before you cut yourself whether you would rather live a rich, short life or a long and poor one. If you choose the first option, you can pass the creature on to one of your children once you're drained of blood. So while your life might be short and the life of your child short and so on, you'll nevertheless ensure that your family grows in power and influence from generation to generation."

After Cen's story, the cook fell into a depression. When he emerged from it, he devoted himself to the task of killing turtles and searching their guts for the rest of his life.

"Did the cook ever come across another one of those creatures?" I asked my grandmother.

"No," she said. "He did not. More importantly, he never grasped the deeper implication of turtle treasures. If a person is willing to risk their life to make a fortune, there are many ways to make one and no need for something as rare as turtle treasure."

A HULI JING TAKES OFF THE MASK

Wu Sheng from Ningbo loved women and all the shapes and sizes of them. But there was one that he was repeatedly drawn to until something sprang up between them, something deeper than the fitting together of bodies.

Still, Wu Sheng was loath to commit.

When he told his regular lover about his reservations, she said, "I did not tell you this, but I'm not an ordinary woman. I am a *huli jing*. I am therefore untethered to a single form. I can imitate anybody and anything after just one meeting.

"My doubling is so precise that even if my model were in the same room, you could not tell us apart. Isn't this a much better deal than buying someone's smile for the night?"

Wu Sheng agreed it was. So, he tested the huli jing's claim by giving her the name of a former lover with whom she was familiar.

Just like that, the form of the former lover—no different from the real one, not by texture or taste, or sight or quality of voice—stood before him.

At first, Wu Sheng was very happy with his new situation. But soon he began to worry. He could not detect any difference between the copy and the original. Yet, he felt that something undetectable but essential was missing from the huli jing's disguise. A final degree of satisfaction eluded him, close but ever out of reach.

Wu Sheng said to the huli jing, "You've played many different roles for me. I'm grateful. But in the end, they've all been illusions, haven't they? Therefore, I can't help but feel that I'm missing out on something real."

"It's a fine distinction that you're making," said the huli jing. "A valid one perhaps. But you misidentify why my mimicry seems off. It's because *you* didn't see these women to begin with. You mistook the projections of your mind for the women themselves.

"The pale bark of poplar trees, the grass's green, the gold of the fields, the high jade mountains.

"You see all of this through the frames of your peculiar senses and prejudices, through your memories and associations, your misattributions of eternity. Half of it is story, the other half barely observed.

"You strike flint, hoping it'll light all your tomorrows. You seek a final color in the world's temporary ones, an eternal elation in an hour of pleasure. This is your mistake.

"What's worse, what informs your delusions are further delusions. The stories of great beauties and love affairs in history that provide your measuring stick are fabrications too—exaggerations, fictions, and mistellings.

"Here is the truth. There are lovely times to be had. Yes. Of people enjoying one another's bodies. There are times of dancing and singing. But in a clap, it's over.

"Most of the names are forgotten. The days too. The houses become dark. Funeral jade is buried alongside rotting bodies.

"All this happens quicker than you think—the length of time it takes an arm to stretch out and draw back—as if burnt by flame. No matter how certain the convictions, there always comes a time for people to part. Regardless of whether it's after years or minutes, it's always the same.

"A hand holds yours at the edge of a cliff. Your hands let go. You jump. After that, it's all empty. The fervent kissing and lovemaking seem like a feverish, spring dream.

"Even if couples manage to spend their whole lives together, they also clutch to illusion. They see each other how they looked when they were young, while the gray hair climbs up the body and the flesh sags. Even what they saw when they first met—the good-looking black eyebrows, the pink cheeks—they were illusions in their way too.

"So, Wu Sheng, I say this to you. How come the only illusion you have a problem with is the one I created?"

The huli jing's words profoundly affected Wu Sheng. Even after she left him years later, he never again returned to his libertine ways.

PART III

THE END OF THINGS

A CONVERSATION WITH A FRIEND ABOUT THE END OF THINGS

In a passage to *A Guide to Rare Books*, Qian Zeng discusses the special fondness that the spirit world has for literature—since it is likewise full of lives untethered to bodies.

As an example, he relates the story of how the spirits of Wukang Mountain became so attached to the books of the scholar Zhao Qingchang that they howled in broad daylight and shook the trees when his descendants sold off his collection after his death.

Since losing something to which one is attached is always painful, one feels sympathetic to the spirits' distress. On the other hand, their unwillingness to let go of the world is exactly why they remained stranded in the realm of the living. Change is the nature of all things. What gathers scatters. What scatters gathers. Thoughts become flesh; flesh becomes thoughts. Keeping this larger view in mind allows one to maintain composure.

Spirits sometimes become attached to things other than books too, such as the idea of "home." For instance, the old residence of Zhang Luan, the Ming dynasty emperor's father-in-law, was abandoned, and the main hall was sold to my late grandfather. Shortly thereafter, my grandfather brought in a crew to dismantle the building so that he could sell off the stone and wood.

As soon as the work began, the air filled with weeping and whispering. The frightened workman said the sounds came from the thick pillars in the corners of the room, as if they were buried deep inside the wood like insects in amber.

One day, while having a larger conversation about the dangers of attachment, I and my former classmate and friend, Dong Qujiang, discussed these two accounts. I said to him:

"According to the Buddhists, the physical world is an illusion created by the waking mind, similar in kind to the illusions created by the dreaming mind.

"While one daily encounters mountains, rivers, forests, and lovers, they're unreal in an ultimate sense. Because we too are unreal in an ultimate sense, except for that part of us that is beyond the powers of our mind to fully comprehend, at death we dissolve—back into our original nature like a wave smoothing back into the ocean.

"This is to be sure a kind of annihilation—even if something eternal remains. So the thought of it disturbs many people. Like the ghosts we've discussed, they don't want to let go. I'm fine with such dissolution though. Even if the I that presently says "I" vanishes, I find consolation in imagining others acquiring my possessions. I find solace in the thought of someone holding one of my books or pieces of art with affection and, upon seeing my personal seal, declaring: 'This was once owned by Ji Yun, who had a little something to say.' That is more than enough for me."

Dong Qujiang laughed. "Well, my friend," he said, "what you're saying sounds brave, but it nevertheless reveals that you can't let go of the desire to persist—even if it's in name only. Don't mistake me. I'm not saying that gathering antiques and art or the reading and writing of poems or the touching of beautiful things has no place while we're alive. But once we're done here, let us be done. Let what we've gathered, including our names, fill the bellies of worms and rats. Let it become one with soil and sea. Because this philosophy guides my life, I don't sign my books with my seal. Nor anything else in my house. Nevertheless, I own much. When I walk up a meadow, my eyes own all that I see: every color of every flower that flares. And in night's darkness, the bright moon functions as my personal lamp. If I hike a mountain, that's mine too, and also the river currents in which I bathe. There is no rent paid in these moments. And when I look elsewhere or move on, there is nothing lost."

In Dong Qujiang's view is more wisdom than in my own. I am grateful to have had such friends.

Of course, there are strange things in this world of ours for which there is not yet a theory. As for those who insist all principles of existence have been discovered, and that all phenomena have been recorded, come now, they are simply being ridiculous.

—Ji Yun, Investigator of the Strange
(1724–1805)

STORY NOTES

Part I
Strange Nonfictions

Secrets of Hanlin Academy

Hanlin Academy, the most important academic and research center in China, was the Harvard of its time, with an ancient pedigree dating back to the eighth century. Its elite scholars performed many tasks for the emperor. They trained new scholars, interpreted the Chinese classics, administered the imperial exams that one had to pass to become a government official, and carried out special projects.

Meat Vegetables

The idea of "paying off debt" makes this story an even more meaningful account for a Chinese reader.

The concept of debt frequently pops up when rebirth is discussed in China, where it is seen as a major driving force determining one's next incarnation. Because the Zhou does a favor to the woman he kills, she is reborn as his son, thus paying off her debt to him.

Guests from the Sky

The xian nü (仙女) mentioned in this story is also known as the Chinese "fairy." Like its Western counterpart, this fairy entity is seen as part of a distinct race of divine beings. Typically portrayed as female, they are associated with woods or uninhabited mountain ranges. As well, they are reputed to have magical power over natural phenomena.

The obvious similarity between Western and Chinese fairy lore is interesting by itself, but a further connection makes "Guests from the Sky" even more fascinating. It can be read as an early alien abduction tale, just like many Western fairy stories. Here are some points of comparison:

Like aliens, the xian nü are often said to come from the sky, or from heaven realms.

Like modern accounts of aliens, they are associated in the story with strange lights or orbs in the sky, and they transport —via teleportation—human beings to these orbs/lights which turn out to be dwellings.

Both aliens and the xian nü demonstrate the ability to paralyze human beings.

Both aliens and the xian nü express a strong interest in having sex/breeding with human beings (go figure).

Finally, encounters with both types of beings result in extreme illness. In alien abduction accounts, this sickness is attributed to radiation exposure. In this tale, it's attributed to occult energies.

Ultimately, one then can equally understand classical fairy abduction stories as early alien abduction tales or, conversely, alien abduction tales as contemporary iterations of fairy abduction tales.

In either case, we're presented with a phenomenon that, while interpreted through the respective cultural frames of a given age, remains surprisingly the same.

Windows That Were Not Windows

There are several theories about why "substitute ghosts" seek substitutes to repeat their deaths (a process called "zhua jiao ti"). In addition to the ideas discussed in Ji Yun's piece, another major theory is that the substitute ghost derives a twisted sense of empowerment by visiting upon others what happened to it—as a kind of cycle of abuse, analogous to what sometimes occurs to victims of violence.

Several scholars, such as Rania Huntington, as well see the actions of this figure as a perversion of the idea of repaying karmic debt, "bao." There is also a similarity between the substitute ghost and the Jewish possessing ghost known as the "dybbuk."

In some versions of the dybbuk myth, it temporarily possesses a victim in order to drive them to repeat some unclean act committed by the dybbuk when it was alive (such as murder), as if fulfilling a compulsion. When the victim does so, the dybbuk leaves.

Checkpoints

The work of the Tang dynasty writer Han Yu (768–824) heavily influenced the development of Chinese prose, as well as Neo-Confucianist philosophy.

Specifically, he advocated a prose style that was simple and transparent and that avoided excess literary ornamentation. Among his own literary contributions is *On the Ways of Spirits*, referenced in this piece.

Interestingly, Ji Yun mentions Han Yu in another piece as

well—"The Rat in My Friend's Room." The reference to Han Yu there is comic, however, and takes the form of a discussion of Han Yu's infamous libido and his love of libidinal aids.

A God of Our Own

Stove gods, also known as kitchen gods, were believed to serve as intermediaries (not unlike saints in the Christian tradition) between a family and the Jade Lord—the first of the Chinese gods. They not only looked after a family's welfare but also reported regularly to the Jade Lord on their behavior.

The Delicacy

The Great Imperial Banquet referred to in this account took place about seventy years after the Manchu people founded the Qing dynasty.

It was hosted by Emperor Kangxi during his birthday as a way of making peace between the then-present rulers of China, the Manchu people, and the Han people—who had ruled China during its previous dynasty.

The Imperial Banquet included six feasts over three days at which over 300 dishes were served—many of them exotic. Over time, the banquet became as iconic as Thanksgiving meals in the West. To this day, its dishes are highly sought after, and many cooking competitions are named after it.

The Fields in Which We Wander

According to traditional Chinese thought, a human being possesses several souls. While the exact number was sometimes debated, generally two main types were recognized: the hun and the po.

The po soul was thought to enter the fetus first to form its animal mind and drive its physical development and functions. Later, the hun soul would enter the infant, bringing with it the essence of a person's personality. The hun was seen as driving a person's psychological and spiritual development.

Upon a person's death, their hun soul(s) ascended into the afterlife realm before rebirth into a new body, while the po soul accompanied the old body to the grave before dissolving.

While the concept of an individual possessing multiple souls might seem unique to the Chinese, it is in fact a common concept world over. One sees it reflected, for example, in the ancient Jewish idea that the soul has three parts: the "nefish"—an animal component associated with the body and bodily desires; the "ruach"—a mental and emotional component associated with the individual human personality; and the "neshamah"—a spiritual component associated with the divine spark.

As an interesting side note, Western ideas about the multiplicity of the soul were translated later on, via secularization, into Sigmund Freud's model of the ego, id, and superego and theories about hemispheric lateralization (aka the concept that our left and right brain hemispheres comprise distinct personalities and ways of being—as outlined in such works as Iain McGilchrist's 2012 *The Master and His Emissary: The Divided Brain and the Making of the Western World*).

The Setting of a Clock

This account interestingly parallels contemporary Western paranormal accounts, in which watches and clocks stop, break, or otherwise are strangely affected by a death—thus behaving like symbols although they are real-world artifacts. Indeed, the collapse between subjective and objective meaning and artifacts is central to occult thought.

The Repeater

Throughout history, the Chinese have conceived of the divinity that governs life in several ways. Two concepts are relevant to this story:

a) divinity as an impersonal conscious force, referred to as "tian" (Heaven);

b) divinity conceived as a personal, anthropomorphic god, "shangdi."

These two terms are frequently used interchangeably, depending on whether one wants to draw attention to the divine as a human-like personality or as an impersonal and generative cosmic force beyond human comprehension. In this piece, Ji Yun uses the term "shangdi" (上帝).

The Shard and the Hunter

Over the ages, many Chinese artists have embraced, or at least toyed with, the idea that to make a work of art involves investing it with life force or consciousness and that sometimes such investment can lead to the work coming to life. This bears some relation of course to the Tibetan (now popular culture) concept of tulpas.

Playmates

The Chinese often forbid using the word "buy" with figurines that are associated with divinities or divine powers, such as the shrine dolls in this tale. To do so would reduce a sacred artifact imbued with life to the status of a mere commodity. One typically says instead that one has "led" the object home. Thus, sacred statues or dolls are often wrapped with a colorful thread that is symbolically used to "lead" the figure to your home.

Yeren Stones

Associated with the Western Hubei province in China, as well as the Himalayan regions near Tibet and Nepal, reports of the "yeren" (a Chinese word meaning "wild man"), also known as "yeti" (a Tibetan word meaning "bear of a rocky place"), stretch far back into China's history. Some Buddhist beliefs in Tibet and Nepal hold the yeren to be a divine being, a kind of primitive god of the forest. Ji Yun's naturalistic account of the yeren, however, is similar to most other Chinese accounts—in terms of the yeren's apelike description, hair color, horsey sounds, ability to laugh, and fondness for carrying large stones.

Remembering Those Whose Names Are Forgotten

To appreciate why calligraphy is so revered in China, it is important to understand a few things.

First off, calligraphy is seen as a dynamic rather than static art. To gaze upon calligraphy is to witness the spontaneity of an artist expressed through brushwork that has encoded the effects of place, time of year, mood, and hundreds of other things on the artist's state of mind. It is therefore experienced by the viewer similarly to how an audiophile experiences music on a top-end speaker. When music is recorded, one doesn't just record the sounds of the instruments but also the way that the waves of sound move, reverberate, and bend around objects or people in a space. In the case of the highest quality recording equipment, if a person walks across a room in which music is being played and recorded, their passing is recorded as well because of the way the sound bends around them. Therefore, when playing back a piece of music, a listener would feel a spectral presence glide past.

Secondly, unlike Western handwriting, calligraphy is

understood as a kind of painting due to the ideographic nature of the Chinese language. The characters of Chinese don't represent sounds, as is the case of the English alphabet, but rather ideas—so much so that frequently Chinese characters are pictographic (in other words, like Egyptian hieroglyphs, they look like the things they are representing). For example, "Rén" (人), which means human being, looks like a person. "Mù" (木), which means tree, looks like a tree. Not only does calligraphy constitute a type of painting, but it represents a style especially esteemed for most of Chinese history—a minimalist style seen famously in Chinese landscape paintings—full of space, silence, and suggestiveness. Such a style, perfectly matched to the use of black ink on rice paper, traffics not in realistic mimeticism but rather in the portrayal of essences, spirits, and archetypes. It seeks to portray a world distilled, paring away the noise of variation so that the artwork, in a small number of well-chosen strokes, miraculously reveals the Tao that gives rise to all things.

The Secret of the Whole Design

Note 1: One could consider this piece as an early example of copyright concerns—and, moreover, an ironic take on the subject, given the charges that the Chinese are especially disrespectful of intellectual property rights.

Note 2: The *Yongle Encyclopedia*, referred to this piece—also known as *The Great Canon of Wisdom* or *The Vast Treasure of Knowledge*—was a cherished and invaluable compilation of works on diverse subjects assembled in 1403 at the command of the Chinese Ming dynasty emperor Yongle. The largest paper encyclopedia ever assembled, it was produced through the efforts of over 2000 scholars working around the clock over a period of six years—collecting, transcribing, and editing over eight thousand texts, dating from ancient times into the early Ming dynasty.

A Messenger Rides from One Camp to Another

Note 1: "Liezi" in this fable refers to Master Lie, a fourth-century BCE Taoist philosopher. Highly regarded in Taoism, his book of fables and sayings, the *Liezi*, is considered one of the three foundational holy books of Taoism (the other two are the *Tao Te Ching* and the *Zhuangzi*).

Note 2: Ji Yun briefly references Liezi's fable at the beginning of this piece. While we filled out details in this fable for modern Western readers, it is still well-known in China, where it has given rise to the idiom, "to cover a deer with firewood." You tell someone not "to cover a deer with firewood" when warning them to treat real life more seriously.

A Spell for Dice

The reason that the word "donkey" is associated with medicine in this piece is that the donkey (especially the black donkey) has a special place in traditional Chinese medicine and was used in many highly regarded medicines.

Donkey fat, for example, was used for coughing and deafness.

Donkey penis was used for skeletal and circulatory issues —and to help with breastfeeding.

Donkey meat was used to treat fatigue and depression, donkey blood to treat intestinal issues, donkey skin to treat menstrual issues, and donkey hair was used for migraines and issues related to cold exposure. In other words, make sure to always have some donkey on hand.

Horse in Snow

Lord Guan Yu was a great warrior who lived around 200 CE. After his death, he began to be worshipped as a minor god. And to this day, he continues to be worshipped by Taoists, Buddhists, and Confucians alike. Thus, it's common to see small shrines to him in public places.

The Realness of Paintings and Demons

The *Bowuzhi*, or *Notes and Reflections on Things in the World*, is one of the earliest Chinese collections of zhiguai. Like Ji Yun's compilation, the *Bowuzhi* is also filled with accounts of strange things—both natural and supernatural—drawn from fields ranging from biology to myth and history.

Among some of the most interesting accounts are wind-propelled flying "carriages" encountered by the first king of the Shang dynasty, King Tang (1675–1646 BCE), arrowheads made from scorched bronze, freeze distillation of alcohol (concentrating alcohol through freezing it and removing the ice), and the earliest account of the yenü 野女—a mysterious, all-female tribe of naked, white-skinned "wild women" warriors who lived in the forests of what is now known as Vietnam.

The *Bowuzhi*'s author, Zhang Hua (232–300 CE), is as interesting as his collection. A Western Jin dynasty scholar, poet, and dabbler in practices both proto-scientific and magical, he was a celebrated "fangshi," or master of esoterica. As such, he was skilled at several methods for predicting the future and was a collector of rare and hard-to-obtain books about strange phenomena and the occult arts.

After his death, stories about Zhang Hua began to appear in other writers' zhiguai. For example, in Liu Jingshu's *Garden of Vast Curiosities*, Zhang Hua proves that a fish dish is dragon meat by showing how it produces a rainbow when steeped in vinegar.

A second anecdote, also in *Garden of Vast Curiosities* illustrates additionally the metaphysical principle of "ganying," sympathetic resonance. It tells of a copper bowl owned by a man that would suddenly begin ringing every morning and every night—as if being intentionally struck by someone—although no one was near.

The man who owns the bowl contacts Zhang Hua. After investigating the anomaly, Zhang Hua says, "I have figured out what sets your bowl ringing. You see, everything that exists is spiritually entangled with something else. And the ringing of your bowl is due to its sympathetic bond with the Luoyang bell tower. When the Luoyang bell is struck in the morning and at night, your bowl rings with it. It's beyond a human being to sever such bonds. But you can use tools to reshape the bowl's metal so that it vibrates silently."

The man follows Zhang Hua's advice, and the bowl ceases to disrupt his sleep.

The Future in the Past

The name "Jia" simply means somebody. Traditionally, in China, if you're telling a story and you don't know a character's name, you call them "Jia." If there's a second character whose name is not known, you call them "Yi." If there's a third somebody, you use the name "Bing;" and if there's a fourth somebody, you name them "Ding."

Spirits in the Belly

Note 1: As this story makes clear, in addition to the hun/po model of the soul, there are many other Chinese beliefs, of varying popularity, about the spiritual entities that may occupy the human body. These range from ghosts and fox spirits to gods of all kinds. For example, one ancient belief holds that the body houses minor gods who receive communications and spiritual insights from major gods that they pass onto the human hun soul.

Note 2: Underlying the logic of this piece is the Chinese belief that some people are born owing their lives to others because of debts incurred in previous lives. To this day, it's common to hear Chinese parents sigh and complain: "My whole life has been devoted to getting this child of mine on the right track. I must owe him from a previous life."

Note 3: Another interesting aspect of this piece is that the ghosts reside in the belly—versus say the head or the legs. This location calls to mind phrases like "listening to one's gut," and of course the image of an embryo in the womb. Such belly ghosts made frequent appearances in ancient tales and one even finds examples in literature today, such as Can Xue's "The Child Who Raised Poisonous Snakes" (1992).

The Shao Yong Method

Shao Yong (1011–1077), also called Shao Kangjie, was a Chinese philosopher active during the Song dynasty. He believed that the most basic level of reality was mathematical, an observation that contributed to his "observing plum blossoms" method of prediction, which is also known as the image-number method. This method takes into account all the factors in a given environment, including oneself, and seeks to decipher them just as one might decipher the different elements of a given dream.

Not every moment is capable of being analyzed this way— just as only some of one's dreams strike one as particularly meaningful. Moments that *can* be productively analyzed are usually signaled by a person being asked a question or by a question suddenly occurring to them. Such moments can also be signaled by sudden and often dramatic occurrences or coincidences that intuitively strike one as omens. The name "observing plums" method in fact stems from such an intuitively meaningful moment. The story goes that Shao Yong was admiring a clutch of plum blossoms when he witnessed two birds fighting over a branch. The birds' struggle eventually caused them to plummet to earth. Just as they hit the ground, Shao Yong realized two things:

1. The moment was an important one in which something divine was trying to communicate with him via using the things of the material world as a kind of language.

2. Everything that exists corresponds to some number and Shao Yong could interpret this divine language if he made use of this fact.

With these things in mind, Shao Yong immediately began to assign numbers to the different elements involved in the scene he'd just witnessed: including the two birds, the day of the month, the time of the day, and the color of the sky. He then combined these numbers through addition and subtraction. This yielded a sum. He matched this sum to one of sixty-four hexagrams (each made of six stacks of broken or unbroken lines that correspond to either yin or yang energy) in *The Book of Changes*. Also known as the *I Ching*, this is a book of divination regarded as one of the five Chinese classics. After analyzing the matching hexagram, Shao Yong predicted that the next night a strange woman would pass by his garden and pick a flower. This would cause the gardener to chase her and cause her to trip and injure her leg. His prediction came true.

While the modern mind understandably has trouble accepting many of the concepts in this anecdote, the eighteenth-century German philosopher Gottfried Wilhelm Leibniz credited Shao Yong's mathematical ideas with his development of a binary arithmetic that later served as the basis of binary computer code. Like Shao Yong, Leibniz thought that the key to understanding reality lay in understanding its basic mathematical nature. Thus he argued that all things that exist can be represented as ones and zeros (just as Shao Yong saw everything as made up of combinations of yin or yang energy).

Ultimately, both computer code and Shao Yong's *I Ching* method generate predictions via reducing complex ideas and phenomena to binary sequences. The Shao Yong method uses the binary code of yin and yang energy—represented by the stacked, broken or unbroken lines that make up hexagrams—while computers use the binary code of 0's and 1's. One could therefore profitably think of the *I Ching* as a kind of ancient computer in a book or, conversely, of the computer as a kind of modern divination manual—at least when it comes to predictive modelling.

To quote the philosopher Zhuangzi: "If we see things solely in terms of their differences, then even our inner organs are as distant from one another as the states of Chu and Yu. But if we see things from the point of view of their interconnection, then all things are one."

Paper Horses, Wooden Houses

There are two concepts useful to keep in mind when reading this piece. First, both fragrance and smoke were commonly thought during Ji Yun's time to be a kind of spiritual essence, just as ice evaporates into water vapor. Therefore, the burning of an object released its spirit to travel to the spirit world (as in the case of the paper horse).

As Ji Yun indicates though, a second school of thought holds that such burning isn't necessary because everything that is in the physical world is mirrored in the spirit world, although slightly altered—through a mysterious principle of magical correspondence. Thus, coffins are houses in the netherworld, paintings are actual landscapes, and one can bury one's loved ones with simulacra of whatever one wants them to have in the hereafter and it will appear there.

A Qing Dynasty Near-Death Experience

The near-death experience recorded in this account is virtually indistinguishable in its key details from many of those that have been recorded and written about world over—in both ancient and modern times. The shared characteristics include a sense that one's consciousness has left one's physical body, a sound like howling wind, the ability of thought to shape reality, a sense of the porosity of time, and the ability to decide whether to return to the world of the living or not—often influenced by the need of others.

A Question Put to the Office of Ghosts and Yin Realm Matters

The Taoist Wei Boyang referenced in Ji Yun's tale lived sometime during the Eastern Han dynasty (which lasted from 25 to 220 CE).

He is best known for writing down the formula for gunpowder in 142 CE, and significantly contributing to the development of Taoist internal alchemy, a practice devoted to spiritual transformation and achieving immortality.

The "lustrous body" described in Ji Yun's tale refers to a famous account in which Boyang formulated pills that allowed a person to became one with the Tao—in mind and body—and thus immortal. Boyang invited three of his disciples to take the pills with him. However, before they did, he theatrically speculated that the untested pills' actual consequences might be death.

Terrified, Boyang's disciples begged him to first try the pills on his beloved dog, Yu. And Yu, after gobbling a pill, fell over —seemingly dead.

To his disciples' surprise, Boyang just sighed in response and said, "Well, while this is not a good sign, it would nevertheless be a shame for me not to go all the way after putting so much effort into my formula. Besides, the Tao teaches us to look beyond appearances and into the inner nature of things." He then swallowed a pill, after which he also dropped dead.

At this point, a disciple loudly announced, "I'm not taking one of those pills. The purpose of alchemy is to help you achieve immortality. Obviously, our master's formula fails at this task."

A second disciple countered, "Not once before has our master failed us. Therefore, I think we should be faithful and follow him in this hard thing too." He then gulped a pill and also fell. The remaining disciples immediately threw away their pills and rushed to town for help.

The students who fled were not aware that Boyang had withheld a crucial piece of information: his formula worked and wasn't dangerous. A brief spell of unconsciousness was just part of its process, as was the need to overcome one's fear of death. He had simply wanted to test his disciples' courage. In fact, almost as soon as they left, Boyang, the dog Yu, and the faithful disciple regained consciousness and their bodies became pure lustrous light. After that, they ascended into the subtle realms.

The Scroll of Ghosts and Fiends

Luo Pin (1733–1799), also known by his pseudonyms of "Two Peaks" and "Monk of the Temple of Flowers," was a wildly celebrated Qing dynasty painter whose original vision profoundly influenced later artists, as did his distinctive ink-wash style, which he used to paint plum blossoms (a family specialty) and inhabitants of the spirit world, who he infamously claimed that he could see.

Luo Pin is equally famous for elevating portrait painting to a high art rather than a purely commercial activity. The uncanny ability of his portraits to capture the distinctive humanity of each subject revolutionized portrait painting in fact, shifting the predominant style from mythological and archetypal to individualistic and psychological.

It might seem ironic that Luo Pin was celebrated for his realist portrait style while also concerning himself with painting spirits. However, his claim to see spirits was not unique to him. Taoists and Buddhists had long held that the ability to see spirits was a natural consequence of spiritual development or a side effect of having been contacted by a spiritual entity.

In Luo Pin's case, his gifts were triggered by several paranormal experiences. This included a dream visit by his wife, Fang Wanyi, while they were separated for business reasons. In the dream, she informed him that she had died—long before the news that this had actually occurred reached him by normal means.

Different Maps of the Same Places

This story's conclusion echoes a common Chan Buddhist belief that there are multiple ways to perceive reality, ways which correspond to the state of a perceiver's consciousness. One famous Tang dynasty anecdote, for example—told by Chan master Qingyuan Weixin—holds that there are three different understandings of mountains and rivers that a Chan practitioner holds over the course of his life.

It goes like this:

"Before devoting myself to Chan Buddhism for thirty years, I simply saw mountains as mountains, and rivers as rivers. After my study, I saw that mountains are not mountains and rivers are not rivers. But then at the end of my life, after purifying my understanding, I now see mountains once again as mountains, and rivers once again as rivers."

The journey of perception detailed in this anecdote is one in which a person moves from seeing things as separate to seeing their separateness as illusion and their interdependence as THE really real thing—to finally arriving at the point where a person understands that individual expression is not only real but fulfills the potential of ultimate reality.

A person moves, in other words, from seeing the material world as THE real to seeing it as an illusion while the spiritual world is THE real, to finally understanding that each dimension of reality completes, fulfills, and expresses the other.

PART II: FABLES AND PHILOSOPHIES

Apricot Spirit

Note 1: While a relatively light fable compared to some other pieces in this collection, "Apricot Spirit" is nevertheless a significant work. It exhibits Ji Yun's fraught but clear progressivism toward gender identity, just as stories like "Jade Chicken" exhibit his progressive attitudes towards animal rights—a progressivism relative to his time of course. As such, "Apricot Spirit" also draws readers' attention to long-standing conversations about queer and trans identity that have rippled across Chinese fables of huli jing and tree spirits, and tales of reincarnation and body swapping, since ancient times.

Note 2: In the Chinese language, "he"(他), "she"(她) and "it" (它) are all pronounced "tā" when spoken. Thus, in speech, the distinction between "he/she/it" is minimized, and so too consequently are the differences between male and female gender identities, and also the differences between human beings and other life forms. In this way, the apricot tree spirit's argument is supported by the Chinese language.

The Girl with Flowers in Her Hair

That this story's incident takes place on the evening before the first day of Spring Festival (the Chinese New Year period—which lasts around twenty-three days) is thematically significant. Spring Festival is traditionally when people reflect on their achievements and successes from the previous year. The broom seems to have done just that by celebrating its growing sentience—albeit in a peculiarly foolish and destructive way.

Part III: The End of Things

A Conversation with a Friend About the End of Things

Dong Qujiang's comments about ownership in this piece possibly reflect his familiarity with the story of Fayan, an eleventh-century Buddhist monk—as preserved in *Records of the Sayings of the Ancient Worthies*, a collection of Chan Buddhist wisdom. In the story, Fayan has trouble comprehending the Buddhist teaching that distinction and non-distinction are the same, as are object and subject, and the seer and the seen. He's given the metaphor of a person who has just drunk water and who consequently acquires an immediate innate ability to know whether the water is warm or hot inside them.

This metaphor is meant to illustrate that the water the

person has swallowed is simultaneously distinct (since it is distinguishable from the body that it's inside) and non-distinct (its temperature can be sensed only because it is part of the body).

Fayan understands the metaphor intellectually, yet still feels like he is missing something crucial. One day though, in a moment of sudden enlightenment, he finally grasps the full meaning of the metaphor. Afterwards, he writes the following poem:

> *A patch of sunlit field at mountain's bottom.*
> *I bow to this brightness.*
> *I see an old man enjoying the beauty too.*
> *"Do you own this field?" I ask.*
> *"Every day," he says, "I watch the rustle of the pines."*
> *"Every day," he says, "I find the bamboo shifting*
> *in the wind a marvel."*

READING GROUP DISCUSSION QUESTIONS

1. What questions does this collection leave you asking? What topics does it lead you to want to know more about?

2. Many zhiguai writers held that the distinctions people typically make between supernatural and natural phenomena are overly strict. In fact, both types of phenomena are governed by the same deep principles. Thus, reflecting on both can open our mind and expand our consciousness. In the spirit of this attitude, what are some natural phenomena or scientific facts that you've learned (or experienced) in your life that dramatically changed how you understand reality?

3. Ji Yun's intention for these stories was to get us to think about strange phenomena and what they might imply about reality. What kind of phenomena does Ji Yun cover in this collection? What do these phenomena imply about reality or how it works?

4. Are there strange phenomena you've encountered?

5. While our ways of understanding reality have shifted dramatically from magic, religion, and metaphysics to scientific and technological frames and metaphors, still certain themes and plots have stayed consistent in literature. Do any of Ji Yun's stories remind you of contemporary science fiction, fantasy, or horror stories (or movies)? Which ones and how?

6. Several of Ji Yun's pieces discuss dreams. What is your view of dreams?

7. Many zhiguai writers did not distinguish between truth and fiction the same way we do. Consequently, they often mixed together autobiographical accounts, fables, urban legends, and scientific anecdotes in the same collections. Their rationale for doing so is that any story, whether fiction or nonfiction, could potentially offer insights into significant truths. What are some fictional stories you've encountered that you felt had profoundly true things to say? What deep truths do you think the fables in Ji Yun's book (in Part II) are trying to communicate?

8. The Confucians of Ji Yun's time were socially conservative. While Ji Yun shared some views in common with them, in other ways he challenged social conservatism and showed himself to be progressive in terms of animal rights, women's rights, empathy toward the poor and the dispossessed. In what ways does Ji Yun seem progressive in this collection?

9. In Ji Yun's zhiguai that record the experiences of others, he sometimes expresses skepticism about the truth of the tales being shared. On the other hand, he is convinced that other events illustrate genuine metaphysical and paranormal principles. Keeping in mind that true skepticism involves not forcing

a materialist explanation on a phenomenon when a non-materialist one is a better fit, and vice versa, do you think Ji Yun is skeptical enough about the events of these tales?

10. What stories were the most memorable or the most powerful for you and why?

TIMELINE OF JI YUN'S LIFE

1724 (birth): Ji Yun, also known as Ji Xiaolan or Ji Chunfan, is born on July 26th in Xian County, Hebei Province. Immanuel Kant is born this same year in Germany. Meanwhile, in America, Benjamin Franklin turns eighteen.

1727 (3 years old): Ji Yun meets his father, a mid-level bureaucrat, for the first time when he returns home from a faraway post.

1730 (6 years old): Ji Yun is declared a genius based on his performance on the "tongzi" test, a special test given to young children to gauge their analytical and literary abilities.

1740 (16 years old): Ji Yun marries Ma Yuefang. Their first child, Ruji, is born that same year.

1747 (23 years old): Ji Yun is ranked number one in the prefectural examination. This is the lowest level of the three civil service examinations that determine one's eligibility for national government posts. The other two are the provincial exam and the national exam. All three require a candidate to write essays on topics ranging from philosophy and literature to statecraft. And all three require a broad breadth of historical knowledge, as well as critical thinking and literary abilities. Only the top-ranking students from the lower exams can take the higher.

1750 (26 years old): When Ji Yun is twenty-six, his mother dies. In keeping with tradition, he enters a three-year period of mourning. He takes a break from his career (and exam preparation) and remains in his hometown with his family.

1754 (30 years old): At the age of thirty, Ji Yun takes his final examination, the national exam. He ranks number seven out of all Chinese test-takers. His friendship with the emperor of China, Qianlong, begins.

1762 (38 years old): Ji Yun is appointed as the Superintendent of Education for Fujian province.

1765 (41 years old): Ji Yun's father dies. He enters another three-year period of mourning.

Early 1768 (44 years old): Ji Yun comes out of mourning and is appointed to the post of Magistrate of Guizhou Province. Later this year, he is promoted to the faculty at Hanlin Academy, the intellectual heart of China and its top academic institution.

Late 1768 (44 years old): Ji Yun suffers a major setback when he is accused of tipping off a relative that he is going to be charged with bribery. For this, he is banished for three years to Urumqi, a remote borderland of wild prairies, coniferous steppes, and deserts that lies in the far northwest of China in Xinjiang Province.

1771 (47 years old): Ji Yun is pardoned and returns to the emperor's side. On his return journey, he writes the *Xinjiang Za Lu*, a travel memoir comprised of 160 poems that is held in high regard to this day.

1773 (49 years old): Ji Yun is appointed Chief Editor and Chief Librarian for the *Siku Quanshu* (四库全书), the largest collection of Chinese literary works ever assembled.

1779 (55 years old): Ji Yun is appointed as Special Advisor to the emperor and also as Vice Head of the Department of Rites, a position in which he oversees foreign affairs, Confucian rites and rituals, and civil service exams.

1782–1785 (58–61 years old): Ji Yun serves as the Head of the Department of Public Works, the Head of Department of Personnel, and then Vice Head of the Department of War.

1789 (65 years old): Ji Yun writes the first volume of his zhiguai, *Personal Accounts and Records of Others: Written During a Luanyang Summer*.

1791 (67 years old): Ji Yun finishes the second volume of his zhiguai: *As It Was Confided*.

1792 (68 years old): Ji Yun finishes the third volume of his zhiguai, *Locust Tree Notes*

1793 (69 years old): Ji Yun finishes his fourth volume of zhiguai, *Listen Wildly*.

1796 (72 years old): Ji Yun is promoted to the posts of Head of the Department of War and Imperial Censor-in-Chief.

1797 (73 years old): Ji Yun is promoted to Head of the Department of Rites.

1798 (74 years old): Ji Yun finishes his fifth volume of zhiguai, *A Luanyang Summer II.*

1799 (75 years old): Ji Yun's good friend Emperor Qianlong dies.

Early 1805 (80 years old): Ji Yun is appointed as Grand Counselor to Emperor Qianlong's successor, Emperor Jiaqing, and also as Director of Imperial Education.

March 14, 1805 (death): Ji Yun dies before his eighty-first birthday. Four years later, Edgar Allan Poe is born.

INTERVIEW EXCERPTS

What drew you to this project?

We're big horror and weird literature buffs, particularly of the East Asian variety, and particularly in a metaphysical key.

Everything from Kiyoshi Kurosawa and Sion Sono movies to Junji Ito and Yuki Urushibara manga, as well as the surreal prose nightmares of Can Xue and the weird work of writers like Tang Fei, Chen Qiufan, and Han Song.

And as fans, it struck us that not a lot was known about Chinese work in these areas in the West. Usually, if you talk about this sort of thing, attention goes to Japan or Korea—even though the Chinese influence on these literatures is massive.

Plus, we love Ji Yun—his mind, his writing, his sense of humor, his backstory. Although only a fraction of the over 1200 tales he authored can be claimed to be weird tales or horror, they cover almost every type there is, all the while developing the mythology of key Chinese horror figures and tropes. To boot, he shares fascinating examples of occult and horror creative nonfiction.

Where do zhiguai fit into China's weird tale history?

Zhiguai can in part be traced back to the Chinese Taoist philosopher Zhuangzi (369–286 BCE).

He coined the term to refer to storytellers of the strange aka: "guai," a word which came to mean a strangeness rooted in a reality radically beyond the everyday, but which is nonetheless claimed to be true by the teller. Specifically, Zhuangzi discusses a man who tells a "zhiguai" about a cosmically gargantuan and mathematically sublime fish. We're talking a fish hundreds and hundreds of miles long, with a head so big that your eyes and mind can't fully comprehend it. To top it off, this fish—the "kun"—periodically transforms into an equally massive bird, the "peng." While readers today of course have a hard time accepting such a tale as true, it must have seemed plausible at a time when all kinds of bizarre new creatures were being discovered daily, from blue whales to giant squids. And it established a tradition of tales of strange plants and animals being shared in zhiguai collections alongside supernatural phenomena—plants and animals that when described would fill the reader with awe.

Even more significantly for contemporary world weird literature though, and related literary flavors, Zhuangzi also shares a strange tale of his own: "The Parable of the Butterfly." He doesn't explicitly name it as "zhiguai." Nevertheless, it is China's most famous early weird tale and sets important precedents for zhiguai collections: the inclusion of parables that express allegorical truths (a la Plato's "Allegory of the Cave") and the inclusion of paranormal dreams.

In this parable, Zhuangzi recounts a dream in which he is a butterfly. It's a very striking dream to him because it feels as real as his waking human life, although his thought processes and perceptions are specifically those of a butterfly.

The narrative ends in a trippy way too by Zhuangzi asking the reader what he really is—butterfly or man—and wondering about the distinction that exists between things and about the principles underlying their transformation into one another. It's an amazing work, one that's just as thought-provoking today as it was thousands of years ago. And its basic plot carries over to modern movies like *The Matrix* and *Existenz*, in which a character discovers that they might be a virtual reality avatar living in a virtual world.

What more can you ask for from weird prose than for it to not just unsettle your sense of reality during your reading but also afterwards?

And here's the kicker. Zhuangzi's weird tale possibly ties into the contemporary global weird tradition by way of Franz Kafka.

How so?

Well, Kafka's most well-known weird work is *The Metamorphosis*, in which the previously human character Gregory Samsa inexplicably and problematically wakes up as a roach (or a dung beetle, depending on the translation that you're reading). Kafka's story, in other words, updates and amusingly/horrifyingly perverts Zhuangzi's tale. It presents a metaphysics drained of deeper spiritual meaning, and decentered and alienated human beings without hope of connection to one another or to the universe they live in—a kind of negative Taoism. This is probably not a casual coincidence. At least we don't think so. Because Kafka was a huge fan of Taoism and Taoist aesthetics. So, you have this cool circular situation where Taoism influences Kafka whose work is today heavily influencing contemporary Chinese writers of the weird, the surreal, and the strange.

After Zhuangzi, the term "zhiguai" is consistently used to refer to tales, and even non-narrative elements like lists, that create an atmosphere and emotional effect of radical strangeness with metaphysical implications, particularly tales that are claimed to be true—literally or allegorically. Some of these are weird in a capital W way, and others are weird in a more generic sense—as a synonym for strange, odd, or baffling. These include everything from scientific and botanical anomalies (just think how "weird" a black hole is or quantum physics) to supernatural events. In fact, collections of these materials are classified in libraries as philosophy and history, and assembled by historians as a shadow counterpart to their more orthodox work. This was famously done, for example, by the historian Gan Bao (fl. 315 CE).

Known as the "historian of the supernatural," Gan Bao was a key model for Ji Yun's work. Like Ji Yun, he was inspired to compile his collection after his family had several paranormal experiences in order to explore "shendao," the ways of spirits. And like Ji Yun, Gan Bao blended paranormal creative nonfictions and legends—a genre-busting intermingling of hearsay and history, personal encounter and rumor, that he defended by arguing that even orthodox histories are tainted by exaggeration and fiction without wholly losing their truth value.

From Gan Bao on, zhiguai are in most cases united by certain traits. They're strange in a way that shocks open the reader's view of reality. And they're meant to at least attempt to record the true—even if it's the allegorical sort or not 100% verifiable.

This changes roughly around the eleventh century when zhiguai's entertainment value starts to become more important to some writers than its truth-telling function. Consequently, there's a huge influx of comedic zhiguai, "adult" zhiguai, and other sorts. From that point forward, a debate rages. Should zhiguai be a genre of fiction that entertains by way of strange happenings? Or should they be a genre of nonfiction that cracks open the mind by way of strange, true narratives that make their readers realize the limitations of their previous understanding of the universe?

In the eighteenth century, Ji Yun joins this debate and

argues that zhiguai should strive for truth and not simply entertain. However, today this debate is still ongoing. Some people think of zhiguai as any paranormal or supernatural story, true or not true, weird or not, and are indifferent to their truth-telling function. And others, like us, are more interested in zhiguai as a very specific type of creative nonfiction, true tales about destabilizing weird or paranormal events or phenomena that can't be fully understood and which incite awe by hinting that reality is much vaster and more mysterious than our conceptions allow.

How do "zhiguai' compare to other forms of horror writing today?

The closest contemporary counterparts to the type of zhiguai that Ji Yun was writing are "true" glitch-in-the-matrix and paranormal tales, many of which are weird in the same way as weird fiction. As in some of Ji Yun's work, you'll frequently find the tellers of these autobiographical tales desperately seeking to name and describe, and thus order and tame, their experiences yet ultimately unable to fully do so. That's part of the unique drama of the genre: the rational mind grappling with the irrational. This is something Ji Yun's tales share in common with the work of Western authors. Because of the connection between zhiguai and contemporary weird and paranormal literary nonfiction, we even put together a second "little sister" book of weird/strange/horror nonfiction related to *The Shadow Book*. Transparently entitled *Zhiguai*, it translates modern Chinese glitch-in-the-matrix tales, paranormal tales, and weird memoir in order to make this connection apparent.

But as we mentioned previously, the term "zhiguai' has a few different meanings. While for Ji Yun, the term is mostly reserved for weird and paranormal nonfiction, for many other writers and readers it has a broader definition. First off, it is used in China today to refer to classical strange and paranormal Chinese tales, nonfiction and fiction alike. And because such tales had a massive influence on modern Chinese fiction, "zhiguai" is also used sometimes to refer to modern, paranormal Chinese fiction.

To make the whole thing even more complex, there are two related terms that you'll come across pretty frequently in horror circles in China, which also center on the concept of "guai." "Guai qi" (which translates to "strange and weird" or "weird weird") and "guai tan" (a play off "kwaidan," the Japanese term for strange tales) are used to refer specifically to weird fiction proper, as initially defined by H.P. Lovecraft. This is a very well-known genre across East Asia, thanks to the popularity of Junji Ito, H.P. Lovecraft, and Franz Kafka, and of course the long tradition of zhiguai.

While "zhiguai" has been discussed as a possible umbrella term for all weird fiction too, it looks like "guai qi" will win out as the preferred term.

At the end of the day, we think this whole conversation about terms is cool and exciting. Through it, many Chinese lit folks are thinking very hard not just about what to call Chinese weird fiction but also about what might define it. They are also adding to a more general, global conversation about horror, weird, and paranormal creative nonfiction. The creative nonfiction part of the conversation is very timely given that current memoirs like Carmen Maria Machado's *In the Dream House* and Augusten Burroughs' *Toil and Trouble* are exploring this territory. And it's a very revolutionary way to think about creative nonfiction—while being at the same time a return to something that was long prized in Chinese culture.

How much of zhiguai are "weird" in an H.P. Lovecraft or Junji Ito sense, versus just being weird in a way that is a synonym for odd, strange, or paranormal?

Well, first off, people have very different ideas about how

to define the weird versus say the uncanny, the strange, the numinous, the sublime, and so on. But in general, that depends on how a particular author treats zhiguai. For those who just treat zhiguai as paranormal comedy or satire, very little. However, you'll find a lot of weirdness in zhiguai intended as nonfiction. Zhiguai which, in other words, go back to the genre's roots. This material after all frequently claims that the world we live in exceeds the ability of our everyday reason to grasp it and, further, claims that our world is full of unseen threats and invisible dimensions. At the same time, it also claims that reality is more transcendentally awe-inspiring than we ever imagined. This can't help but fill one with that special blend of dread, angst, and sublimity that marks the weird.

Going back to the specific case of Ji Yun, he's obviously a very different writer from H.P. Lovecraft and some of our friends tease us when we compare the two and insist that M.R. James is a much better fit for the sake of comparison. They have a point. After all, you'll find nothing approaching Lovecraft's nihilism in Ji Yun, and his stripped-down prose is the opposite of Lovecraft's baroque excesses. Still, there's a lot of overlap that we think is useful to think about. Both men, for example, were passionate travel writers and antiquarians whose interest in folklore, ancient rituals, old philosophies, and material artifacts heavily colored their writing. Both were fond of theories that combined the supernatural and the scientific, and were fascinated by metamorphosis and the limits of human perception. Lovecraft even nodded to some connection between his work and that of the East Asian weird by heavily praising the work of Lafcadio Hearn, who retold Japanese strange tales, as an exemplary model of the weird. Finally, both Ji Yun and H.P. Lovecraft saw the weird tale as a vehicle to awaken us to dimensions beyond the everyday, and to suspend the sense of being constrained by the limitations of time and space, a matter that Lovecraft expounds upon in his essay "Notes on the Writing of Weird Fiction." Many of the same things that are true of Lovecraft and Ji Yun are also true of Junji Ito. In fact, Ito is an interesting blend of the two. His work shares the pessimistic fatalism of much of Lovecraft's while his depictions of the weird also share distinctive East Asian traits with Ji Yun's work.

Weird fiction and nonfiction are found the world over. Is there anything that makes Chinese weird nonfiction or fiction unique?

Absolutely. The intrusion of an external and unsettling strangeness beyond human reason into our everyday world, which partially defines the weird as a genre, and the ensuing sense of ontological instability, epistemological uncertainty, and awe, which partially defines it as an aesthetic effect, are in a Chinese context marked by Taoist and Buddhist metaphysics, as well as by China's shamanic roots.

Thus, in the Chinese weird (as well as in related genres) we see a variety of metaphysical principles and ideas play out: the constant transformation of things, which is rooted in a view of reality as incessantly in flux; "ganying" (a supernatural resonance and interconnection between distant things and structures); "renfu tianshu" (a resonance and mirroring between otherworldly or "higher" dimensions and humanity); "ming" (fate); the law of karma; "yūgen" (or 幽玄, an originally Chinese Taoist and Buddhist term that connotes the deep, mysterious, elusive, and wistful beauty of a reality that ever exceeds our mind); Buddhist ideas about the inexpressibility and emptiness of ultimate reality, as well as the illusory nature of the visible world; a belief in fu talismans and sigils and other magical paraphernalia and practices that erase the mind/matter and symbolic/literal divide; and an embrace of both/and thinking. Additionally, one typically sees too in the

Chinese weird qualities highly prized in Chinese literary art: an artistic use of silence, space, suggestiveness, and a narrative gesture that could be called koanic—in which the reader is moved to radically reframe their sense of self and reality through exposure to strange uses of language and irrational gestures.

It should be added here that we think this description of the Chinese weird maps rather well onto the East Asian weird in general. This is immediately apparent if you take this list and use it to examine a work like Junji Ito's "Enigma of Amigara Fault" alongside Han Song's "The Wheel of Samsara."

A number of the purported sources for these stories are folks in Ji Yun's immediate circle. How common was supernatural belief in this era of Chinese history?

Very common. Even to this day, shamanism plays a big role in China, as it has since its beginning. And for the average person during Ji Yun's time, the spiritual realms were considered as much a part of their natural world as the microbiological and subatomic realms are considered part of ours.

That said, among the intellectual class the acceptance of the supernatural was far from a settled matter. In fact, there was a huge ongoing debate between different factions of intellectuals and scholars, between those who believed in this or that supernatural thing and those who were skeptical of all such things or outright dismissive. Ji Yun obviously sided with the groups open to the supernatural or paranormal.

There's a second way in which Ji Yun's supernatural sensibility stood out too. As the English critic and father of Virginia Woolf, Sir Leslie Stephen put it once, skepticism is always partial. That is, people will tend to be skeptical about some things but not about others. Thus, you have religious people who don't believe in ghosts or aliens, and you have ghost hunters who don't believe in Buddha or the Tao or Jesus and so on. This is all to say that Ji Yun believed in some of the wrong things for even a supernatural-friendly Confucian scholar, such as Tibetan black magic. Even worse, he treats these subjects as worthy of serious scholarship and writes about them sometimes as an experiencer himself and not just as a detached recorder.

To draw an analogy from contemporary culture, it's not unusual for our professorial and scholarly colleagues to confess all kinds of wild things in private about their astrological beliefs, ghosts, precognitive dreams, or what they REALLY think about aliens or UFOs. But not in a million years would most of them write a paper about these things or present on them at a conference. There's a really interesting separation in other words between what we human beings admit in a professional or public setting and what we admit in an individual one. Ji Yun violated this separation.

*Thanks to Sarah Dodd of *Samovar* and Monica Kuebler of *Rue Morgue Magazine,* and Jim Mcleod of *Ginger Nuts of Horror* for the interview and/or article opportunities from which some of the above materials are excerpted.

FURTHER READING

Campany, Robert Ford. *Strange Writing: Anomaly Accounts in Early Medieval China*. Albany, SUNY Press, 1996.

Chan, Leo Tak-Hung. *The Discourse on Foxes and Ghosts: Ji Yun and Eighteenth-Century Literati Storytelling*. Honolulu, University of Hawai'i Press, 1998.

Chi, Yün. *Shadows in a Chinese Landscape: The Notes of a Confucian Scholar*. Edited and translated by David L. Keenan, M. E. Sharpe, 1999.

Chiang, Sing-Chen Lydia. *Collecting the Self: Body and Identity in Strange Tale Collections of Late Imperial China*. Leiden and Boston, Brill, 2005.

Davis, Edward L. *Society and the Supernatural in Song China*. Honolulu, University of Hawai'i Press, 2001.

Dodd, Sarah L. *Monsters and Monstrosity in Liaozhai zhiyi*. 2013. University of Leeds, PhD dissertation.

Gan Bao 干宝. *Soushen Ji* 搜神记. Edited by Wang Shaoying 汪绍楹, Zhonghua shuju, 1979.

Gu, Ming Dong. *Chinese Theories of Fiction: A Non-Western Narrative System*. Albany, SUNY Press, 2006.

Hammond, Charles E. "Tang Legends: History and

Hearsay." *Tamkang Review*, vol. 20, no. 4, 1990, pp. 359-82.

Huntington, Rania. *Alien Kind: Foxes and Late Imperial Chinese Narrative*. Cambridge, Harvard University Press, 2003.

Liu, James J. Y. *Chinese Theories of Literature*. Chicago, University of Chicago Press, 1975.

Liu, Mingming. *Theory of the Strange: Towards the Establishment of Zhiguai as a Genre.* 2015. University of California, Riverside, PhD dissertation.

Liu, Yiqing. *Hidden and Visible Realms: Early Medieval Chinese Tales of the Supernatural and the Fantastic.* Edited and translated by Zhenjun Zhang, Columbia University Press, 2018.

Needham, Joseph. *Science and Civilization in China.* Cambridge, Cambridge University Press, 1974.

Pollard, David E., editor and translator. *Real Life in China at the Height of Empire: Revealed by the Ghosts of Ji Xiaolan*. Hong Kong, The Chinese University Press, 2014.

Schwartz, Benjamin I. *The World of Thought in Ancient China*. Cambridge, Harvard University Press, 1985.

Schwitzgebel, Eric. "In-Between Believing." *The Philosophical Quarterly*, vol. 51, no. 202, 2001, pp. 76-82.

Yang, Xianyi, and Gladys Yang, translators. *The Man Who Sold a Ghost: Chinese Tales of the 3rd-6th Centuries.* Beijing, Foreign Languages Press, 1958.

Zeitlin, Judith T. *Historian of the Strange: Pu Songling and the Chinese Classical Tale*. Stanford, Stanford University Press, 1997.

STATEMENT ON TRANSLATION

Translations are by their nature shaped both by the translator's purpose and sensibilities. In putting together this collection, we hoped to make clear the debt that contemporary speculative and weird prose owes Ji Yun, as well as the importance of the zhiguai form to creative nonfiction—especially its flash and micro veins. We also focused on those works that reveal Ji Yun's rich metaphysical and occult thought. Finally, we sought to translate his work as vibrant and relevant literature, literature that moreover speaks to a popular culture readership.

We balanced fidelity to Ji Yun's original texts with explicitness about many otherwise implicit matters of cultural subtext and meaning. In this, we privileged conveying the meaning, nuance, and aesthetic effects of a source text over word-for-word transcription, following the Yan Fu method of translation —which allows for the insertion of additional background information to communicate in new languages and to new audiences. These additions are called "Yin Chen" (引衬), which means a guiding hand.

Part of this "guiding hand" approach involved titling (and sometimes subtitling) Ji Yun's pieces, a practice observed by most translations of his work. We found this necessary since in their raw form Ji Yun's stories simply exist as biji, untitled and unnumbered notes. We also, in zhiguai fashion, grouped certain thematically-related narratives together, notably in the case of "On the Jiangshi and Other Returns," "The Appearance of the Sha," "The Red Sect," "The Swap," and "Every Body is a Word; Every Word is a Future." We also strove for language as close to modern speech as possible and filled out parables that Ji Yun only references partially (noticeably in the case of Liezi's dream-deer parable in "The Fields in Which We Wander").

ACKNOWLEDGMENTS

A key concept in Chinese philosophy is that nothing exists in isolation. We've certainly found this true in regard to this translation project, which would not exist without certain people.

First off, a special thanks to 陈玉芬, 尚秉祺, 徐继欣, John Alleman, Bil Brown, Frank Xavier Quickert, and Jeffrey Skinner. They taught us how to create virtual realities to inhabit through the occult practice of reading and writing.

Thank you as well to our parents who taught us light—尚秀华, Shirley St. Pierre, 于兆太, Johnny Lee Branscum, Diana Feger, and Edward Lawson—and the dear friends who gave us valuable advice, inspiration, and love: 韩世亮, 尚秀萍, 邵梦, 杨永卫, 苑蔚, 张晶鹏, 周佩蓉, Rajwan Alshareefy, Annette Armer, Cynthia Arrieu-King, Sally Dora Baxter, Shirley Jean Branscum, William Callahan, Eric Clark, Carri Cleaveland, Susan Comfort, Chauna Craig, Patrick Craig, Gina Detrick, Judy Dong, John Erickson, Barry Franklin, Nicole Goulet, Michael Griffith, Ben Gulley, Melanie Holm, Meiko Ko Ishihara, Jialei Jiang, Kate Kean, Dan Keller, Rhonda Lightner, Luther Ledergar, Nicola Mason, Neely McLaughlin, Zahraa Mubarak, Gerardo Muniz, Christian Nagel, Tayseer Abu Odeh, Gian Pagnucci, Xiubo Cui Pearce, Robert Penner, Mia Petty, Curt Porter, John Possman, Heather Powers, Eric Roper, T Stacy Reynolds, Dawnette Shellhammer, Manuela Da Silva, Peter Sorrell, Angela Sweitzer, Jason Tabbutt, Virginia Tabbutt, Sabrina Wu, Shonda Wade, Ruth Wainaina, David Watkins,

Jacquelyn Watkins, Dan Weinstein, Emily Wender, and James Wilson.

Additionally, we are indebted to the students we've been lucky enough to teach, who in the process have taught us so much in return. Mad love to our Indiana University of Pennsylvania students, and to our Kiski Area High School Chinese language students. You rock hard.

Finally, a grateful thank you to the following journals and all the lovely, hardworking people behind them for publishing some of the pieces in this book: *Cincinnati Review*, *Copper Nickel*, *Lunch Ticket*, *New England Review*, *Passages North*, *River Teeth*, *Strange Horizons-Samovar*, *Wigleaf, and 3:AM Magazine*.

And, above all, we bow to Ji Yun 纪昀 for leaving the world the gift of his work.

TRANSLATOR BIOGRAPHIES

About Yi Izzy Yu

In 2011, Yi Izzy Yu left Northern China for the US, with nothing but $500 in her pocket and a love of traditional Chinese stories that she inherited from her grandmother. Living in a rented room in the small Pennsylvania town of Indiana, late at night she would comfort her homesickness by eating shrimp chips and reading Ji Yun's stories in their original Classical Chinese. It was in these moments that the thought first came to her that it would be cool to do a popular-culture English translation of Ji Yun's work that focused on its contribution to speculative fiction and nonfiction.

About John Yu Branscum

One day in a Kentucky public library, a young John Yu Branscum picked up a collection of "Zen Tales," thinking "Zen" must be an alien planet like Gor (immortalized in the B-movie "sword and planet" novels of John Norman). By the end of the first koanesque tale, he realized that the book he'd picked up was not science fiction. But by then it was too late. Eventually his reading of the Zen tales, and the cognitive rewiring that ensued, led decades later to his teaching college in the small Pennsylvania town of Indiana and reading Ji Yun stories at night. Little did he know (at least not for several months) that a street over, a young woman named Yi Izzy Yu was eating shrimp chips.

Dear Readers:

If you adore Ji Yun's work like we do, please leave a review online somewhere, such as Goodreads or Amazon. We'd love to know how you feel about the individual pieces or the book as a whole.

Best regards,

Yi Izzy Yu
John Yu Branscum